Elemental
Threat

Elemental Threat

Richard Henry Opper

Oak Tree Press
Claremont, CA

Oak Tree Press

Oak Tree Books may be purchased for educational, business, or sales promotional use. Contact Publisher for quantity discounts.

First Edition, July 2002

Cover Design by One 2 One Direct
www.121Direct.net

10 9 8 7 6 5 4 3 2 1

Library of Congress Cataloging-in-Publication Data
Richard Henry Opper-1952-
Elemental Threat / By Richard H. Opper.—1st ed.
P cm.
ISBN 1-892343-22-3 (alk. Paper)
1.   Indian reservations—Fiction. 2. Explosions—Fiction.
3. Montana—Fiction. I. Title
PS3615.P65 E44 2002
813'6-dc21

2002008640

Acknowledgements

First, I thank all those friends and good sports who read my manuscript long before it had taken recognizable form. They provided the support and input that helped me turn this story into a book. Among them are Deb Akers, Tom Bateridge, Doug Sepkowitz, Joel Higgins, Becky and Doug ("Hey, this is as good as any of the S_ _ _ I read.") Latka, Ruth Mueller, Nettie Meyers, my sister Carol Powell, and brother, Gary Opper. Forgive me if I have inadvertently omitted a few loyal readers and friends from this list. I also thank the members of the Sioux and Assiniboine Tribes on the Fort Peck Indian Reservation who provided me with some of the history I incorporated into this book. To them I offer my hope that I have done justice to some of the tragic stories they so willingly shared with me. Jeanne Heuser provided a great deal of editorial assistance, and I am grateful for her support. My friend, editor, and writing mentor, Susan Risland, has taught and continues to teach me how to write books. I offer my heartfelt appreciation for her help and patience. James Crumley, Jon Jackson and Jenny Siler, three fine Montana writers, were gracious enough to read my manuscript and say nice things about it. I thank them for their unselfish support of new writers like myself. My publisher at Oak Tree Press, Billie Johnson, has been a joy to work with, and I thank her for the enthusiasm with which she tackled this project. Finally, I thank my wife, Sally Mueller, whose relentless integrity continues to inspire me. Someday I hope to be as good a writer as she is a person, though that is a lofty goal indeed.

CHAPTER 1

This should feel more awkward, Robert Botkin thought as he steered the grain truck across the field of ripened wheat. His friend, Frank Kicking Bird, was bouncing along beside him in a borrowed combine, a thick hose from the back of his machine sprayed dusty grain into the bed of the truck Robert was driving. Robert knew there was something significant about having his lover's husband spew seed into his own back end, but he didn't have a clue as to what it all meant.

Bits of chaff stuck to Robert's forehead and his skin itched all over. The hot afternoon sun had baked the sky into a dull enameled glaze. The glare drained color from the fields and made the air thick and heavy.

Frank was allergic to grain dust, or so he said, and his ruddy face was hidden behind a dust mask and goggles. Heavy earphones hugged his large head. Robert watched him furiously pounding out a beat on the combine steering wheel, sweating heavily despite the over-worked air conditioner in his cab. *I'll bet he's listening to the Stones, probably "Sympathy for the Devil*," Robert thought as he tagged along beside his friend. With Frank, Robert always felt like he was tagging along. They were spiraling towards the middle of a quarter section that Frank had irrigated with a center pivot system, a 1,300 foot-long aluminum arm studded with sprinkler heads that moved on wheels like a second hand around a giant clock. The corners of the field grew mostly sagebrush and native grasses that hung low with fat seed heads.

Grain began to spill over the sides of Robert's truck. He honked twice to get Frank's attention, but Frank just kept pounding away on his steering wheel. After a third futile honk, Robert nudged the truck into the combine, jarring Frank from his musical trance. Frank coasted to a stop, stepped out, stretched, pulled off his dustmask, and approached the window of Robert's truck. He was wearing Wrangler jeans that looked new and a red cowboy shirt with pearl snaps, a yoke in back, and dark sweat rings under the armpits. "Pleased to meet you," he said. "Hope you guessed my name."

"I'm puzzled. What's the nature of your game?"

"I tell ya," Frank said. "I lose myself in that song. The Stones could play rock and roll."

"Could? They're not dead you know."

"Shit almighty it's hot!" Frank changed subjects frequently, particularly when he didn't have a response. He slipped a hand under his long, black braid and scratched his back. The earphones hung around his neck like a stethoscope.

"You ought to try sitting in this oven for a change, you think you're hot now," Robert said.

"Me do that kind of grunt work? No way. That's for white people." He slapped his meaty hand on the windowsill of Robert's truck and looked over the field. "We just got a little more to do. Let's leave it till tomorrow. It's getting late."

"Sure enough, Chief. There's only about six hours of day-light left." Robert would have gladly worked twenty hours that day. Anything to avoid going back to the house with Frank where Anna would be waiting.

"Six damned, hot, dusty hours. Let's knock off."

"What if it rains tomorrow?"

"It won't."

"How do you know?"

"I can feel it in my bones. The Great Spirit tells me we're in for a dry period."

"You lie like a dog."

"The paper showed a high pressure ridge the size of Venus centered over eastern Montana."

"That's more like it."

"Let's head back to my place. I'm ready for a drink."

"You're always ready for a drink. Hop in." Robert pushed the remnants of his lunch onto the floor: a plastic sack holding a few remaining bites of a ham and cheese sandwich, an empty can of Coke, a crumpled bag of chips, an apple core. He wondered how he could feel such as sense of dread, almost as if his world was about to come crashing down around him, on such a hot, sunny, seemingly innocent day.

Robert drove two miles over rutted tracks while tall sage scratched the truck's underbelly. The country was drier and harsher than Robert's native South Dakota. Here, they grew more sage, the skies were often clogged with dust, cattle required more land to forage for grass, and the farmers depended upon irrigation to get a crop. The eastern Montana sunsets had more fire, and so did the people. Still, Robert missed his ranch. He longed for the solitude of work, the quiet evenings spent planning his next day's activities while he watched his sheep and cattle and, often, a few deer graze outside his kitchen window. He enjoyed the feel of his sore muscles relaxing at the end of the day, and missed the freedom of having his thoughts to himself.

Unlike Robert, Frank allowed his moods to dictate how hard he'd work on his ranch. Sometimes he would put in long hours, and often when he was by himself, he'd accomplish as much as a small crew. But knocking off early was not at all unusual for him. They pulled up to Frank's house, a flat roofed, box-like structure that was always hot in the summer and cold in winter. It sat alone on the prairie about fifteen miles north of Poplar, Montana, which was the tribal headquarters for the Fort

Peck Indian Reservation. Years ago, Frank and Robert had been schoolmates in South Dakota. Frank returned to the reservation his Senior year of high school, and never again set foot in South Dakota, or so he claimed. At least twice a year, Robert would spend a couple of weeks with Frank on the reservation.

Frank took the earphones from around his neck and left them and the portable CD player on the front seat of the truck. Robert followed him inside.

"We're home, Anna," Frank called to his wife. Anna stepped shyly from the kitchen. She was thirty years old, ten years younger than Frank and about five years younger than Robert. She hadn't yet developed the bulge around the middle that affected her husband and many other residents of this corner of Montana, especially on the reservation. Maybe that was because she was only half-Indian. Besides her mom's Sioux blood, she was a quarter black and a quarter Detroit White Trash, as Frank was fond of saying. Her father had been stationed at Malmstrom Air Force Base near Great Falls where Anna's mom was working at the time. Anna never met her father, or even saw a picture of him. He left the state before he found out that Anna's mother was pregnant. The only presents he gave to his daughter were a milk chocolate complexion as smooth as pond water and a dark, smoky passion which Robert found irresistible.

Anna was wearing a long denim skirt and a white blouse that stuck to her arms and ribs where she was sweating. Her raven black wavy hair shone like it was wet. Small beads of perspiration dotted her upper lip and hairline. The sight of her dark eyes and thin lips sent a current of electricity down Robert's spine. When he was away from her for a long time, which he often was, he'd forget how much or even why he loved her. But seeing her now reminded him that he was willing to pay any price to be with her—even if it meant losing his best friend. Or losing more than that.

Anna nodded to Frank and Robert before returning to the kitchen. Robert's stomach contracted at the sight of her leaving the room and he felt physical pain over her absence. Sometime that evening he and Anna would tell Frank that she was leaving him for Robert.

"What a warm greeting." Frank said. "Ah, the joys of married life. When are you gonna try it?"

The knot in Robert's stomach tightened and he thought he might throw up. Before he could respond, Anna returned with two open cans of Bud. "You were saying, dear?" Her smile had a peculiar mix of warmth and intelligence, but it was a mirthless smile. It seemed as if her mouth and eyes were telling different stories. She handed a can to each of them, turned swiftly and headed outside. Her skirt kicked up a small breeze that cooled the sweat on Robert's face but did nothing to cool the fire in his belly.

"She hasn't been too happy with me since she saw me with Verna at the Dew Drop Inn last week," Frank said.

"I can't imagine why."

"She never did care much for Verna."

"What does Anna think about you sleeping around?" He was fishing for some justification for falling in love with his friend's wife. Maybe Frank wanted to get rid of Anna. If that was true, Robert realized, Frank would want to be the one who decided when and how to end the relationship. *I'm dead*, he thought as he watched Anna through the window as she weeded the carrot patch in the garden behind the house.

"She's probably relieved," Frank said. "I think she's got a lover, too. We haven't been real intimate, Anna and me, for a long, damn time." He drained half his beer and wiped his thin, brown lips with his sleeve. "It don't mean we don't love each other. It's just that we've entered a new phase." Robert's discomfort with the subject was growing more acute with each sentence. He was relieved when Frank turned away to put Jethro Tull's *Aqualung* CD on the stereo. A band of green lights on the amplifier danced in time to the music as Frank made some adjustments to the equalizer. Clumps of matted cat hair dulled the green shag carpet, even though there had not been a cat in the house for a couple of months. Sections of the *New York Times* littered the sofa.

Anna had many interests, her most recent ones being

architecture, psychology, and archeology. Her books and magazines were stacked on and under the coffee table and in piles on the sofa.

"Follow me," Frank said. "Let's fix something to eat."

"This place is disgusting! I'm not going to eat anything from this kitchen. The cleanest things here are the cockroaches." Dirty dishes were stacked in the sink. Robert's shoes stuck to the linoleum floor, and it sounded like he was pulling apart strips of Velcro every time he took a step. "Can't we order pizza or something?"

"Sure, if you don't mind waiting two days for it to get here. They have to ship it Federal Express."

"I think I'd better get drunk before I eat."

"Good idea. Alcohol kills germs." Frank scratched at the long space between his nose and his upper lip. His lips were as thin as if they had been drawn with a brown pencil. His eyebrows turned down where they almost met in the middle of his forehead, making him look angrier than he usually was. He could turn them down even more severely by tightening the muscles above them. The trick served him well, especially in the Tribal Council meetings he'd attended as a member for ten years. Robert had sat in on several council meetings, and it was clear that Frank could scare the crap out of other council members when he wanted to. Most of the tribal members appeared to hate Frank, but in a nod to his intelligence and passion, they elected him chairman two years ago.

Anna and Robert were the only two people who didn't cower under Frank's glare. Robert had heard the story of Frank and Anna's first romantic encounter so many times, he felt like he'd been there. "Cut that shit out!" Anna told Frank the first time he'd tried to stare her down. Frank thought that was the funniest thing he'd ever heard, and he laughed for five minutes after she said it.

"What's so funny?" she asked.

"I think—" He paused to laugh some more and, wiping his eyes, said, "I think I want to marry you."

Then Anna started laughing. Uncontrollably. Harder than

she'd ever laughed before. Until her sides ached.

"What's so goddamn funny?" Frank said, more confused than angry. "I don't propose every day, you know."

She looked at him, started laughing again, and finally said, "Okay."

"Okay, what?"

"Okay, I'll marry you." They both laughed for a long time after that. Two hours later they stopped by a liquor store for a bottle of Old Crow on their way to the Justice of the Peace, where they laughed through the ceremony.

A year after they were married, Anna enrolled in law school at South Dakota State University where she spent three years studying environmental law. She graduated third in her class, but hadn't practiced law or taken the bar exam in the years since her graduation. While she attended school, other tribal members teased Frank about not being able to keep his wife at home. But after he broke bottles over the heads of a few who didn't back down from his stare, the teasing stopped, or at least went underground.

Now, in his kitchen, Frank picked up a wooden spoon, held it like a flute, and played along with Ian Anderson. Two extra speakers were mounted high in separate corners of the kitchen.

"I think I'll take you up on your suggestion to kill some germs," Robert said, getting a beer from the refrigerator. "You ready for another?" He felt like drinking hard today.

"Have you ever known me to say no?"

He shook a can of Bud and tossed it to Frank who pointed it at him before opening it. Across the kitchen floor shot a spray of foam that dried quickly to thick syrup in the heat.

"Grab one for Anna and let's go outside. It's too fuckin' hot in here."

They moved outside to the garden around the back of the house where the corn stalks clattered like bones in the breeze. Anna was bent over harvesting carrots, putting them into a metal colander and piling the green carrot tops at her side. The sight of Anna in that position stirred another wave of sexual desire in Robert. She stood up, brushed the dirt from her knees and accepted the beer. Robert took the colander from her, making sure his fingers grazed hers in the transition, and he began to pull carrots. "How many do you want us to pick?" he asked. Frank had begun to pull carrots too.

"Not too many," she said, holding the can to her forehead. "They're sweeter after a frost."

Frank and Robert moved to the tomato plants and began pulling pigweed from the moist black soil. It had rained hard two nights ago, and the weeds came up easily by the roots. No one talked for a while, which was fine with Robert. Anna sipped her beer while Robert and Frank worked their way through the tomatoes. Color returned to the land as the sun sank lower on the horizon. The tall grass of the prairie took on a reddish hue that made the sky seem bluer than before. The wind had died, and grasshoppers bounded out of Robert's way as he crawled in the garden.

"Let's drive to the lake to watch the sunset," Anna said.

"Good idea," Robert concurred.

Frank also agreed to the plan. He went inside and returned shortly with a backpack and a bottle of Cabernet. "Let's take your car, Robert. Gimme the keys. I'll drive."

Robert tossed him the keys and crawled in the back seat of his 1976 Ford station wagon. Anna climbed in the front next to Frank and they were off to Fort Peck Reservoir. Gravel rattled against the underside of the wagon as Frank navigated the forty miles to the lake. Robert caught occasional glimpses of the Missouri River to their south, marked by dense, serpentine bands of cottonwoods. Heads of whitetail deer popped up as the car went by, and small bunches of antelope romped the prairie, seemingly caught up in the sheer joy of running.

Frank parked by a boat ramp on the northeast corner of the reservoir. They decided to hike a half-mile to the top of a clay butte that rose a couple of hundred feet above the prairie floor. The temperature was about ten degrees cooler near the lake and was dropping even more in the waning sun of the late afternoon, but Frank was sweating profusely by the time they got to the butte. "We should have driven the car over here, saved us some steps," he said.

"Nonsense, dear. You're just out of shape."

"Bullshit! I'm in superb shape. I just sweat more than you."

"And pant more, honey," she said with a wink.

Anna's movements were effortless. She seemed to glide rather than walk up the butte. Her thin legs showed little strain as she ascended the steep, rocky path. When they got to the top, they sat facing west on a table rock on the edge of the butte's summit. The sun had just touched the horizon as they settled themselves. A few thin clouds formed deep, crimson gashes in the sky. The sound of crickets made the land seem more alive than it had been in the heat of the day. Below them stretched an enormous man-made reservoir, a pool of blue water 135 miles long that spread out over a quarter million acres of prairie. The entire lake was backed up behind a four-mile long berm of dirt. A couple of fishing boats rippled its otherwise glassy surface.

"I don't know about you, but I'd be nervous about living downstream from the dam," Robert said. "All that water…"

"I don't really think about it," Frank said, still panting.

Uncomfortable with the silence, Robert continued with the questions, this time for Anna. "What are you studying this week?"

"You'll make fun of me. It's kind of obscure."

"No I won't,"

"Yes I will," Frank said at the same time.

"Shut up, Frank," Robert said. Then, turning to Anna, he said, "Go ahead and tell me. He's too out-of-breath to tease you anyway."

"I'm learning about radioactive waste disposal."

"You're finally thinking of cleaning your kitchen?"

"Robert!"

"Sorry."

"I've been studying about half-lives, isotopes,

transportation modes, burial methods, and stable geologic structures."

Frank took three water-spotted wineglasses from his backpack and passed one to Robert and another to Anna. "No wonder I was so tired hiking up the hill. I was carrying all the weight."

"You can say that again, dear," Anna said, patting his stomach.

"Let me help you lighten your load." Robert held his glass to Frank, who filled it generously with wine that looked shockingly red in the waning sunlight. Mosquitoes buzzed in their ears and the wine sloshed in their glasses as they slapped at the bugs with their free hands.

"Why nuclear waste?" Robert asked, trying to postpone the impending confrontation with Frank. The only thing he dreaded more than confronting Frank was losing Anna. Both options were awful, and he longed for simpler choices. "Well?" he said to Anna, who also seemed lost in thought. Anna's passions always had a purpose. Too bad she never pursued any of them to their conclusion. She lacked confidence despite her beauty and intelligence. Robert assumed that being an Indian and a woman contributed to her self-destructive tendencies, but he'd never discussed it with her.

"I think it's an issue all of us on the reservation may have to live with soon."

"Or die with," Frank added.

"Or die with," Anna agreed, her voice barely a whisper. She sipped her wine, set the glass on the rock and looked at the scarlet and gold sunset. The surface of the reservoir doubled the sunset's colors. A slight breeze carried the smell of water from the lake.

"What the hell's that supposed to mean?" Robert asked, picking a mosquito from his wineglass with a dirty finger.

"Official tribal business, white man," Frank said.

"Don't give me this 'official business' bullshit. Tell me what's going on."

"Don't push this one, my friend," Frank said. "Let it drop for now."

"What about you, Anna? Are you going to fill me in?"

"Not now," she said, tossing back her hair with a shake of her head. "This one's his call. He's the council member." Her face reflected the reddish hue of the sunset.

They finished the bottle of wine in silence. Robert's irritation faded slowly like the dying rays of the sun. Frank pulled a flask of whisky from the backpack, took a swallow and passed it to Anna. The sun had just sunk below the surface of the lake as they began talking again. Anna had a knack for storytelling. Her voice was soft and melodic and Robert used to encourage her to get a job on the radio, but she was intimidated by all that technology in the studios. He suggested that Frank teach her about the technology since Frank knew more about sound systems, communication devices, and computers than anyone he'd ever met.

"You're single," she said. "You've never tried to teach a spouse anything. If you had, you'd know how stupid your suggestion was."

He let it drop. He didn't like talking about Frank and Anna's marriage anyway.

Despite the colorful sunset and panoramic view of the lake, Robert wasn't enjoying the evening. His friends had called him a stupid white man, and his stomach was still in knots over the prospect of talking to Frank about Anna when they got back to the house. The alcohol was helping though. He wanted more.

As night stole color from the sky, Anna told a story about a fox hunting a rabbit. Two or three times the fox had the hare cornered, but the wily rabbit always managed to escape. Robert loved the sound of her voice so much that he often forgot to pay attention to her words. She would get angry and accuse him of ignoring her. But he wasn't being rude; he was just lulled into a trance by her voice. It was beginning to happen to him again tonight. Try as he might in the weeks that followed this evening on the butte, he couldn't remember how the rabbit managed to escape. The drinks may have had something to do with it. *It's a shame she doesn't have children*, he thought as she told her story. Just the sound of her voice could calm the worst tantrum. *Maybe someday she'll have mine.*

When she finished, Frank said to her, "Tell me about your new lover."

"Frank!"

"You're my wife. I'm curious."

"Why do you always get this way when you drink?"

Robert's head began to throb, and he reached for the flask. It was empty.

"I don't always get this way," Frank said. "I usually become a mean son-of-a-bitch. This time, I'm just curious. What's this guy like? What do you like about him?"

"I think a change of subjects is definitely in order," Robert said. "Let's head back. By the time we get to the car, Frank'll be so winded, he'll forget what he asked you about." Frank didn't push it. *Thank God*, Robert thought as he stood to stretch his legs. Again Robert began to miss his ranch. After his mother had died and his former girlfriend returned to her native New Mexico, the ranch was all that was left to comfort him. He had healed himself through it even as he healed the land and turned it into one of the most productive ranches in his state.

A streak of lightning split the black sky as they made their way down the butte. "I thought you said it wouldn't rain today," Robert said.

"That's just heat lightning. Nothing to worry about," Frank replied. Just then, they heard the distant rumble of thunder. "Goddamn newspapers. You can't trust 'em. You'd think the weather reports were put out by the goddamn Chamber of Commerce."

That's just like Frank, Robert thought. *Blaming someone or something else when he's wrong.* Several more streaks of lightning forked through the southwestern sky as they made their way to the car.

"The storm's headed right for us," Robert said.

"Fucking weather reports," Frank grumbled.

"At least the lightning helps us see where we're going," Anna said.

Robert drove home as the three of them watched the oncoming storm in silence. The thunder was soft but continual by the time they returned to the house. Frank was the first to enter. He flicked on the light and collapsed heavily on the sofa. Anna curled up next to him, fitting snugly under the arm he'd draped over the back of the couch. She looked so cozy and soft. Robert was jealous. He pictured her curled up under his arm as he leaned over to kiss her forehead. He imagined the smell of her as he pulled her a little tighter. He could see himself lifting her face with a finger so he could bring his lips to hers. And he could imagine the feel of her breasts through the thin material of her blouse—

"Wake up and get us a beer, Robert," Frank said.

Robert tilted his head like he was trying to drain the daydream from it. "Okay, but if I get stuck to your kitchen floor, come get me."

"We'll throw you a rope."

He returned with three beers and sticky soles. "We'd better get that grain under shelter before the rain gets here."

"I suppose you're right, goddamn it to hell," Frank said. "Here's the keys."

"Wait a minute," Robert said. "Let's draw straws to see who drives the truck to the garage." The combination shop and garage was about 100 yards from the house. It was a barnwood shack with holes in its roof, but it would keep most of the rain off the grain.

"You got any money on you?" Frank asked.

"I'm not paying to get out of it."

"No. We'll flip for it. Give me three coins."

Robert tossed him two pennies and a dime.

"No, you idiot. Give me a quarter."

He gave Frank and Anna each a quarter. "I've only got two."

"I don't give a fuck what you flip with, man."

"Odd man—or woman—has to move the truck."

Another clap of thunder gave the task some urgency. They flipped their coins in unison. All of them had tails. The second time, Anna had tails and the two men had heads.

"Sorry, Love," Frank said, tossing her the keys.

"I think I'll use this break effectively," Robert said, heading to the bathroom.

"It's broken," Anna reminded him.

He stepped into the damp night air on his way to the outhouse. The crickets were making a racket outside. The stink of the outhouse overwhelmed the smell of damp earth and ozone from the approaching storm, but considering the condition of Frank and Anna's house, the outhouse seemed one of the most sanitary places around. Honestly, he preferred it to their kitchen.

It was dark inside. He was woozy from alcohol and the smell of the outhouse, but he managed to pull down his pants and sit in just the right spot. A sliver of moon appeared in the hole at the top of the door. Holding his head as still as possible, he watched the moon slide past the hole on its way across the sky. It didn't take long, maybe a minute or two. Then there was nothing. Only blackness. The crickets still buzzed loudly just outside the door.

He suddenly realized that Frank had kept his quarter after the coin toss that Anna had lost. Robert shook his head and smiled at Frank's behavior. *So that's why he needed a quarter instead of a penny*, he thought as he heard the truck door open and slam shut.

Suddenly, the world erupted in a blinding flash of light. It was as if a piece of the sun had dropped into the yard. The light seared his flesh and eyes with a heat so intense that it burned into his soul.

There was no sound. He watched the outhouse disintegrate, and then something that felt like wind hit him so hard it knocked his breath away.

The light began to dim around the edges of his vision. He was looking through a camera shutter until there was just a pinpoint of light at the end of a long tunnel.

He tried desperately to crawl his way to the light, but it stayed for only a second. Then it was gone and the darkness overtook him.

CHAPTER 2

The sun in Robert's eyes woke him up, and he lay quietly for a few moments blinking in the afternoon glare.

"I thought you'd never come to, man," Frank said.

Robert lifted his head and looked around, confused and in pain. He had not awakened in Frank's yard in the middle of the afternoon since his college days. He could see from where he lay that the front half of Frank and Anna's house, including the room that looked out over the garden, had been torn completely away. The kitchen and the bathroom, two of the most useless rooms in the house, seemed to be intact. Then he remembered. *The explosion!*

What was it that had caused the night to literally blow up in his face? And where was Anna?

"Looks like you might of broke a couple of ribs, judging by the bruises on your side. Got a nasty cut on your head, too. Not very deep, but it bled like a son-of-a-bitch. You look like hell. I can't find your pants anywhere."

Indeed, Robert was without pants or shoes. His shirt, or what remained of it, hung in strips from his shoulders. His chest was scabbed in dried blood from many small cuts and scrapes.

What the hell happened last night? He wondered. *And where was Anna?* His grogginess made it difficult to sort his thoughts.

Frank was on his stomach next to him. The ground was wet from what had obviously been a hard rain the night before. "I thought you were going to drown like a turkey last night," Frank said. "I had to rest your head on that," Frank pointed to the remains of his portable CD player. "To keep your face out of a puddle. How you feeling now?" He squinted into the sun.

Robert's head throbbed and his ribs ached. He was light-headed and thought he might be suffering from shock. "Like I lost a fight. Badly," he said. "What about you?"

"No pain at all."

"That's because you drank so much last night."

"I wish that were the case, my friend."

Robert felt the blood drain from his face. A red triangle of fear with sharp points lodged in his stomach. He was scared to hear what Frank had to say next, but he asked anyway. "What are you trying to tell me?"

"My legs don't work."

"Oh my God!" Robert stood up as quickly as he could. Swaying dizzily and holding his aching ribs, he hovered over Frank, whose shirt was torn and bloody. He ripped open the rest of Frank's shirt and discovered a patch of crusted blood encircling a dime-sized area of torn flesh in his lower back. "Jesus, Frank! You've been shot!"

"No, man. I got hit by a piece of the house, which, I might add, is even more of a wreck now than it was before the bomb went off."

"What do you mean, a bomb? Who the hell would want to bomb your place?"

"Someone who wants me dead, I'd guess."

"That's crazy! It doesn't make any sense." Robert was lost in his fear and confusion. "Who'd want to bomb you?"

"I intend to find out. I promise you I will get to the bottom of this, legs or no legs."

"Why are you so calm?" Robert said. "Someone just tried to kill you!"

"I've had half a day more than you to deal with it."

"Half a day to get used to being paralyzed and losing your house? That's a pretty quick recovery. We've got to get you to a doctor, fast. And where's Anna? Did she go off to find some help?"

Frank's eyes watered as he lay silently. His mouth moved as if he was trying to speak, but no sounds came out.

Again, Robert felt the blood drain from his face. He slumped to his knees, ignoring the stabbing pain in his ribs and landed on the earphones he'd left in the pickup. He covered his head with his arms to shut out the terrible realization dawning on him.

Not Anna! She can't be dead. He couldn't imagine the world without her. Their lives were supposed to be tied together forever. That was the plan. She couldn't be dead. "I don't believe you. Where is she? Tell me!"

"Part of her's still in the truck."

"Oh God, no!" He began to sob. "No! No! Tell me it's not true!"

"Part of her's behind the house. Some of her's in the garden. I haven't found the rest. But then, I don't get around so good now."

"Stop it, Frank!" he screamed. "Just shut the fuck up. I can't listen to any more of this!" His shoulders bobbed as he pictured her face and remembered the sound of her voice. His love for her poured out of him and spilled on the ground like blood. He could feel the life force drain from his body in his grief. His head drooped onto Frank's shoulder.

"Cut that shit out!" Frank yelled. "I don't want you getting my shirt wet. I fucking hate it when people cry. Especially men!" He shuddered lightly. "And I don't like to be touched by a man, either. Get your head off my shoulder."

"Goddamn you!" Robert yelled. "Your wife was just murdered, and you're worried about your shirt? To hell with your shirt! It's shredded and it stinks." He punched the ground with his fist, which doubled him over in pain. It felt as if someone had just stuck a knife between his ribs. "If I wasn't so banged up, I think I'd beat the hell out of you."

Frank grabbed him by the shirt and pulled him close. His arm was as strong as ever. "I'm angry, my friend. Real fucking angry." His eyebrows didn't dip in the middle like they did when he was trying to scare someone. "I don't want to lose it by feeling sad. I'm going to use this anger to find the bastard who did this, and I'm going to make him pay. Do you understand?" He let go of Robert's shirt.

"And I'm going to help you find that murdering bastard."

"The fuck you are. Like I told you last night, this is official tribal business."

Robert remembered their discussion about nuclear waste. "You're in no position to be ordering me around or doing things on your own, you gimpy son-of-a-bitch. She was my friend, too. And I want to kill the bastard who did this, too. I'm going to find out why she died. I'd rather work with you than against you, but I'll get to the bottom of this one way or another."

"You're a stubborn S.O.B., almost as stubborn as me."

"So we're working together?"

"Fuck you."

"Fuck you, too, my friend." With Frank, a fuck you, delivered in the right tone, was as good as a handshake.

Robert stood up slowly holding his ribs and looked over the damage.

A fine coating of wet grain from the back of the destroyed truck covered the ground like mulch. He could see the trails where Frank, in his crippled state, had snaked his way across the property. The area around the remains of the truck was particularly disturbed. Frank had evidently explored that area thoroughly. It was probably the place where he'd first discovered Anna's remains.

Another trail led to and from the house, another to and from the garden. Lots of tracks circled the place where he, Robert, had lain unconscious, oblivious to Frank's pain. A couple of mice skittered in the grain, making much smaller tracks than Frank's. They were having a marvelous day, enjoying the windfall brought on by the tragedy.

A two-foot deep crater marked the place where the bomb exploded. The grain truck's cab had been blown twenty yards away and lay on the ground, twisted and mangled like a crushed tin can. Robert started crying again as he thought about part of Anna still in there and Frank crawling over to find her.

"You need a doctor right away," Robert said. . "I'm not going to move you since you have a spine injury. You shouldn't have crawled around so much."

Frank grunted, but did not protest Robert's decision to leave him behind.

"I've got a fifteen mile drive to town, assuming my car still works." The bomb had blown out the windows on the passenger side of his station wagon. He wiped his eyes with his sleeve. "I'd better get started. What do you need before I go?"

"I need some shade over my head. It's gonna get hot soon."

Robert struggled to pile rocks on both sides of Frank's head, holding his ribs with one hand as he worked. He found an old blanket in the remains of the house, and he spread it across the rocks for shade, piling more rocks on top to keep it in place. The kitchen sink still worked, so he used it to fill a small bucket for Frank to drink from.

"Anything else?"

"Yeah. A bottle of whisky for my pain. I'd get it myself, but I'm tired of crawling around. And get some pants on, goddamn it!"

He found some sandals and a pair of jeans in the bedroom. They were much too short, and he had to suck in his stomach to fasten them.

They were Anna's.

* * * *

Sheriff Charlie Broadbow's office in Poplar smelled moldy, as if the doors hadn't been opened in a long time. A desk fan hummed loudly as it stirred the hot air.

"Sit down, Robert," the sheriff said. "I've got a few questions to ask you."

"Ask me later, Charlie. Get on the phone now, then we'll talk."

"No, I want to talk first. I thought you might give me some insight." Charlie leaned back in his chair until he almost tipped over. His oversized head came to rest on the wall behind him, pushing his face forward and doubling the number of his chins. His hands were folded across his belly, which was as smooth and sculpted as a dish of soft ice cream. His fat bottom lip covered his upper one as he smiled at Robert.

"There's time to talk later. Frank needs to get to the hospital right away. He can't move his legs."

"Hospital? You didn't tell me this was a medical emergency. Hang on." Charlie called the Indian Health Service to order an ambulance. He started yelling into the receiver. "I don't give a goddamn what you're doing now. You get your ass in that ambulance right this minute!" He slammed the phone down, and soon afterwards, Robert heard the unusually reassuring sound of a siren.

"Now we can talk," Robert said. "What did you want to know?"

Charlie put his face up next to the bowl that housed his pet fish, Golda. His face, when seen through glass and water, looked even bigger. His eyes were hockey pucks, and the pockmarks in his cheeks looked like craters, his mouth a fleshy cave. "Why don't you start by telling me what happened."

Robert's eyes started to water again as he thought about the bomb that ended Anna's life and paralyzed Frank. He wanted a drink. Instead, he cleared his throat to help the words get past the lump that had formed in it. Then he retold the story of helping Frank harvest wheat, the evening of drinking, and then the explosion. He had to pause as he thought about the inordinately high price Anna had paid for losing something so simple as a coin toss.

Charlie watched intently as Robert told his story. "I'll send the Bureau of Indian Affairs cops out there to investigate since Frank's house is in their jurisdiction. I'm just a county sheriff." Charlie bounced his fist a couple of times on his desk. "They aren't going to be able to find Frank's house, much less conduct a competent criminal investigation. I already know what the tribal cops'll put in their report. They'll say the truck was carrying some dynamite in the back end, and a spark accidentally set it off."

"But that's BS. Frank wasn't carrying any dynamite. Why would he be doing that?"

"I don't know. Maybe he was planning to go fishing. Dynamite's a great way to catch fish from ponds. The point is that it doesn't matter to the BIA boys. That's what they'll say so they won't have to look any farther."

"But you and I know it was murder, right?"

"That brings up another point I wanted to discuss with you, Robert. I don't know how to bring this up delicately, so I'm just going to flat out ask you." He strummed his fat lower lip a couple of times. "I heard you were screwing Anna. Any truth to the rumor?"

Robert turned his back to the sheriff and drew in a deep breath. He nodded slowly. "For about the last six months."

"When'd you get a chance? You live 400 miles away."

"I've been here twice, she's met me in a few places. Here and there." He turned back towards Charlie. "Don't tell Frank if you can avoid it."

"He's the one who told me."

"Oh, shit!" He buried his face in his hand. *So Frank knew all along*, Robert thought. *Why hasn't he shot me yet?*

Frank's infidelities were practically legendary around the reservation. No one knew why Anna put up with him, and a lot of people hoped she'd leave him. Robert had heard people say this about her. But maybe she was like many people on the reservation and its tribal council who felt a reluctant attraction to

Frank. He had an odd form of integrity and intelligence that people could not help admiring. He had no respect for other people's personal space or property. But the future of the reservation and the people who called it home had no fiercer guardian than Frank.

Most people would be happy that Anna had found a chance for happiness by falling in love with another man. *But why did it have to be me?* Robert wondered yet again. The hardest thing was not being able to talk to Frank about it. Robert hated secrets, and yet, he hadn't been able to force himself to discuss the situation with Frank before the accident. It came down to whether Robert loved Frank or Anna the most, and since Robert hadn't told Frank that he was in love with Anna, the question remained unanswered.

Now there was only Frank to love, and Frank made that pretty difficult.

"Why'd you bring this up?" Robert asked.

"Does it have anything to do with the fact that she's dead?"

Robert's cheeks burned with anger. "Of course not!" *How dare he suggest that I'd kill Anna! I loved her*, he thought. *I'd rather have killed myself.*

"Now if you don't mind, or even if you do, I'm going to go see a doctor, too. I'm a little banged up myself."

"It wasn't an unreasonable question on my part," Charlie said.

"Think you can fuck another man's wife on this reservation and keep it a secret?" Charlie yelled as Robert limped his way to the clinic.

People in the street didn't bother to look up.

CHAPTER 3

Before the accident, Frank was built like a buffalo, with strong arms, a barrel chest, a stomach like a sofa pillow, and skinny little legs. The injury that cost him the use of his legs exaggerated those dimensions. He drove his wheelchair the way teenagers drive cars, using his strong arms to push himself along at breakneck speed even as his legs withered.

While he waited for his home to be repaired, Frank devoted considerable energy to remodeling the shack he rented in the nearby town of Poplar. Already, he had managed to convert his rental from a dump into a disaster, all while sitting in a wheelchair. He had littered the front yard with carcasses of old trucks, broken what little furniture there was, and scorched the kitchen walls with a grease fire that, by rights, should have burned down the whole house and killed Frank in the process.

The man possessed boundless reserves of energy. At all hours, the sounds of the Stones, Led Zeppelin, the Doors, Janice, Jimi, and an incongruous song or two from Joni Mitchell blared from the shell of his house. There were nearly 800 people living in Poplar when Frank moved to town. Robert predicted the population would surely decrease because of

Frank's presence. Sure enough, two neighbors had already moved away because of him.

A couple of weeks after getting Frank settled into his new house, Robert returned to South Dakota. Fall had arrived almost overnight and the mornings now sparkled with frost.

Four years ago Robert's widowed mother had died, leaving him in sole possession of nearly 1,000 acres of farm and ranchland near the town of Millington in south central South Dakota. He'd spent much of the past four years undoing his father's life work, converting back into range land most of the land his dad had plowed and seeded to wheat.

His dad had died in a tractor accident while tearing up virgin sod that Robert believed should have been spared the touch of the plow. Just before Robert left for college, he watched his dad tip a tractor while plowing the side of a hill near his house. The tractor had thrown his father downhill and, as he scrambled to get out of its way, it had rolled over him like a large mechanical predator, crushing his skull and severing both arms he had thrown up for protection from the machine he thought would be his economic salvation..

Now, as Robert looked at the hill from his kitchen window, he couldn't help wondering why his dad had to pay such a high price for one bad decision. It was the same question he asked of Anna, who died because she lost the flip of a coin.

Under Robert's stewardship, the native grasses on the ranch were reclaiming more acreage every year. The place had more deer and antelope on it than any similarly sized ranch in the state. He raised bands of sheep and cattle that grazed together in what he called his "Desegregation Project." Robert made little money but spent even less, turned a profit every year, and drove away most of his friends and neighbors through his unconventional management of the place.

Although the ranch was comfortable, Robert was restless when he returned. The chores he had loved now felt like work, the cold days stung rather than invigorated, the livestock seemed like pests.

After four months, he was ready to return to Montana.

Here, he had too much time to think about Anna and no one with whom he could share his grief. He knew that his relationship with Anna had a toxic quality to it that both frightened and excited him, and he had tried many times to stay away from her. But all it took was a call from her, and he would find himself pacing the floor of a motel room waiting for her to show up.

After Anna's death, Robert became obsessed with the task of making sense of her loss. The love and desire left in absence was like organic debris from a flood. All the feelings were jumbled, thrown together in a haphazard way that was impossible to sort out.

He thought of killing himself to end the tedium of trying to understand the riddle of her death. He imagined blowing himself up in a truck so that he could have known what she went through in that last moment of consciousness.

Yet he knew that made no sense, and sense was something he desperately needed now. He had to understand the reason for her death, even if it was "official tribal business" as Frank had so patronizingly put it. So he decided to leave the comfort of his ranch to join forces with Frank to find her killer.

One of the few friends Robert still had in Millington was Sammy Carter, a recovering alcoholic in his mid-thirties, about Robert's age. Sammy had worked on just about every ranch in the county at one time or another since he had left his own family's ranch at age fifteen. The last few years, he'd spent about half his time at Robert's place, feeding cattle and running the place when Robert was gone. He was a good worker, especially now that he had given up drinking. He was also one of the few people around who did not think Robert's unconventional ranching practices were crazy. He was happy to hire on to look after the place while Robert returned to Montana.

"Don't get yourself killed," he said as Robert climbed into his car to leave.

"Don't worry. Whoever I'm looking for probably doesn't even know I exist."

"I meant by Frank."

Robert hadn't told anyone about his affair with Anna except Charlie, the sheriff. But he had told Sammy lots of Frank stories over the years.

"That guy is one colorful dude. He almost makes me miss drinking," Sammy would say, shaking his head.

Robert showed up unannounced at Frank's rented house in Poplar with two cups of coffee and a box of powdered sugar doughnuts. It was a bright early-January morning, and dawn still painted the eastern horizon with chilly pink and blue washes from a broad brush.

It was a colorful, if unsettled, beginning to a new year. He went inside to discover Frank asleep in his wheelchair next to the computer. On the screen was a full color picture of a woman servicing two men who stood on each side of her.

Frank had evidently been trading pictures over the computer with Internet friends from around the globe. Frank's online name was "FRANK K B," plain and simple.

Robert played with the keyboard to check out Frank's profile. He wanted to see what kind of lies Frank was exchanging with his faceless girlfriends in Oklahoma City, San Diego, Kansas City and other places across the country. He'd listed himself as Frank Kicking Bird, and his profile said he was a forty-year-old, bad-assed, pot bellied, ill tempered Assiniboine living on the Fort Peck Indian Reservation. A surprisingly accurate description, Robert thought.

The computer chirped like a bird as an Instant Message flashed across the screen. It said: "Still there, honey? I'm not nearly through with you!"

Fascinated, Robert typed "What do you have in mind next? Be explicit!" Then he moved the pointer to the "Send" button and clicked the button on the mouse.

"Who the fuck is this?" came the angry reply. "Frank would never use a work like 'Explicit!'"

Robert exited and shut off the machine, which said "Goodbye!" in a pleasant voice just before the power went out.

"Good-bye—" Frank muttered. "Oh it's you," he said, rais-ing his head. After a belch, he said, "I was hoping you'd never show up again."

"Thanks for the welcome." Robert's shoes stuck to the lino-leum floor as they had in the old house.

"At least you had the decency to bring breakfast." Frank grabbed the box of doughnuts.

"So, are we ready to solve the crime?" Robert hadn't talked to Frank since the week after the murder, but he'd consulted often with Frank's physicians and Charlie, the policeman in Poplar. Charlie Broadbow maintained an interest in the case even though it was technically outside his jurisdiction.

"Quiet! I fucking hate to talk during breakfast." He sprayed powdered sugar on the rug as he spoke. When he'd eaten four doughnuts, he pointed to a corner of the room and said, "Grab that bag and throw it in the back of the pickup." Then he took off for the truck in his wheelchair.

"Where are we going?" Robert called to Frank.

"You'll see."

Frank's truck was a canary yellow, rusted 1966 Dodge short bed pickup. He had rigged it with a series of wheels and levers that allowed him to work the clutch, gas, and brake with his hands instead of his feet. Cracks webbed the windshield, and the window on Robert's side was shattered. Empty Bud-weiser cans rattled about the floor.

"We've got about a forty-five minute drive." Robert did not ask him again where they were going. Frank probably wouldn't have heard him anyway, since he already had on the earphones. The tinny sounds Robert heard coming from the earphones were from the band "Traffic." Robert pulled the plug on the earphones so he could hear the music better.

"Anyone else fuck with my music like that, I'd kill them on the spot." Frank removed the phones from his ears. "For you, I want to take my time, think up a slow torture." He scratched his armpit. "I'll let you off this time if you reach back and get me a beer from the cooler."

"Frank! It's 10:30 in the morning."

"So what? I got doughnuts to wash down."

Robert opened the sliding window behind him and reached back into a box that held a dozen loose cans of beer. The air was cold and damp, and he was glad he wore gloves. Icy clouds softened the eggshell sky, now drained of its pastel colors, and dry leaves rustled below the bare branches of cottonwoods along the creeks. Robert handed a beer to Frank and zipped up his insulated denim coat.

They bounced over blacktops, county roads, abandoned oil field roads, and tracks on the prairie. Robert tried to take a sip of his beer but it was frozen. He noticed that Frank had completely removed the top of his beer with a can opener. A minute later, Frank threw the empty can out the window and asked Robert for another one.

"Don't throw things out the window," Robert said. "I don't care if this is your reservation."

Frank slammed the truck to a halt, pulled his body awkwardly through the sliding window and grabbed another beer from the back end.

He sat back heavily in his seat and after removing the top of the can he said, "I'm not too thrilled to see you, my friend." He belched loudly, patted his belly like he was proud of it and continued. "You got no business here, this is a tribal matter, you don't know what the fuck you're doing, and you're a white guy."

"I'm happy to see you too, Frank." It was best not to argue with him when he was in one of these moods, which he usually was, but Robert couldn't resist. "This is not just a tribal matter, it's a personal matter. I don't give a shit about tribal business." Robert noticed that he cussed more when he was around Frank.

"Bullshit, you don't. How come you like to sit in on our Council meetings if you don't give a shit? You're a goddamn wannabe."

"You're a friend, Frank. I just wanted to see what you did with your life when you weren't screwing around on Anna." Robert threw this last sentence at Frank like it was a rock.

"Don't you talk about Anna. Don't you ever fucking bring

her up again!"

"You'd better get used to it. She's the reason I'm here. And I plan to find out who killed her."

"We got that in common," Frank said, apparently backing away from the argument. "Hand me another beer so I can begin to warm it up, and let's roll."

Frank threw the beer on the dashboard near the defroster and put the truck into gear. Robert turned around to see the dust roil behind the truck as it lurched toward its destination.

Thirty minutes later Frank stopped the truck and peered at something in the distance through a set of binoculars.

"See that over there?" He handed Robert the glasses.

Robert got out of the truck, stretched his legs and looked over the clumps of sagebrush that held little pockets of dirty snow behind them. He spotted an old mesh fence surrounding an area roughly five acres in size. Much of the wire mesh was either lying on the ground or had rusted away. Loops of razor wire drooped from the top railing like curls of hair. Behind it was an old wooden fence that was missing several planks.

"What am I looking at, Frank?"

"Sometime back in the late '60s, a mining company leased this part of the Rez. They promised jobs, jobs, and more fucking jobs, and we rose to the bait like dumb, hungry fish. My dad was on the council back then and he cast the only vote against the lease. That was the last vote he ever cast on the Council 'cause they threw him out afterwards."

Frank took a dirty handkerchief from his pocket and rubbed his nose with it. "He never got over his bitterness about it. Two weeks later someone found him dead in his car on that very spot. Right over there near the fence."

"Do you still think he was murdered?" Robert sighed. He had been over this ground with Frank many times before.

"Of course he was murdered, you idiot!"

"What about the hose that ran from his exhaust into his car?"

"Those dumb tribal cops," Frank said. "What the fuck do

they know? He was a fighter, my old man. He was planning to kill the mining project, not himself." Frank squinted at the area for a moment.

"What happened to the project?"

"Somebody salted the core drillings with high grade coal. Turns out that there was a little coal, but it was so soft you could not get it to burn with a blowtorch. The company that leased the site abandoned it a couple months after they began their operation. I haven't been here since my old man died, but it looks like a few other people have, judging from the tracks. Grab that sack from the back."

Robert pulled a heavy duffel bag from the pickup bed and set it on the ground. He zipped it open and pulled out what looked to be a couple of insulated astronaut suits. "To quote *Annie Hall*, 'What are we doing, Frank? Driving through plutonium?'"

Frank spit out the truck window. "Maybe. Call it a hunch. You'd better pee now. You'll never find your pecker after you get into these suits. Hand me an empty beer can."

The two men struggled into their suits. Frank took longer because he could not use his legs. They drove closer to the site and stopped the truck. Robert grabbed Frank's folded wheelchair from the pickup bed and set it up. Then he pushed Frank awkwardly fifty yards to the fenced site.

The ground was frozen, which made it easier to push the wheelchair, but clumps of sagebrush and pockets of dirty snow slowed their journey.

"I got these suits at an Army Navy store in Albuquerque a couple of years ago. They're supposed to keep out radiation, but I don't know if they still work." Frank spat on the ground. "Better put on our helmets. I don't know what kind of shit we'll find in there."

Frank looked like a character from *Dr. No.* The helmet covered his entire head and Robert could not see his eyes through the darkened Plexiglas window.

"Can you hear me?" Frank said. The helmets were equipped with small microphones. Only Frank's worked.

Robert kicked in a few rotten fence boards and the two of them marched and wheeled their way into the abandoned dumpsite. Scores of barrels littered the ground. Some were still stacked in pyramids, but others had collapsed after the rusting corroded barrels on bottom could no longer support the weight. There must have been close to a thousand of them on the site. Some had had their tops and bottoms removed and a half dozen or so spokes had been welded inside each cylinder.

Frank pointed to them and said in a tinny voice through his microphone, "Birdcages."

Robert had no idea what he meant. In the middle of the site were a dozen concrete-lined trenches, each about a hundred yards long. Some of them appeared empty except for a layer of snow. Others were partially filled with dirt that had mostly washed away, exposing another supply of partially buried barrels. A couple of aging bulldozers sat rusting nearby.

Frank nodded to a tin shed on the east side of the site next to an old truck scale. "Let's check it out," he said. His voice sounded like it came from a cheap radio. "Maybe the rapists left a card."

At first, Robert thought the ping was just the sound of the barrels expanding in the afternoon sun. But the second time he heard it, he saw a little tuft of dust erupt near Frank's wheelchair. A cool logic took over and he wheeled Frank as fast as he could behind a stack of barrels.

A third shot penetrated a barrel and slammed into the wooden planks behind them. Viscous liquid, in all likelihood some of the most toxic stuff on earth, drained from the container and stained the dirt between them.

Robert lifted the wheel of Frank's chair and spilled him onto the ground. "Stay low!" he shouted. But the sounds of his words were stuck in his helmet.

Frank crawled surprisingly quickly to the edge of the stack and looked around it while Robert peered from the other side. Ping! Another shot hit a barrel inches to the right of Frank's head. Black liquid drained onto the leg of Frank's suit. He crawled back to Robert.

"There's two of them," he said. "Dressed like us in these monkey suits. I can't believe we didn't hear them drive up. Must be 'cause we've got our heads in these buckets."

Robert spelled "GUN?" in the dust between them. Frank just shook his head.

"I got beer, I got doughnuts, I got four dollars and seventy-six cents. But I don't have a fucking gun."

Another ping. This one slammed harmlessly into the barrels where Frank had been before he crawled over to Robert. More liquid spilled onto the ground. Robert again looked around the barrels, noting briefly the irony of using containers of toxic waste for protection.

He saw a man on the other side of the rotting wooden fence looking for them through binoculars. Another man began moving slowly towards them and was putting on the same kind of helmet they wore. He was only about a hundred yards away, and Robert saw something in his hand reflect the sunlight. Probably the stainless steel barrel of a pistol.

Robert wrote "Stay!" in the dust and took off at a dead run for the tin shed.

A wave of panic washed over him when a slug tugged his suit near his calf. It felt like he'd snagged it on barbed wire. Luckily, it didn't break the skin. He hurled himself into the door at full speed.

The lock gave so easily that he almost went through the wall on the opposite end of the shack. He knew his only advantage was that ninety percent of the time, the attackers couldn't see Frank and him. That advantage would disappear in about two minutes when the man passed through the rotting fence.

The inside of the shed looked like a small high school chemistry lab. There were a couple of Bunsen burners and beakers on a table. A box of wooden matches sat nearby. Dark colored bottles lined the shelves above the table, and heavy, empty containers that looked like sculpture molds lay on the floor. Robert opened the one drawer in the desk, and quickly looked over its useless contents of pencils, log forms, paper clips, and an old pack of Pall Malls.

He ran to a closet and found some more radiation suits. He arranged one on the ground outside the shack to look as if it were a person laying down. He was planning to ambush their attacker at the fence, but the man entered the compound about thirty seconds earlier than Robert had anticipated. The man in the suit fired four rounds into the dummy. Then he went down like he'd been tackled. Frank had hit him in the knees with a crowbar. How Frank got there so fast was a mystery.

What the man's face looked like before Frank worked him over was also a mystery. Frank hit him a dozen times before Robert was able to stop him.

"Fucking dump your shit on my land, will you?" Frank was shouting. "Think you can fuck us just because we're Indians?" Another blow to the man's head sounded like a watermelon splitting.

Jesus, Robert thought. *This guy's face looks like a pasta dish with tomato sauce.* "We still have another one to go!" Robert shouted, the sound echoing uselessly inside his helmet. He pointed to where the attacker's truck was parked and held up a gloved finger.

Frank shook his head and said through his microphone, "The other one's not going to bother us for a while."

Robert looked through a broken slat and saw a cone of dust pointing away from them as the intruder sped off. Charlie Broadbow's official Ford Bronco cop unit was parked a half-mile away on the other side of the dumpsite.

Robert felt like throwing up as he looked at the remains of the man's face. This was the first dead person he'd seen since his mother's funeral, and she definitely looked more peaceful in death than this poor guy. He kicked a few barrels on top of the dead man to cover him up.

"Serves the bastard right, getting buried in nuclear waste." Frank jabbed a hole in one of the barrels with his crowbar, causing a stream of brown, brackish liquid to drain on top of the corpse. "And this prick probably isn't the one who really deserves to die. He was only trying to kill us, not poison the reservation."

Robert thought of several retorts, most of which were critical of Frank's priorities, then he noticed how badly his hand was shaking. He saw Frank look at his hands too, and he put them behind his back. Frank's hands were steady, despite the fact that he'd just beaten a man to death.

"Let's go tell Charlie a bunch of lies. I suppose he'll be curious about why we're here."

In the dust, Robert wrote, "So am I."

"Grab my carriage, white boy. I'm ready to travel in style."

God! Robert thought. *It's good to be back on the Rez!*

CHAPTER 4

Robert was winded from pushing Frank to the truck. It was hot inside his suit despite the cold air outside, and he wasn't sure the breathing unit was working properly. Frank carefully stripped off his suit, refusing Robert's help, and he threw it on the ground. Robert did the same, shivering as the cold air hit his damp sweatshirt.

"This is one time I won't complain about your littering," Robert said as he helped Frank into the truck.

Charlie Broadbow pulled up next to the pickup in his Bronco. "What kind of trouble are you boys in, now?" Big puffs of steam came from his mouth as he spoke. "I saw the dust from your rig about an hour ago, so I decided to come see what the commotion was about." He spat on the ground. "No one ever comes out here. You two must be up to something no good."

"We're just out for a leisurely Sunday drive," Frank said from the truck.

"It's Tuesday. And the guy who just took off? The one who was shooting at you. Was he just enjoying a bit of target practice?"

"That guy in the funny suit?" Robert said. "He told us he has sensitive skin and he didn't want to burn."

Charlie started his Bronco and crooked a finger to indicate they should follow. Robert and Frank talked all the way back to town.

"There never was any coal to speak of, like I said. The company knew that all along," Frank said. He was holding a frozen can of Budweiser between his thighs, which was about the only thing his legs were good for.

"Why'd they go through the trouble and expense of developing the site?"

"Two reasons. First, it gave them cover to build the dump, which is what they planned to put here all along I suspect. They could throw up a big goddamn fence without raising suspicion. Since they had the permits and a reason to build, no one questioned them—except for my daddy, of course." He tilted the can and shook a few drops of beer into his mouth. "And he's dead."

"And the other reason?" Frank had a habit of losing his train of thought halfway through a list, and Robert often had to remind him of where he was in a conversation. Maybe it was because Frank's brain worked faster than his mouth. Or maybe it was the beer.

"People here don't trust disturbed sites. Whether it's an abandoned home site or an old broken down tribal business, it makes people uncomfortable. Like it's contagious or something. So we stay away. We don't build our homes next to it. We don't drill our wells near it. We don't graze our cattle on it." Frank belched loudly. "You white people build apartments on old cemeteries. But we don't do that kind of shit, either out of respect or superstition, or maybe both."

"I didn't know that."

"There's a lot you don't know, Robert."

He ignored the insult. There wasn't enough time in a day to respond to all Frank's barbs.

"Listen to me, Frank. I've spent a lot of time here. If I did not know that business about avoiding disturbed sites, how did they know it? How'd they know that people would leave them alone once the bogus mine went belly-up?"

Frank shrugged his broad shoulders and stared ahead at the road.

"Don't you see? They must have had inside help to get the site."

Frank turned and stared at Robert for a long time, but his hand on the steering wheel kept the old Dodge pointed down the middle of the road.

"You're saying that someone from the reservation actually helped those bastards arrange to dump their shit here?"

"Just a theory."

"Poison their own home?" Frank said.

"Maybe."

"My father had an expression that translated loosely into 'Don't shit where you work.' He meant that you shouldn't sleep with your co-workers, but I think it applies here pretty goddamn good, too."

Robert continued. "Maybe the person who helped them hated this place for some reason. Maybe he made enough money through the arrangement that he could move away."

"I hate it here too most of the time." Frank poured down a few more drops of beer. "But I sure as hell wouldn't poison the place."

"Maybe he was desperate. Desperate for money, desperate to get out. I don't know why he did it."

"Sick fucker!" Frank grumbled. "Wait till I get hold of him. He'll envy the bastard I did today." He punched the dashboard with his fist, expanding a crack in the vinyl.

"Don't get carried away just yet. It's only a theory." Robert opened his window a bit to get some air as they sped towards town. They were still following Charlie's Bronco, and the cold air was heavy with dust, so he rolled it back up, but he could not close it properly, and the wind whistled in it as they drove.

"I'm never surprised by people's greed," Frank responded, as if he hadn't heard what Robert just said. "I've seen people do horrible things to each other to make a buck. But I'll never understand how someone could sell out the reservation. I don't care how much he got paid. This is their home. Spiritually, if not physically."

"Careful, Frank. That love of the reservation is what got you elected Tribal Council Chairman. Even though they all hate your guts."

Robert suddenly had an image of Anna pulling carrots from the garden. Once he got past the stab of pain at her memory, he thought about how strange it was that the same soil that grows food can also be used to bury toxic wastes.

"When did you learn about this site?" Robert kicked off his shoe and rubbed his foot to get more circulation to it. The heater in the truck did not work well. "And how did those two men know to find us there?"

Frank chuckled to himself. It was the first time Robert had seen him smile all morning. "I was playing around on the Internet maybe six months ago, just before all this shit happened. I did a word search for 'Fort Peck Reservation' and it turned up the names of four companies that had done or were doing business here. The only one I'd heard of was Crown Pipe Mining Corporation, which is the company that got the original mining permit for the site. They don't exist anymore. I searched the archives at tribal headquarters for the permit application and guess what?"

"Let me take a stab at it, Professor. Someone stole the file."

"Very good! No pamphlets about the company. No corporate profiles, no annual reports, no names, no addresses, nada."

"I'm shocked," Robert feigned surprise. "Actually I would not expect them to leave much of a trace if they're guilty."

"I put an ad on the 'Net asking if anyone knew about 'Crown Pipe Mining Corp.' Said I wanted to string up the owners by the balls."

"You get any hits?" Robert asked. Now that his sweat had

dried, he was beginning to shiver.

"Got my wife killed." The corners of Frank's mouth turned down as he said it.

Robert looked down at the floor of the truck. Neither man spoke for a couple of minutes.

"I did find out a couple of things," Frank said after a while. "A fellow from Yakima told me about a company called Pipe Butte, Inc. that applied for a mining permit on his reservation in the late 1980s. They were rejected because after an initial ore strike, there was no evidence of the precious metals they wanted to mine."

"Sounds like a long shot, Frank."

"I thought so, too. But the company had a similar name, and it sounds like they salted the site just like they did here. I just couldn't let it go. I still blame those bastards at Crown Pipe for killing my daddy."

"So what'd you do, threaten the president of the company?"

"Well, yes. I did."

"Frank D. Kicking Bird. I presume the 'D' doesn't stand for 'Discretion?'"

"'Dumbshit' would be more like it. Sometimes I have a temper, Robert. In case you hadn't noticed."

Was that a threat? he wondered.

"I did some research through the 'Net and found a corporate file on Pipe Butte, Inc. The chairman of the board is one Christopher Buckley from Southeast Harbor, Maine. Age fifty-seven. Graduate of Harvard Law School in 1964. Finished second in his class. He became President of Pipe Butte in 1988, ever since the corporation was first registered with the SEC. I tried to find out more about him, but I hit a wall. The bastard's got a lock on it.

"Anna suggested we appeal to his vanity. She called the company and said she was a reporter for Money Magazine. She asked to set up an initial on-line interview with the company president for a feature story she was doing on 'New Resource Companies with a Future.' Buckley jumped at the bait."

"What'd you learn, about him?"

"Anna was asking him a few standard questions on-line over the computer. Then the old fart starts flirting with her. With me sitting right there. The nerve! Course, he didn't know I was there. So I told Anna to go with it and flirt back. Maybe she'd find out more about him. It was all very interesting, let me tell you. I learned a lot."

"Like what?"

"Like for a quiet person, she was really a very good flirter. Surprised the hell out of me."

"I mean, what did you learn about Buckley?" Robert already knew how sexy Anna could be.

"They arranged a phone interview. He gave her his work number. When she called him a little later, all he talked about was how much he wanted to get in her pants."

"Not very politically correct, is he? I thought sexual harassment was passé."

"I guess that makes me old fashioned, too," Frank said. "Something came up and Buckley said he had to go. He told her to call him back in two hours. When she did, a secretary put her on hold for fifteen minutes. Anna suddenly hung up and told me, 'He's on to us, Frank. He just traced our call.' I think she even said 'Damnit,' or something like that."

"Was she right?" Anna had good instincts about almost everything except what to do with her own life.

"To check it out, she called Money Magazine and asked for 'Martha Boileau.' That's the name Anna used when she interviewed Buckley. She always wanted to be French. The secretary at the magazine said that there was no one at the company by that name."

"So? What does that prove?"

"She also told Anna that she was the second person that afternoon who'd asked for Ms. Boileau. So, yeah. Anna was right. Buckley had called the office to check her out."

"He shouldn't have been surprised. Everyone on-line lies about themselves. Except you, of course, you 'Ill-tempered, pot-bellied big-assed—'"

"'Bad-assed,' please!"

"Whatever—'Assiniboine from the Fort Peck Reservation—'"

"It gets people's attention."

"Speaking of getting attention, what did you do next?"

"I was so mad, I did something you might call impulsive."

"Everything you do is impulsive," Robert said, glancing over his shoulder at his friend. Frank was having a great time working the steering wheel, clutch, brake and gas with his hands while sipping his thawing Budweiser. He'd replaced his radioactive helmet with a Red Sox baseball cap. His braid came out the hole in the back.

"I sent Buckley an E-mail. It said something like, "Hey, you fat, old fart. Ever heard of a company called Crown Pipe Corporation? Still poisoning reservations and killing off old Indians?"

"Oh, oh."

"He never wrote back. But I heard from him a week later."

"How so?"

"He blew up my truck and my wife."

They pulled in front of the police station next to Sheriff Charlie Broadbow's Bronco. "Let's not be too forthcoming with old Charlie," Frank suggested. "I don't think he's ready for the truth just yet."

Robert pulled the wheelchair from the back of the truck. Frank moved himself gracefully from the truck to the chair and the two of them went inside.

Charlie was feeding Golda, his pet goldfish, when they entered his office. "What the hell kept you boys?" He turned to Frank. "You drive slower than an old woman now that your legs don't work," he said. "Takes all the fun outta my job. I can't give you as many speeding tickets. Not that you'd ever paid 'em, anyway."

Charlie finished feeding his fish, and he emitted an enormous sigh as he sat down with great effort behind his desk.

"I only believe in donating to good causes, Charlie," Frank said. "Why should I help fund you by paying your damn tickets?"

"A real fucking philanthropist, right Frank?"

"Is this why you called us in, Charlie?" Robert said. "To discuss what a great human being Frank is?"

"No, it isn't. That's a subject we could exhaust in about two seconds." He unconsciously rubbed a sausage-shaped forefinger up and down Golda's glass bowl. "I was wondering what you two sorry-assed—"

"That's 'bad-assed, '" Frank said, exchanging a wink with Robert.

"Whatever—bad-assed idiots were doing at the old mine site besides getting yourself shot at."

"I was looking for clues to my father's murder."

"For Chrissake, Frank. That was nearly thirty years ago. And it wasn't a damn murder. It was suicide."

"That's what the death certificate says. But I still don't believe it."

"Believe it." He turned his head to Robert. His jowls caught up with the rest of his face a moment later. "And you, Robert. What the hell were you doing there?"

"What do you think I was doing, Charlie? I was looking for investment property."

Charlie slapped his palm on the desk so hard that some water spilled out of Golda's bowl. "'Scuse me, darlin,'" he said to the fish. Then to Frank and Robert, "I'm really not in the mood for games."

Charlie kept Golda at the office and fed her so often that she was becoming as fat as he was. He loved that fish more than anything, except, perhaps being a cop.

Come to think of it, Robert thought as he sat in the office, *I've never seen Charlie with a woman other than his sister.* Frank was the first and last person to point out a link between Charlie's avoidance of women and his love for the fish.

"I know why you feed that fish so much," Frank said about a year ago when he woke up in the jailhouse after sleeping off a drunk. Robert had just come to get him and they were standing in front of Charlie's desk.

"Why's that?" Charlie said without looking up from his newspaper. A minute earlier, he'd tossed the keys to Robert to unlock the cell.

"You're hoping to get her big enough so you can fuck her."

Charlie flew over the desk without touching anything on it and landed a punch on Frank's jaw that sent him into the wall fifteen feet away. Frank hit the wall so hard his head and elbows left dents in the plaster.

"She's a boy, goddamn it!" Charlie said as he drug Frank's nearly lifeless body back to the cell. Frank was out for two hours.

Robert came back to pick him up just as he was coming to.

"What'm I in for?" he said, rubbing the lump on his jaw.

"Disturbing my fucking peace," Charlie said.

From then on, Frank gave Golda a wide berth, as if the fish had punched him instead of Charlie.

Robert, too, was wary of the fish and even today, he was hesitant to make eye contact with her.

"I'm sorry, Charlie," Robert said. "But you're not going to get a straight answer from us. Not yet anyway."

"You sorry, white bastard. I'm considering charging you with criminal trespass."

"I don't want to spoil your efforts to intimidate me, but a couple of nights in the jail isn't all that much of a deterrent. It's a lot cleaner than Frank's place, and the food's better. Go ahead and lock me up if it'll make you feel any better. But Frank and I have a few more things to find out. And we're going to do it whether or not you harass us."

"You know what I think?" Charlie said.

"I know it can't be too complicated," Frank replied.

"I think you boys are going to be making my life miserable

for a while. And the thing I hate most is that there's not a damn thing I can do about it."

"Thanks, Charlie," Robert said. "We'll try to stay out of you hair, I promise."

Frank wheeled his chair to the door. "If you stay out of ours," he said.

Robert stood up to join him.

"In case you didn't notice," Charlie yelled to the two men as they left. "I saved your two sorry-assed lives today."

"That's 'bad-assed,' Charlie!" Frank yelled over his shoulder. "That's B-A-D-A-S-S-E-D. Bad-assed!" Charlie watched the two figures grow smaller as they walked and wheeled their way to Frank's for a drink. They left Frank's truck in front of an expired parking meter.

CHAPTER 5

"We need to get the owner of Pipe Smoke to the reservation," Frank said. "Show him our brand of hospitality."

"That's Pipe Butte." Robert stretched lazily in his sleeping bag on Frank's floor. Most of his time was spent wrapped in a sleeping bag to ward off the cold inside Frank's house, which was beginning to resemble the place Frank owned in the country. He had already knocked out several windows in a drunken rage, ostensibly over phone company charges but no doubt fueled by his wife's murder, his partial paralysis, poverty, and the fact that outsiders had poisoned the reservation.

"Tell me again, what's the guy's name who runs Pipe Butte?" Frank asked.

"Buckley. Christopher Buckley.

"Why don't we fly out to Maine and pay Mr. Buckley a personal visit?"

"You're crippled, Frank. And that's his turf. Bad idea."

"Well, what if we threatened to—"

"Shush! I'm coming up with an idea."

"Last person told me to shush, I kicked his—"

"Shut the hell up a second!" Robert shouted.

This time, Frank listened. Robert crawled out of the sleeping bag, stood and paced noisily across the sticky floor. Then he turned to Frank. "You got any friends on the council?"

"I wouldn't call them friends."

"Anyone owe you a favor?"

"They all do. But only one or two realize it. Petey Red Elk would probably help me out. Especially if it got me off his back for a while."

"Okay. Who publishes the tribal rag, the—"

"The *Wotanin Wowapi*?"

"Yeah, that one," Robert said. He resumed his pacing.

"That'd be Mason What's-his-name, Tomlinson. What're you getting at, Robert?"

"Would he ever do you a favor?"

"Probably not. He's only printed nasty shit about me since I got on the council."

"Let me see that look," Robert said. "The one you use in council meetings."

Frank narrowed his eyebrows until they pointed straight down to the middle to his nose.

"That's perfect. Give him that look and he'll do anything you say. Here's my plan. First we visit the newspaper office and get Tomlinson to—"

Robert talked for twenty minutes straight, by far the longest stretch of time that Frank had let Robert talk without interrupting him. When he finished, he crawled into his bag once again and lay on his back, staring at cracks in the plaster ceiling.

"So what do you think?"

After a moment, Frank said, "That's a goddamn good plan, boy." He clapped his hands together and leaned forward in his wheelchair with his elbows on his knees. "If I didn't know better, I'd think you want this bastard as much as I do."

"It's true."

"You act like it was your wife got killed instead of mine."

Here was another opening to talk about how his feelings for Anna, and how desperately in love with her he was. Should he just bring it out in the open and face the consequences? He waited a minute before deciding it would serve no purpose to discuss it with Frank. But a nagging voice in his head accused him of taking the easy way out because he was scared.

"Get dressed," Robert said. "We're going to the newspaper office."

"I am dressed." Frank was wearing a pair of faded sweatpants and a shredded T-shirt with a logo over a faded word Robert could not make out. He threw on a coat.

Robert grabbed his jacket and they marched and wheeled their way through the cold, dry afternoon air to the tribal newspaper office. Robert entered first and saw Mason Tomlinson asleep at his desk.

Frank wheeled his way to the desk and peered at the editor's balding head. "Whew!" he said. "Must have been some drunk he was on last night."

He banged his fist on the desk. Mason jerked up his head so fast that he almost fell over backwards. He was in his mid-thirties and looked to be half-Indian.

"Local editor found sleeping off a hangover at 11:00 a.m. on Wednesday, January 15," Frank said.

"Who the hell are you?" Mason said, rubbing his eyes.

"Frank Kicking Bird. This is my friend, Robert."

"Oh yes," Mason said. "Current Tribal Chairman offered a motion at last Monday's council meeting to secede the entire reservation and all its tribal members from the United States of America. 'But wouldn't that be, in effect, a declaration of war?' Council Member Red Elk asked. 'So? Who gives a s___?' Frank replied'." Mason put his head back on his arms, which were folded on top of his desk. "Great rhetorical comeback, Mr. Chairman."

Frank shrugged. "It seemed like a good idea at the time."

"Only to you. No one else voted for it," Mason mumbled

into his arms.

"We didn't come to discuss politics," Robert said. "We have a favor to ask you, Mr. Tomlinson."

He lifted his head and said, "I'm not in the mood to be handing out favors, gentlemen. But don't think I don't appreciate your stopping by. Pardon the double negative. Let me put it in a more positive way. Please leave."

Robert nodded to Frank who lowered his eyebrows and assumed his famous glare. It was one of the most severe expressions Robert had ever seen.

"My God!" Tomlinson said. "The man looks just like a chicken."

"I must be losing my touch." Frank shook his head.

"Please, boys. Get out, will you? I have a bad headache."

"Here's the deal," Robert said. "We need a front page article about Frank's death."

"Nothing would please me more, Mr.—?"

"Botkin. Robert Botkin."

"Right, Mr. Botkin. I'll treasure the day I can write that story. But as you can see, he is still very much alive although only partly functional." He pointed to Frank's wheelchair. "Now please. I have some pressing business." He put his head back on the desk.

Frank started to reach for him, but Robert stopped him with a shake of his head.

"Hear us out," Robert said. "There's an abandoned coal mine north of here about fifteen miles or so."

"Yet another failed tribal business. Now that's headline news for you."

"It's actually a nuclear waste disposal site."

Mason jerked up his head like he had when Frank had pounded the desk. "You're kidding?"

"No, sir. I'm not. And the three of us are the only ones on the reservation who know about it."

"Not for long." Mason stood up to make his way to the

nearby computer terminal. He stopped after two paces and grabbed his head. "I'm seeing triple this morning. Must be the barometric pressure."

"Wait, Mason," Robert said. "We have a chance to catch the guy who did this red-handed, but we need your help."

"What are you asking?"

"We want to lure him to the reservation. We're pretty sure he's shopping for more space to dump his wastes, but he'll never do business here as long as Frank is chairman."

"Where do I fit in?"

"We need you to print a front page story about Frank's death."

"So kill him."

"You're a funny guy, Tomlinson," Frank said. "I'm beginning to realize you're only half the prick I thought you were."

"Half a prick, huh? Like that's a compliment?" Mason squinted hard and ran a hand over the top of his balding head. "Seriously, I can't willingly print a false story, even if it's to catch a big-time polluter."

"You go to print now about the dumpsite, without enough evidence, and this bastard who killed my wife will go free. I'll have to fly all the way to Maine to kill him!" Again, Frank pounded the man's desk. "Where is Maine, anyway?"

"Whoa, slow down! He killed your wife? I thought she died because some dynamite accidentally blew up in her truck."

"She found out he was responsible for the dump site, so he killed her," Frank said. "Or maybe he was trying to kill me. But if you print any of this in that rag of yours before we're ready, I'll have to kill you too!"

Mason appeared unconcerned. "Idle threats, Frank. Don't waste them on me." He rubbed his forehead with his thumb and forefinger. "What's in this for me if I hold off on this story? Why should I go along with your plans?"

"Because if you don't," Frank began. "I'll…"

"Hold it," Robert interrupted. "Listen, Mason. I realize this is asking a lot of you."

"You got that right."

"You're gambling that if you're patient, you'll get to write a once-in-a-lifetime story, a chance that you'll blow if you don't help us now."

"Like I said, I couldn't *willingly* go to print with a false story about Frank's death."

"And I said I'll kill you if you don't help us. Or at least beat the shit out of you."

"Wait," Robert intervened. "Let Mason continue. I think he's headed somewhere with this." Then to Mason, "you said *willingly?*"

Mason nodded slightly to him.

Robert searched the office until he found some duct tape in the lower left hand drawer of Mason's desk. He peeled off a couple of feet of tape and wrapped it around Mason's wrists.

"Tighter, Botkin," Frank said. "A twelve-year-old could get out of that."

"Sorry. I'm a little new at this assault business."

Frank shook his head.

Tomlinson guided them through the process of developing a newspaper piece. "You guys owe me big time," he said. "I get first crack at this story when it's ready to go to print."

"Okay by me. How about you, Frank?"

"Write whatever you want. I don't give a shit."

"What if you guys are making all this up?" Mason said. "Ah, hell," he said, answering his own question. "Frank can be full of shit," he said to Robert. "But he doesn't lie."

Frank knew computers well, so he took over the typing. "Just wait till we give you the go ahead. Jesus, man! Your computer is so slow I'd beat it in a race, and I'm paralyzed."

"This isn't the *New York Times*, Frank. It's the *Wotanin Wowapi*. I was using a Corona manual until two years ago."

Frank and Robert conjured up a story about Frank dying from exposure a week ago following a long battle with alcoholism. He was last seen alive, according to the bogus article, at the Antelope Tavern, a local establishment where he'd been quarreling with several patrons.

"Kicking Bird had been confined to a wheelchair since an automobile accident last August that killed his wife, Anna." The article went on to speculate that the loss of his wife contributed to his latest bout of drinking which ultimately led to his death. Frank tried to veto the speculation about the cause of his drinking. "Too sentimental," he protested, but the other two conspirators overrode his arguments.

Mason was a tough editor, insisting upon the use of proper grammar. "Hey, this reflects on me," he said. "I won't publish sloppy stories in my newspaper."

Frank laid out the story in columns the same width the newspaper used. He matched the newspaper's font and type before printing it on blank newsprint Mason had in the office. Robert cut up the columns and painstakingly laid them out so they would fit exactly over the lead article in the previous week's issue about a scandal in the Indian Health Service. He saved some room for Frank's picture, which Mason had on file from when Frank was first elected to the tribal council.

"We need a catchy headline," Robert said. "How about 'Council chairman drinks himself to death?'"

"Nah. Too unflattering," Frank said.

"What about 'Grief over wife's death drives council chairman to suicide?'" Robert tried again.

"Too sappy," Frank said.

"Type 'Council chairman found dead,'" Mason said. "That way, people will want to find out how you died. Put it in twenty-four-point type."

When they were finished, Frank said, "Goddamn, that's sad. He was so young, and he had so much to give."

"A month from now when this has all blown over," Mason said, "you can use Mark Twain's famous quote."

"Which one is that?"

"'Reports of my death are greatly exaggerated,'" Mason

said. "Now hurry up. I'm getting tired of sitting in this chair."

By one o'clock, they had made a dozen copies of the doctored paper on the Xerox machine. Their work was seamless and convincing.

"That should do, Mason," Robert said. "Thanks again for your help."

"We're not done yet," Mason said. "Open that tool drawer over there. No, the one just below where you found the duct tape." Mason pointed with his chin. "I've got some sandpaper in there."

"There's a little piece here. It's been used, though. Why do you need it?" Robert said.

"Bring it here. Now sand a little spot on my cheekbone till it just starts to bleed. That'll be where Frank punched me. It's better than having him really do it. Ouch! Take it easy."

"Sorry," Robert said. "There, that looks pretty convincing."

"Want me to take another inch or two off your nose?" Frank said.

"No. Just tape my mouth and get the hell out of here. My intern from Fort Peck Community College will be here in about an hour. I'll just sleep till he arrives. Then we'll call Charlie Broadbow and let him deal with this. But I suggest you make yourself scarce in the meantime."

"Oh, man. Charlie's going to be pissed. He's already mad at us for making his life difficult." Robert put a strip of tape over Mason's mouth. Then he grabbed the doctored papers and headed to the door where Frank waited for him.

"Bye Mason. Thanks again for your help."

"Mmmmfffff, mmmfffff!"

"I never could understand that guy," Frank said as he wheeled his chair into the street. "I gotta go send a fax. Then let's pay a visit to Petey Red Elk."

Back home, Frank pulled his wheelchair up to his computer and hooked to the Internet. He began typing and clicked his mouse a couple of times. "Ah, here it is. The fax number. He scribbled it down, signed off from the Internet, and began composing the following letter:

Dear Mr. Buckley.

      My name is Peter Red Elk, and I'm on the Fort Peck Indian Reservation Tribal Council. I have a friend on the Yakima Reservation in Eastern Washington who told me you were interested in finding a site on his reservation to do some mining or other activities. I think you would find Fort Peck to be quite accomidating—

"You misspelled 'accommodating.'"

"I did that on purpose. Petey could never spell worth a damn. Now let me finish."

      accomidating to your interests. We have nearly 2,000,000 acres of land with very few people living on it. Whether you're interested in mining, manufacturing, waste disposal, or any other business development, we would be very eager to talk to you about it.

      I wanted to get hold of you sooner, but Frank Kicking Bird, our Tribal Chairman, was very much against recruiting such a business on the reservation. Long ago his father committed suicide. Frank was convinced it was murder and he blames it on a coal mining company. But now Frank's dead, too. He drank himself to death last week just like his father. So the council put me in charge of getting businesses to locate here. Here's a copy of the article about Frank's death.

      We'd love to have you come out to our reservation to show you the area. Please feel free to call me at (406) 555-0069.

Sincerely, Peter Red Elk
RR 20T, Poplar, Montana"

"I suppose that sounds believable," Frank said, admiring his work on the letter. "Sincere, in a good-old-boy, uneducated way. Let's ship it."

Frank was one of the few citizens on the reservation who owned a fax machine. The Bureau of Indian Affairs offices and the schools owned several. So did Sheriff Charlie Broadbow, but his was still probably in the box at the office.

"Ready for the next volley, Captain."

Frank slipped the papers into the fax and pushed some buttons.

"It's a miracle this fax stuff actually works," Robert said.

"Not really. The technology is pretty simple. It's been around for years. They were just waiting for the market to develop before they introduced it. Now let's get over to Petey's. If I know Mr. Buckley, he'll be calling in about ten minutes to check us out."

No one was at Petey Red Elk's house when they arrived a couple of minutes later. The wheelchair hardly slowed Frank at all. He could enter and dismount his pickup as fast as ever using only his arms.

"What do we do now?" Robert asked.

"We go in, of course."

"Why not add breaking and entering to our list of crimes? We're on a roll, Frank."

"God-damn untrusting son-of-a-bitch!" Frank yelled. "Locked his fucking door. Where does he think he is? Chicago?"

They heard the phone ring inside the house. Robert threw his shoulder into the door and it flew open, showering the floor with wood splinters from the broken jamb. Warm air from the house greeted them as they stepped inside.

"Serves him right for locking the goddamn thing," Frank

said as he made his way to the phone.

"Didn't you tell me back at the dump site that people here don't disturb other people's property?"

"Sometimes we make exceptions. Or I do anyway." Frank picked up the receiver. "Hello, this is Petey," he said, trying to imitate Red Elk's voice. After a minute he continued. "Put me down for a dozen. Make that two. Yes, you can bill me with the shipment. No, don't thank me, it's a wonderful cause. And please call me again next year, too. Yes. You, too. Have a nice day." He hung up the phone. "Petey just bought himself two dozen lightbulbs from the handicapped. He's got a big heart, that guy."

Robert began picking up the wood splinters. The living room floor was covered with a red and gold shag carpet. The sofa, done in similar colors, was worn but clean. Robert could see no books or magazines in the room, but there was a large console television set with foil flags attached to the antenna.

Robert wedged the largest splinter back into place in the doorframe so tightly that it was hard to tell it had been broken. The phone rang again and Frank answered it after three rings.

"Hello, this is Petey. Well, hello. Yes, sir, that was quick. I didn't expect to hear from you for a couple of weeks."

Frank gave Robert a thumbs up sign, which Robert returned.

"No, sir. No, sir," Frank continued. "Well, I was planning to be in Billings that day anyway to sell some stock. No, sir, *livestock*." Frank pulled the phone from his ear and stared at it incredulously, as if it had just said something stupid. Robert rolled his eyes.

"You're bringing who?" Frank said. "That's wonderful. We'll hold a feast on the reservation for the four of you. I can introduce all of you to the council. No, really. It's our tradition to do that when a group like yourselves visits the reservation. Really? Are you sure? Then I'll bring the council members to Billings to meet you and your colleagues. We'd like to be a good host to all of you. Okay, I understand, then. Don't worry about it, sir. That would be just fine. Friday afternoon at 1:35.

That's all right, I don't need the flight number, it's a small airport."

Robert pumped his fist. He was surprised it was that easy to lure Buckley to Montana.

"You must have to get up awful early to get in that soon. Oh, I see, you'll be coming from Denver. Doing business there. Rocky Fats? Whatever. I'll be there to meet you at the airport. I know a good lunch place in Billings. They've got the greasiest burgers and coldest beer in town. Only the locals go there. You're sure you don't have time to run up to Poplar and meet with the council? It's only three hundred miles from Billings. Okay. Maybe next trip. You what?"

Frank waved his hand at Robert to make sure he was listening, an unnecessary gesture.

"Sure," Frank continued. "I can do that. I might have to send you a Xerox, though. The newspaper office only keeps one copy of each issue, and most people around here throw theirs out pretty quick. Or they use it to train their puppies. I don't suppose you want one of those copies, do you? No, sir, I was just kidding. Sad deal about 'ol Frank. He was quite a character. Okay, then, sir. I look forward to it too. Bye."

Frank smiled broadly when he'd hung up.

"A little thick on the 'sirs,' don't you think?"

"I wanted to appear properly kiss-ass. The guy was planning to bring some colleagues, but when I threatened to parade them before the council, he backed down. He doesn't like publicity when he's planning to pollute, I guess. He thinks he's meeting Petey in Billings for a couple of hours before he flies back to wherever. But I think we should bring him back to the Rez."

"You sure kissed his ass but good."

"Hey, he's a special guest. I wanted him to feel welcome."

"We'll show him a little reservation hospitality, all right," Robert said. "He's going to have a very memorable trip."

CHAPTER 6

Robert drove to the airport on a crisp January morning to meet Buckley. He was comfortable in his old Ford station wagon with the faded imitation wood paneling on the sides.

The winter had been dry and the only snow he saw was clumped in dirty piles on the leeward side of fences and houses. The sun filtered through cottonwood branches along the Missouri River and speckled the ground with a quilt of pale light. As he climbed out of the valley, the hills and bluffs were bathed in slanted morning light that cast long shadows to the west, making them look bigger than they were.

Little hills trying to look like mountains, Robert thought. *Kind of like Frank and me.* He wondered if he was in over his head.

The thought of meeting Buckley had sustained Robert for the past couple of weeks. He believed Buckley was responsible for killing Anna, paralyzing Frank, and ruining Robert's dreams, and he was curious to see how he'd react to this evil man. Robert seldom reacted violently. When his soul, battered from some loss, needed to recover, he would bury himself in chores. Nurturing the land was a form of self-care for him. But he had never experienced anything like this, and the physical effort of running the ranch provided no relief from the pain of losing Anna.

Robert found himself fantasizing about killing the man who took Anna from him a little over four months ago, even though before the bomb, his most vicious thoughts were usually of breaking a stick over a lazy cow's butt. He thought about confronting Buckley, savored the image of Buckley's face becoming a mask of horror when he realized Robert was going to kill him, and then emptying the contents of a pistol into his chest. The fantasies gave him a measure of relief, perverse though he knew it was.

Robert turned south onto the three hundred mile stretch of prairie that separated the Missouri and Yellowstone Rivers. He thought of Anna, how her lips felt when they touched his, the way her skin smelled first thing in the morning, the color of her face in the reddening sunset that last night on the butte above Fort Peck Lake. He noticed that his hands were gripping the steering wheel almost hard enough to snap it, and he realized that he'd been this tense for four months.

He got to Billings about forty-five minutes early and pulled into a turnout on top of the rimrocks that overlooked town. The trees below him had lost all their leaves and he could see houses peeking from underneath the branches. A line of bare cottonwoods traced the rambling Yellowstone River, and to the southwest, he could see snow in the far off Beartooth Range.

He and a former lover from New Mexico had once driven along these same rimrocks. His love for her was simple and pure, and it generally brought out the best in both of them. Had it not been for the fact that she was as connected to the high southwestern deserts as he was to the northern Great Plains, they'd still be together. Their relationship had only a fraction of the passion and none of the toxicity of his relationship with Anna.

Robert had had a hard time persuading Frank to stay home on this particular trip. They both wanted first crack at Buckley. Robert's main argument was that Frank would probably kill

Buckley in the airport, they'd both be thrown in jail, and then they'd never be sure if Buckley was actually responsible for the bomb that killed Anna.

"So?" Frank said. He didn't seem at all troubled by the scenario that Robert described.

"So, let me pick him up peacefully, deliver him to you, then you can question him. He'd recognize you anyway. There was that picture of you in the bogus article about your death."

"That's a bullshit argument. All Indians look alike to white men, especially to the rich ones."

Frank reluctantly agreed to stay home, but as a safety measure, Robert stole the keys to his pick-up to make sure Frank would not follow. Frank was staying in his bombed-out house in the country to avoid running into Sheriff Broadbow. The Bureau of Indian Affairs employed the tribal police on the reservation, but they weren't much of a threat because they rarely ventured into the countryside. Despite their fancy, federally-funded brick building with the bulletproof glass, the Bureau of Indian Affairs police were as competent as the Keystone Cops.

Charlie Broadbow was a much better officer than he appeared to be. He had no tolerance for stupid people, so he spent much of his life in an irritable mood. "You want to know how dumb those guys are?" Charlie once said to Robert. "Ask them where the town of Lustre is. I grew up there. It's in the northwest part of the reservation, smack in the middle of their jurisdiction."

When Robert asked them about it, the BIA cops spent a long time arguing about whether it was in western Montana or northern Wyoming.

Robert killed half an hour on the rimrocks before he drove to the airport and entered the terminal. Frank had downloaded a picture of Buckley from a corporate report he'd gotten over the Internet, so Robert knew the man's face.

Christopher Buckley was the first passenger off the plane, a tall man with a straight back. His hair was in stunning transition from rich brown to distinguished silver. He had a sharp, angular nose and full, sensuous lips above a jutting chin with a dimple in the middle. He carried a black briefcase and was rolling a small overnight bag.

The sight of him stirred Robert's rage. Buckley's arrogant expression and pompous chin, especially the chin, drove Robert wild with hatred. Buckley glanced briefly around the terminal and, seeing no Indian, sneered ever so slightly.

Robert stepped up to him and said, "Mr. Buckley."

"Yes. Who are you?"

"I'm Robert. I'm here to welcome you to Montana. Please follow me," he said, amazed at his self-control. "We're going to drive to the reservation."

"Just a minute. Where's Mr. Red Elk?"

"Probably sleeping off a hangover. Now come on. We've got a five hour drive to the reservation ahead of us."

"I most certainly will not," Buckley said, raising his voice slightly. "I came here to do business with Mr. Red Elk. We're supposed to meet here in Billings. I don't have the time to go to the reservation, and I'm certainly not leaving here with a stranger. I don't even know you."

People were streaming by them on their way to the baggage claim. Robert put his left hand on Buckley's shoulder as if he were getting ready share a secret with him. Then he turned and buried his right fist in Buckley's stomach.

Buckley doubled up and made great, dry heaving sounds. Robert patted him on the back as if to comfort him. "Don't worry folks. His ulcer's acting up. He'll be all right in a moment."

Robert pulled a miniature tape player from his pocket, bent down to Buckley's level and turned it on. The volume was turned low, but you could still hear Buckley's voice as he talked with Anna.

"I bet you taste sweet, darling," he said.

"I'll give you references," Anna said.

"I'd rather find out for myself."

"You are forward, Mr. Buckley."

"Let's meet soon, darling."

"For an interview, hmmm?"

"For a taste."

"And your wife would no doubt approve?"

"Ms. FBFH?"

"FBFH?"

"Frigid Bitch from Hell."

"A poor, horny man who doesn't get enough from his wife. What an original story," Anna said sarcastically.

"Oh, my. You're not going to be easy. Now I want you twice as much."

"The others are easier?"

"Much."

Robert clicked off the recorder. "Sorry it's such a poor recording. It's only a copy. The original's in safe hands though," Robert whispered in the man's ear. "Your choice. Join me or I'll ship a copy of the tape to Ms. FBFH."

Buckley slowly straightened himself. "You think the fact I screw around is a secret?"

"No, but it will make for great reading in court. The woman on the tape is dead, and you're the prime suspect, though nobody but you and I and a friend of mine know that yet."

"I never met her in person. I didn't know she was dead, and I damn sure didn't kill her." He gently rubbed his stomach. "I should kick your bloody ass for sucker punching me like that."

The crowd of passengers was thinning now. "I'm willing to hear your story," Robert said. "But you're going to have to tell me in the car." Robert felt his cheeks quivering as he stared at Buckley's face. There were a few hairs in the cleft of Buckley's chin that his razor had missed.

"I might have some thoughts on your adulteress' murderer. Oh, excuse me, did I offend you," Buckley said, feigning concern. "Of course she was your lover. No one gets as upset as you are about a dead woman unless she's his sister or he was fucking her." He nodded towards the door, and they both began to move with the remaining crowd.

Robert knew he would hate this guy even if it turned out that Buckley had not killed Anna. He led Buckley outside. Buckley put his hands under his armpits to keep them warm and blew out clouds of steam as they walked. They both got in the front seat of the car and Robert pulled up to the pay their parking fee.

"One word and you're dead."

"Suppose I call your bluff?"

"I'm not like you, Buckley. I have nothing to lose. No family, no money, no prestige, no future, no pride. I'd be just as happy if you did make me kill you."

"I'm going to talk this through with you, but I'm not going to drive all the way to the reservation."

Buckley behaved himself as Robert paid the money and they drove through the booth. Then he said, "Let me get this straight. Some woman was murdered in Montana, and you think I killed her?"

"She was not just 'some woman,'" he said through clenched teeth. "Her name was Anna."

"I'm sorry for your loss, but I have a few problems of my own," Buckley said. "Why don't you just turn around and forget this silly little kidnapping escapade? You're not cut out for this sort of thing."

Buckley was right, and Robert knew it. "Let's talk over here." Robert pulled out at the same place he'd stopped earlier along the rimrocks. He reached inside his coat pocket and grabbed the butt of his .38 pistol. Then he whipped around and hit Buckley squarely in the face with it.

Buckley's head rocked back like he'd been shot. Blood dripped from his lip, and he was out cold. "I'll make this your problem, you arrogant bastard!" Robert said.

He taped Buckley's mouth shut and secured his hands behind his back with duct tape. "This is the most useful stuff ever created," he said to the still-unconscious Buckley. "Give me duct tape over Velcro and Post-Its any day."

He struggled to heave Buckley into the back seat. Robert got out of the car, opened the back door, and arranged Buckley so that he was lying in a fetal position on the seat. Then he hopped back in and began to drive. Twenty miles north of Billings, Buckley began to stir.

"Stay down," Robert said. "I don't want to explain to anyone what I'm doing on the road with a taped-up man in the back seat."

The wind blew hard enough that it took an effort to hold the car on the road. "You can't believe how open the country is around here. You can see in every direction for miles. Those are the Beartooths to the southwest. The Bull Mountains to the north. In between, there's nothing but prairie. Too bad you can't see it. Except for a few towns like Billings, hardly anyone lives here."

Robert took a deep breath and looked across the panorama spread before him. "I know what you're thinking," he said. "You're thinking, 'What a wonderful place for a nuclear waste dump.' That alone makes me want to kill you. But I've got other plans for you right now. Sheer torture."

Robert turned to look at his captive who showed no signs of fear. His blue eyes stared back at Robert with what appeared to be a mixture of disdain and hatred. Undoubtedly, his resources had gotten him out of many jams before.

Not this time, Robert thought. Then he said, "Today, I'm going to make you do something you've never done before. I'm going to make you listen. I want you to know about the people's lives you're messing with."

"I've known Frank for nearly thirty years. His dad used to work for my father in the mid-sixties, and we became friends, even though he was four years older than me. He bounced back and forth between schools in my town in South Dakota and the reservation. People in my town hated Frank, in part because he was Indian, but also because he was a hell of a lot stronger and smarter than they were.

"I always admired the guy. I still do, even though some of his traits don't look as good on him now that he's forty. Back then, he used to beat up eighth graders when he was in fifth. He intimidated teachers, which infuriated them because most of them were racists. They tried to flunk him, but he was an outstanding student. The thing that made everyone mad, including me, was that he never worked at school. He just *got* it.

"One night when he was a senior and I was in eighth grade, we were having a beer behind the school yard. Actually, Frank was drinking beer, and I was sipping a Coke. It was a Thursday towards the end of September, deep into Indian Summer, if you'll pardon the expression. The moon was about half full, no breeze, but you could smell the cottonwood leaves rotting down by the creek that ran along one edge of the schoolyard.

"Frank and I were under the bleachers. He was talking about how much he loved pussy. He always talked about that, but he'd get a lot more graphic after a couple of beers. I heard a noise off to our left and shushed him for a second. Then we spotted two people by the schoolhouse about fifty yards away.

"'Can you believe it? They're fucking, man!' he whispered. 'Let's go in for a better look.'

"I tried my damnedest to talk him out of it. I was curious, of course, but I wanted no part of the trouble we'd get in when we got caught. And I knew we would. But Frank began crawling towards them, and I followed him like I always did. We got pretty close and hid behind a dumpster. The woman was bent forward over a bicycle rack and the guy was behind her.

"'Jesus,' Frank whispered in a much softer voice. 'Know who that gal is? She's the new third and fourth grade teacher at school. Been here less than a month. My, my, don't she work fast? And that's Tommy Svent, the sheriff. I can see his uniform on the ground.'

"And then I saw it. The moon came from behind a cloud and its light reflected off his knife. The sheriff was holding it against her throat while he grabbed a handful of her hair with his other hand and twisted her face towards us. Tears streaked her cheeks and she looked in terrible pain. We could now hear him saying the most vile, disgusting things to her.

"I whispered to Frank that we should get out of there before we got killed. I was terrified. But Frank jumped up before I could stop him, and he charged the bastard.

"Again, I followed him, not knowing why or what I'd do when I got there. Frank was at least ten paces ahead of me. The sheriff turned around just as Frank shattered a beer bottle on top of his head. He went down hard and grabbed the gun from his pants on the ground. I hit the sheriff around the waist with my whole body as he stood to fire at Frank, who was now running away.

"The sheriff dropped the gun, but in a second or two, had me in a headlock that cut off my breath. He had the knife in his other hand, and I could tell he was deciding whether he should kill me. Suddenly, his grip relaxed, and he dropped the knife. Frank was holding the remains of the broken bottle against his kidneys.

"'I should cut off your worthless pecker and stuff it down your throat, you son-of-a-bitch!' Frank said. Mind you, this was an officer of the law he was talking to, but Frank didn't scare easy, especially when he was right. 'But I'd rather see you rot in jail for rape.'

"I think Frank had more self-control in those days. Blood was running down the sheriff's face from the cut on his head where Frank had hit him. He started calling Frank every racist name I'd ever heard. 'You better clean up your language in prison, partner,' Frank said. 'I got lots of relatives there.'

"The schoolteacher—I can't even remember her name now, isn't that terrible?—she'd run off by then, and we had no idea where she was. Frank told me to hold the gun on the sheriff. I was happy to do it. The shock had worn off and I was mad as hell by then.

"Frank went though his pants. He cuffed the sheriff to the bike rack, kept his keys and pants but left the wallet. We threw his gun on the roof of the school, jammed on the horn of his patrol car with the sheriff's nightstick to draw attention, and ran like hell with the sheriff's pants and keys in hand while he stood there, buck ass naked except for his red socks. I still remember his repulsive potbelly hanging down. 'I'll always remember you like this!' Frank yelled as we ran away, laughing. We dumped the pants and keys in the creek.

"The schoolteacher refused to testify. She'd have lost anyway, and the defending attorney would have probably made her look like a whore in the process. She did not return to the classroom, and a week later she was gone for good. I never saw her again. Frank was charged with assault and ran off to the reservation where he's been ever since. I wasn't charged with anything because I was white and my father was well liked in the community. I tried to convince people of Frank's innocence, but no one much cared. The sheriff died a year later in a car wreck that I still think Frank may have caused, though I never asked him about it.

"Frank and I have continued to stay in touch. I spend a month or so each year on the reservation helping him farm. Now that people's memories have faded, he could come back to South Dakota any time he wanted to, but he never returned. We don't talk about the rape. In fact, this is the first time I've brought it up in twenty years. But that's not even what I want to talk to you about today.

"What do you say, Buckley?" Robert turned to look at him. "Am I boring you? What's the matter, cat got your tongue?" He was lying on his side, his face towards the front seat. Blood had seeped from under the tape around his mouth and was caked on his chin. He stared back at Robert without expression.

Robert had almost forgotten about Buckley as he told his story. It felt so good to be talking about himself for a change, he didn't care if Buckley was listening or not. There were so many things in his life he wasn't supposed to talk about. Especially the topic he was about to bring up.

"Hearing no protests, allow me to continue." The Big Snowy Mountains rose to the west like a furry animal sleeping on the prairie. A storm was building over them, and he knew there would be snow in the valley soon.

"Frank's marriage to Anna wasn't a good one. It became

obvious to everyone six months after the wedding that he was screwing around on her. Anna was quiet, somewhat exotic in appearance with her mixture of Black and Indian blood, and she was very intelligent. I didn't know her well for a long time. To me, she was just a woman with few options who would counter Frank's offensive remarks with wit and intelligence. Her intellectual passions would flair up and then die just as quickly. She'd pursue them with abandon, but never to conclusion. She was lonely, but wouldn't admit it. She was unhappy, but refused to discuss it. I had little to do with her sad life until I, quite literally, got sucked into it.

"I began encouraging her to talk when I'd call and Frank wasn't around. I felt bad for her. God knows Frank can be a prick. At first she was hesitant to talk much. She'd admit to being angry at Frank's infidelities. Then she started naming them for me. 'The Fuck-of-the-Week,' she'd call them. I knew a lot of Frank's women. I've spent way too much time in local bars with him, getting in fights and sleeping with some of the same women he did. Not at the same time, mind you.

"After a while, Anna started getting bolder in her conversations with me on the phone. She told me how long it had been since she'd had sex with Frank. She told me about the men who'd tried to screw her in graduate school. The funny thing is, we'd never talk about this stuff in person, even if we were alone for long periods. Only on the phone. I started calling a lot more often, hoping to catch Anna alone at home, and I was getting more and more stimulated by our conversations, particularly when she started talking to me about the kind of things that excited her.

"We crossed a line one day, I guess it was about a year and a half ago. We'd been talking with increasing intimacy for at least six months. I knew it was wrong to be doing this with my best friend's wife, even if he did treat her like shit. But watching her open up for what I believed to be the first time was like, I don't know, discovering a new element. I think it went deeper that that though. I've never felt this way about a heavy metal."

Robert laughed at his little joke. He wondered why he was talking so much to Buckley, a man he thought a few hours earlier that he might kill. Robert decided that his need to talk about Anna was so desperate, and his options for listeners so limited, that he was willing to talk to a man who was tied up in the back seat of his car. Besides that, he wanted to put a human face on Buckley's victims. He decided to continue.

"The truth was, I was falling in love with her. One day I asked her if she ever masturbated. She'd been talking about how long it had been since she'd had sex, and how much she thought about it. It seemed like a logical question." He shrugged his shoulders as if to suggest innocence.

"She didn't say anything for a moment, and I immediately regretted the question. I started to apologize, but she cut me off. 'All the time,' she said. And then she started giggling. She sounded so adorable at that moment, I couldn't have resisted her if I'd been there. I got bolder and asked her what she thought about when she masturbated. She hesitated before she said, 'You, Robert.'

"I can't tell you what that did to me. Then she started describing to me, very slowly, some of the things she had dreamed of doing with me. In detail. I could tell she was touching herself as she spoke. I was doing the same thing. At one point, she jammed the receiver in a pillow so I wouldn't hear her as she came. 'Sorry,' she said a minute later, as if I might have been upset.

"After that conversation, we got bolder still. She'd call me collect when Frank was gone, and I'd call her right back. Two, three times a week we'd make love over the phone. I'd have her describe everything she was doing to herself while I'd imagine how she would taste and feel and smell. It was an incredibly erotic experience.

"Hell, old man," he said, glancing at Buckley in the mirror. "This shouldn't surprise you. You're an old pro at phone sex. You wanted Anna yourself. You have no idea what you missed.

"We'd try role playing. Her car died near a biker's bar where I was drinking with friends and she'd wander in helplessly. I'd be a teenage student and she'd be my teacher. Stuff like that. She was incredibly creative sexually. You'd never know by looking at her. All you'd see is a shy, pretty, unhappy woman who looked out of place wherever she was. Frank had no idea how much of her love he'd squandered. I began to almost hate him for it, but I was looking for excuses to hate him so I wouldn't feel guilty about falling in love with his wife.

"This went on for a couple of months. The thrill never left us. One day she said, 'Robert. It's time for us to meet alone.' I argued with her for hours over the next week or two, but she could be incredibly persuasive for a shy woman. I wanted her so badly anyway. The hard part was that I couldn't talk about my feelings for her because she was my friend's wife. Plus, how many people would understand how you could fall in love over the phone? I finally gave in and reserved us a room in the Alex Johnson Hotel in Rapid City. It was just after Thanksgiving, 1994, a little more than a year ago, even though it seems longer than that.

"I got to the room first, and I wished I hadn't. I thought I might lose my mind as I paced the small room, stopping every five minutes to brush my teeth.

"Finally, I heard her knock on the door and I almost passed out. I fumbled with the knob and let her in. Oh, my God, she was so beautiful that night! Her face changed every time I saw her. That night she looked more African American than Sioux. Her hair was as wiry as spun wool and pitch black. Her eyes were, well, not to sound too corny, but they were full of love, almost like they were lit from behind. She wore this red silk blouse that fit her loosely, and a black cotton skirt that buttoned up the front.

"I was overcome with emotion. I dropped to my knees and hugged her hips. I was crying at the time. 'My baby, my baby,' she kept saying as she stroked my hair, bending down to kiss the top of my head. Finally, I lifted up her skirt. I had stopped crying by then, but I couldn't always tell if I was tasting her or my own tears. It didn't really matter though. Whenever we made love, from that moment until the end, it was as if our bodies, our souls were forced together with such intensity they became one. It released such power it was frightening. We'd get lost in each other. I couldn't tell her body from mine, or even if

I was thinking her thoughts or my own when we were together. Do you know how scary that is?"

He took a couple of deep breaths. "I'm sure we weren't the first couple to make love in the old Alex Johnson Hotel. But I bet we were the loudest. Three times the management pleaded with us to keep it down. They offered to buy us a room in another hotel. By the second day, we had almost the whole floor to ourselves, and the sign outside said 'No Vacancy.'

"We saw each other a half dozen times over the next six months. Usually, I'd have someone look after the ranch while I'd drive to Montana and meet her in Glasgow where no one knew her. She'd spend the day with me and get home about midnight while Frank was still out. I don't think he ever knew she was gone. He wasn't home much, and often he'd spend days away from the house.

"Each time we met, the intensity of our passion seemed stronger than before, if you can believe that. Once she came to see me when Frank was off on a trip to DC, and we made love in the schoolyard on an old bike rack just like Frank and I saw the sheriff doing years ago. I was ashamed of myself. Here I was, desperately in love with my best friend's wife, doing things to her that I never thought I'd be capable of. We fed off each other in an almost evil way. She'd get bigger and more alive the rougher I was with her. It's like our love tapped into a vein of something toxic in me that never should have seen the light of day."

He paused to consider a new thought. "I sound like I'm in your business, now, Buckley. It's a lot like uranium mining. Tapping into something toxic. What are you going to do with all that stuff once it's exposed? Maybe we're not all that different, you and I." He rolled the window down briefly and spit into the cold wind. A dozen Black Angus were grazing along the highway. "I hope that's not true. As much as I hate myself these days, it'd be worse if I thought I was like you."

He stopped the car to urinate beside the road. There was no danger of being seen since they hadn't passed a car in fifty miles. He got back in, turned up the heater, and was silent for the next ten miles. Then he started again.

"One day we were making love when she left the bed and stood by the window. 'What's the matter, baby?' I asked her.

"'You were scaring me,' she said. 'Do you have any idea what you were saying?' I told her I didn't, which was true. Apparently, while we were making love, I'd been saying this was a love to die for, a love to kill for. Stuff like that. It brought up the Frank issue. We'd never talked about him before. 'He'd kill you if he knew you were sleeping with me,' she said. 'You know that, don't you?'

"I told her I'd die without her anyway. I meant it. We decided we'd tell Frank about it since we couldn't go on without each other. The separations from each other were too painful, our passion was too intense. The pain of being apart outweighed our fear of Frank and what he might do to us. I'm not sure to this day that I wouldn't have killed Frank to be with her. In fact, that's what I was saying while we were making love. I guess I'll never know what I might have done, thank God.

"We decided to tell him when I came for my annual August trip to help with the wheat harvest. Everything was set. Three months went by. I only saw Anna once in that time, and finally I was there, ready to tell Frank and face the consequences.

"But something happened. Know what that was, Buckley? A bomb that was probably meant for Frank blew Anna into too many pieces to count. And it shattered my life. Half my soul is gone and the other half is still picking up the pieces trying to make things whole again. But it will never be whole again. Do you understand, Buckley? Has this little story put a human enough face on your fucking bomb?"

Robert pulled the car to a stop. The sun was low on the horizon. They'd been driving on dirt for miles, and the cloud of dust from the car was just now catching up with them. "My, my. Look where we are. Recognize this place?"

Buckley sat up and looked out the window. There was frost on the bottom of it. They had pulled to a stop near the dumpsite on the reservation, the place where someone had shot at him and Frank.

"I just got a wild hair," Robert said. "There's a desk inside the shed in the compound. There's a pack of Pall Malls in the top drawer. Get me one, will you? I feel like a smoke."

Buckley violently shook his head no. For the first time, fear showed in his eyes. Robert reached in his coat and pulled out the .38 Special. He held it against the side of Buckley's nose. "Damn you, Buckley. You poisoned this land, killed the woman I loved, and paralyzed my best friend. I'm under a lot of stress and I want a goddamn cigarette. Now go get it for me!"

Again Buckley shook his head. Robert cocked the hammer, moved the barrel slightly and fired. The slug missed Buckley's nose by inches but left a powder burn on his face. It shattered the station wagon's back seat window. Buckley recoiled from the noise. Then he nodded, and Robert let him out of the car.

"Turn around," he said. "Let me untape your wrists, but don't touch that tape on your mouth." He tore off the tape and Buckley marched slowly towards the compound. "I wouldn't change my mind if I were you. I'm a damn good shot."

Buckley slowly made his way the twenty yards to the compound and disappeared behind the fence. A couple of minutes later he returned with the pack of smokes. Robert knew Buckley wouldn't run away. Out here, there was no place to hide, and he'd freeze to death in an hour.

Robert took the pack and tossed it on the ground. "Thanks, but I changed my mind. Go ahead and untape your mouth. I'm all talked out for now."

The tape left bright red patches on Buckley's cheeks. It must have hurt like hell to remove it, but Buckley showed no signs of pain.

"Well," Robert said. "Aren't you going to say anything?"

Buckley hauled back and punched Robert in the mouth. He'd been hit harder before, but it still hurt. It struck Robert as funny and he started laughing.

"Am I mistaken, or am I still the one with the gun?" He actually looked down at his hand to be sure. The .38 was still nestled comfortably in his palm. "You don't hit a guy with a gun."

"You son-of-a-bitch!" Buckley was shaking with rage. "I'm not your man."

Robert pressed a sleeve to his lip and then examined the blood on it. "I suppose you had nothing to with this?" He waved his pistol in an arc towards the compound.

"Of course I did. My company built it and operated it. You already know that. I don't know how you figured it out, and right now, I don't care, but I didn't kill your girlfriend. The man who did that is as much a threat to me as he is to you. I want him as badly as you, and I'll work with you to get him."

Robert scratched his jaw with his thumb, spit blood in the dust and looked up at the sky. "Whoa there, Buckley. This is a strange turn of events." He stuck the pistol in his pocket. "Get in the car. No, the front seat. I want to hear you out on this one. You've had almost five hours to come up with a good lie to save your butt. I want to watch your eyes as you talk to me."

Robert listened as Buckley talked for the next forty-five minutes. It was dark by the time they arrived at Frank's house. The house looked the way it did the day after the bombing, except the spilled grain had blown away.

"Jesus. That was quite a bomb," Buckley said. "I can't believe any of you survived it."

Robert got out of the car. "C'mon. Let's go meet Frank."

It tore at Robert's heart to see the place where Anna was killed. The house looked like a fresh wound; a gaping, mangled shell of what it used to be, much like Robert's heart. Frank was in his wheelchair when they entered.

"What the fuck kept you?"

"We took the scenic route. Frank, this is Mr.—Frank! No!"

He tried to knock the gun out of Frank's hands, but by the time he lunged at him, Frank had already fired a slug into Buckley's belly.

The man doubled over and dropped to his knees. He made gurgling sounds in his throat as he stared at the floor and clutched his stomach.

"Goddamnit, Frank!"

Frank said to Buckley. "That's a Pope John Paul shot. A .38 slug to the lower abdomen. No vital organs destroyed.

You'll wear a colostomy bag for six months, but you'll live."

Buckley's blood began to pool on the floor.

"Breaking and entering, forgery, kidnapping, and now man-slaughter," Robert moaned. "Frank, he didn't plant the bomb! You didn't give me a chance to explain."

"It that his dump site?"

"Yes."

"Then you deserve to die, mother-fucker," Frank said to Buckley. "You treated us like slaves, poisoned our land, lied to us, hardly paid us a goddamn cent, and you killed any of us who got in your way."

"No, he didn't kill anyone."

"Shut the fuck up!" Frank shouted, pointing the pistol at Robert.

Then to Buckley, "I want you to experience some Indian hospitality. You came here to meet with me. That's what you tell the sheriff. There was an apparent domestic disturbance in town. You caught a stray bullet in the gut. You'll stay in the Indian hospital in Poplar for a month to recover. You stray from the story, you leave a day too early, I'll find you later and give you the John Lennon treatment instead of the Pope shot. That's three bullets in the aorta. You understand me?"

Buckley managed to nod weakly.

"Robert, run the good Mr. Buckley into town. Then get your ass back here quick. We've got some talking to do."

CHAPTER 7

Robert returned to Frank's house a couple of hours past dark. He entered through a blue plastic tarp that replaced the door between the living room, which was no longer there, and the kitchen. Frank sat at the kitchen table, staring into an almost empty bottle of Jack Daniels.

"Well?" Frank asked. Even though he uttered only one syllable, he still managed to slur it.

"Well what, for Chrissakes?"

"How is he?"

"A little late for concern on your part, don't you think?"

"He gonna live?"

"He almost bled to death on the way."

"Yeah, I miscalculated. The Pope got medical 'sistance right away."

"He went into shock about ten miles from town and started convulsing. I thought I'd lost him. I had to stuff my shirt in the hole in his gut to stop the bleeding. He'll be lucky if he survives the infection. The hospital said he had no pulse when he got there. But they pumped him full of fluids, put him on a respirator and got him breathing again."

"'At's good, real good, Robert."

"Fuck you, Frank. You shot the poor bastard before he even said hello. What do you care about him?"

The tarp wasn't nailed down tight enough, and it fluttered noisily in the wind. Frank poured himself another glass of whiskey, draining the bottle. "Want some?"

"Sure," Robert said. "I had a rough day."

"'There's another bottle under the sink. Glass on the counter."

Robert washed the glass and poured it half full of whiskey. "How much of that did you drink tonight?" he said, pointing to the empty bottle on the table.

"Most of it, I think," Frank said as Robert sat across the table from him. "I guess I mighta overreacted a bit."

"Putting a bullet through a guy? I'd say so."

"I got a lotta anger in me, Robert. I just don't know what to do with it sometimes."

That was about as honest a statement as he'd ever heard from Frank. Robert was mad as hell about Frank's having added attempted manslaughter to their crimes. He had every intention of telling Frank that he, Robert, would find and punish the man who killed Anna without Frank's help. But with Frank acting so uncharacteristically contrite, he couldn't help but stay a little longer, if for no other reason than to see where the conversation was headed. It was like hanging in to see your last card in seven card stud.

"My wife was killed, Robert. You don't know what that's like. Not really. We had our problems. She never did master the art of living with an asshole like me. But aside from that, she was a wonderful woman. None like her in the world."

"Maybe you should have told her that once or twice."

"What the fuck do you know about my relationship with her?" He threw the empty Jack Daniels bottle across the room and it shattered against a kitchen wall. "What the hell business is it of yours what my relationship with Anna was like?"

Robert wasn't intimidated by Frank's anger. He was still furious with him for squandering Anna's love. Staring back at Frank, he said, "You didn't have to be a rocket scientist to see how unhappy she was. And you didn't have to be too bright to know that you were a big reason why she was so goddamn miserable."

He thought Frank might shoot him for saying it, but he himself was so miserable, he didn't much care. Instead, Frank surprised him by putting his head on the table and crying. Not loudly, but Robert could see his shoulders bobbing up and down. The sight made Robert extremely uncomfortable. In all his life, he'd never known Frank to cry. Robert downed his whiskey and poured himself another. He hadn't a clue what to say or how to provide comfort to his friend, whom he still loved even through his anger. So he just sat there and didn't say a thing.

"I didn't know she was going to die," Frank said after he'd stopped crying and wiped his eyes with a paper towel. He did not look directly at Robert when he talked. "I'd have either treated her better or divorced her so she could have gotten on with her life if I'd only known."

He blew his nose into the towel. "I guess it's better to treat everyone like they're going to die tomorrow. I know that now, but I don't know if I can do anything about it." Frank sipped from his glass of whiskey. "And another thing I learned today—"

"What's that, Frank?"

"It don't feel right."

"What doesn't?"

"Shooting a man. It just don't feel right. I wish I'd 'a never pulled that trigger. My anger just got the best of me. It almost always does. But that's the first time I ever shot anyone."

"It didn't seem to bother you to kill that guy at the dump site."

"That's different, damnit. I did that with my bare hands."

"Pretty subtle distinction, if you ask me."

"Besides, he was shooting at us. He had a mask on, too. I couldn't see the pain in his face like I could in Buckley's. Made me feel so bad, I wanted to turn the gun on myself."

"That makes three of us in the room who wanted to shoot you."

"I worry you might do that one of these days, Robert. Or that I might shoot you instead."

Robert couldn't think of a single response to that one.

"But hell," Frank continued. "No sense crying over spilt milk. We still have a murder to solve." Frank was ready to get back to business. The cry seemed to have sobered him up. "You say that Buckley's not the one who killed Anna?"

"Not according to Buckley. And I'm inclined to believe him in this case."

"Then who the fuck planted the bomb?"

"It was a guy who calls himself 'Newt'. Not after the beloved Speaker, though. He's been calling himself that for nearly thirty years. He used to live on the Fort Peck Reservation years ago. Part Indian. His last name was Nori. Ever heard of him?"

"Nope. He must have changed his name when he left the reservation. No Indian would last long around here with a pussy name like 'Newt.' I'd 'a beat him up myself for good measure." Frank tossed the end of his braid over his shoulder. "What's his interest in all this?"

"Newt's short for 'Neutron.' The guy has this fascination with nuclear power. He was kind of a nerd in school. People were mean to him, and he couldn't wait to get off the Rez. After he graduated high school, he got a job working for one of Buckley's companies hauling—guess what—nuclear waste. Basically, the guy drove a truck, but instead of hauling lumber or garbage, he was transporting toxic stuff, even though he was right out of high school."

Robert took another sip of whiskey. He closed his eyes for a moment and felt the warmth flow through his body as the whiskey went down. He always drank more when he was with

Frank.

"Don't go to sleep on me, Robert. I'm just getting into your story."

Robert shook his head and continued. "So the guy hauls poison for a couple of years, eventually gets a fifteen cent an hour raise and discovers he's not all that happy with life off the reservation. He's living in a drafty trailer in a rough section of Denver, and life's not the bed of roses he expected. The world hadn't yet recognized his superior intelligence. He was still just another lowlife, and he was probably every bit as miserable as he'd been on the reservation.

"Buckley was being paid heavily at the time by the U.S. Government to clean up after its nuclear test blasts. The government was also busy promoting its nuclear program."

Robert stood up and stretched. He went to the cupboard and opened it out of curiosity. A couple of cockroaches, irritated by the light, scrambled over an open package of Fig Newtons. He closed the cupboard door and continued with his story.

"The early nuclear power plants built in the '50s spread a lot of contamination. The operators would vent radioactive iodine and other nuclear gas byproducts into the atmosphere whenever they felt like it. They stored contaminated water in open pits lined with leaky plastic tarps. Spent uranium was stored in canisters near the barracks where the workers slept."

Robert shook his head as he thought about the government's careless attitude that bordered on being criminal. "The United States was on a mission to develop its nuclear program faster than any other nation on earth, especially the Soviet Union. It wasn't going to let safety considerations slow its progress."

He sat back down at the table, took another pull from his drink and again paused while the alcohol circulated through his system. He could smell snow in the air from the wind that blew outside the tarp.

"Are you going to get back to this guy, Newt?" Frank asked.

"I'm getting there. This is all related. You'll see. Back in the 1950s and early '60s, the government could condemn a piece of land and dump anything they wanted on it. There were about a hundred million less people in America, so we had a lot more room. Almost everyone trusted our government back then, and nobody except scientists and the government knew a damn thing about radioactivity and what it did to cells in the human body. So no one questioned them. But the late sixties came around, the dawning of the Age of Aquarius, and all that, and people didn't want that stuff in their backyards anymore. And to make matters worse, strange things began happening near the power plants."

"Like what?" Frank asked. "Three-legged frogs and giant dandelions begin showing up?"

"That's probably exaggerated. But they began to notice a lot of infertility, low birth weight babies, high leukemia and cancer rates among the locals, especially around the Hanford plant in Washington."

"Did Buckley tell you all this?"

"Some of it. I've also done some reading about it on my own, before I knew any of this would affect my own life."

"Man, you're just like Anna—reading all that shit like you're gonna have a test on it. I never much liked homework, myself." Frank wheeled his chair to the kitchen sink where he proceeded to empty his bladder bag.

"God, Frank! Aren't you going to rinse out the sink?" Frank made no comment as he wheeled himself back to the table.

Robert decided not to press it. "Newt was still driving trucks for Buckley at the time, not making a big impression on the world as yet. The guy had no social life at all. When he wasn't reading about the theory of nuclear fission, he spent his time studying corporate reports on the company he worked for."

"What a fucking life. If I was bored enough to read shit like that, I'd of killed myself a long time ago."

"Finally, he decides to take action to improve his lot. He rents a P.O. box, prints up some business letterheads to make him look official, and writes a letter to his boss, Mr. Buckley, who he's never met. Says he has some ideas about sites for storing contaminated materials. He knows Buckley's company is running up against a shortage of dumpsites because he'd done his homework. What's more, he could talk Buckley's language. Hell, he probably knew more about nuclear wastes at that point than his boss did. It must have been a hell of a letter, because Buckley agreed to meet him in Denver a week later."

"How did Buckley react when he was greeted by a kid instead of some big shot?"

"The same way he did when I met him at the airport. He tried to leave with a show of indignation. But Newt was prepared. He got Buckley's attention when he said he was worried about the public reaction to the news that Buckley was storing excess nuclear materials in an unsecured warehouse in downtown Denver."

"I bet he did, all right. Buckley seems to respond real well to threats." Frank placed a hand over his gut and looked pained. "I had too much to drink tonight, Robert. I was upset about the shooting, even if it was a favor to society." Frank no longer seemed drunk. "Would you mind getting me a glass of milk from the fridge to settle my stomach?"

Again, this was new behavior. Frank actually asked rather than ordered Robert to do something for him. Things were changing. Robert washed another glass, being careful not to cut himself on its chipped edges. No telling what kind of infection he'd pick up from an open wound at Frank's house. He went to the refrigerator, and to his surprise found the milk to be sweet and fresh. He poured Frank a glass and delivered it to him along with the carton so Frank could help himself to more of it. The house was so cold, the milk would stay fresh for a long time on the table.

"So what was Newt's proposal?" Frank asked. "To dump shit on the reservation?"

"Yes. You can see why the plan appealed to Buckley. All that open space and no people around. He could secure the land cheaply and no one would ever question it."

"Okay, so he suggested dumping on the reservation. What was Newt's role in making the arrangements for it to happen?"

"He told Buckley who to pay off in the Tribal Council, how to package the deal as a coal mining venture, and helped locate the perfect dump site. Newt basically arranged the whole damn thing."

"Son-of-a-bitch!" Frank yelled, slamming his fist on the table. His glass fell over and a little milk dribbled onto the floor. "Now *there's* a lunatic I could shoot without feeling bad about it!"

Then again, Robert thought, *maybe Frank hasn't changed all that much.*

"So Newt, the former tribal member who changed his name and left the reservation, helps poison his former home," Frank said. "Crown Pipe Mining Corporation was his brainstorm. What'd he get out of all this?"

"He got Buckley to line up a scholarship for him go to college in Denver."

Frank shook his head in disbelief. Though he excelled at it, school was like punishment to him.

"Newt kept working for Buckley while he was in school. He was a good driver and he got the job of hauling enriched uranium to some of the test plants around the company."

"I can't believe this shit. Some delusional, dipshit, pimply-faced kid was getting paid two bucks an hour to haul weapons-grade uranium all over the goddamn country?"

"You got it."

Frank poured himself some more milk. "That's it. I'm never paying taxes again." He drained his glass.

"You never have, have you?"

"No, but now I'm making a point of not paying. Go on."

"What do you suppose Newt studied in college?" Robert asked.

"How about home economics?"

"Nuclear engineering. Now, you want to guess what else he

was doing at the time?"

"Jerking off on the side of the highway? That's what I'd do."

"No, damnit, he was—"

"I know what the fuck he was doing. You think I'm an idiot? He was squirreling away uranium."

Frank was paying better attention than Robert realized.

"So that's why Buckley's put up with our boy for all these years?" Frank said. "Because Newt's been blackmailing him? Threatening to report his company for stealing uranium. They'd probably trace the thefts back to Buckley instead of Newt."

"That's right. Newt was smart. He never took much from any one shipment. Not enough to be detected. Over time, he's socked away plenty. He hasn't driven in years, but he's still on Buckley's payroll. About ten years ago, he knocked Buckley over the head and drove him around in a cargo van for two days to show him the goods. Buckley has no idea where Newt's keeping the stuff. He couldn't see a thing the whole trip. Newt may have been driving him in circles for all he knew."

Robert paused. "I was really disappointed to hear this part of the story. I thought I was the first one to knock Buckley over the head, but seems he's had previous experience."

"How come Buckley doesn't just kill Newt?"

"Newt says he wrote a letter documenting abuses of Buckley's company. The letter will be released to authorities in the event of Newt's death."

"So Buckley has to keep Newt alive to save his own ass. Very clever. Did you find out why Newt planted the bomb at my house?" Frank asked. "Why'd he want to kill us?"

"The guy's a computer nut. He was on-line when you started asking questions about Crown Pipe Mining Corporation. I guess it got his attention."

"What name's he go by on-line?"

"I have no idea."

"You didn't ask Buckley? What the fuck were you thinking? I probably know the guy from on-line. I could look up his profile on the computer."

"It never occurred to me. I'm not the electronic whiz you are."

"Great. Now I have to go ask Buckley, the man I almost killed, if he'll kindly share the information with me. Shit, Robert, I think I could have found him if you had his screen name. Now it's probably too late. I bet he's already destroyed his profile."

"Anyway," Robert continued, "Newt bombed your truck. Buckley said he loves to make bombs. He was probably the kind of kid who'd paint chairs with stuff that blew up when it dried, or maybe he'd fill soap bubbles with gas from a Bunsen burner and set them on fire when they rose to the ceiling. The guy apparently has had a life-long fascination with pyrotechnics. The problem is now that he's bigger, his toys are more dangerous."

"What's enriched uranium going for these days?" Frank asked.

"Plenty. I'd guess maybe ten grand a kilo."

"How much has he got?"

"I don't know, a couple of thousand kilos or so."

"Jesus! That's quite a stockpile. Is he trying to sell it back to Buckley?"

"No. Buckley pays him a couple of grand a month to keep his mouth shut. Nothing exorbitant. Newt's not interested in selling it."

"So what's a lonely recluse going to do with, let's see, that'd be about 2.2 tons of uranium?"

Robert looked at him with a cocked head. "How the hell did you figure out it was 2.2 tons?"

"You said he had two thousand kilos. That'd make 2.2 tons."

God, Frank made him mad sometimes! Here he was, drunk, in mourning, paralyzed, and a fugitive from justice, and he could still make conversions from the metric system easier than most people count change in the grocery store. It was exasper-

ating. "If you can figure that out, then you can sure as hell figure out what he plans to do with the uranium."

"What? Make a fucking bomb?"

"Bingo!"

"I was just kidding! You can't make a nuclear bomb in
your garage, like it was some kind of woodworking project."

"Apparently he can. He's a nuclear engineer, after all. He
got his college degree that Buckley financed. And he does have
the essential materials."

"So we're after a nuclear terrorist? This dipshit who killed
my wife has unlocked the secret of the Bomb? We're trying to
stop him before he blows up the country?"

"That's right."

"Well, shit almighty, buddy. This is getting exciting!"

CHAPTER 8

Robert's love for the Fort Peck Indian Reservation had blossomed over the two decades he'd been visiting it. The vastness of the landscape was humbling. Two million acres of practically deserted prairie stretched far beyond the horizon like an ocean, and he could only guess at the distance of its boundaries. The undulating hills had a sensual quality, particularly in the fall when they took on a brown tone that looked almost flesh-like. The land was more open and harsher than his native South Dakota. The grasses were shorter, the rainfall less, the wind stronger, the land emptier, but the smell of sage and soil were like perfume to him and the skies were bluer than wildflowers.

The Missouri River, looking like it did when Lewis and Clark first saw it nearly 200 years ago, formed the southern border of the reservation. Robert visited the Missouri often to feel the shade of the trees and smell the leaves decaying under the cottonwoods that bordered the river. Years ago, there were more trees along the river, but in the 1930s, the federal government built the world's largest earth-filled dam. They sited it just upstream from the reservation.

Before the dam was built, the river would rise every spring until it overflowed its banks. The waters picked up sediment from the floodplain and deposited it downstream as sandbars where birds nested. The shallow waters flowing over the floodplain would recharge oxbows and other nearby wetlands while providing spawning habitat for the river's ancient native fish— the paddlefish, the pallid sturgeon, and others. The receding floodwaters added debris to the river and nutrients that helped maintain healthy fish populations.

By late summer, the river would slow to a trickle and stay low until the melting snow in the mountains refreshed the river in the spring. Then the river would begin to swell as if it were breathing until it overflowed its banks, and the cycle would begin once more.

The flooding worked well for the river's fish and wildlife, but it wreaked havoc on cities. People in Kansas City and Omaha, hundreds of miles downstream from the river's source in Montana, grew tired of having to navigate their streets in boats every spring and began clamoring for assistance from the federal government to control that goddamned, unpredictable river. So Congress authorized the construction of the Fort Peck Dam in Montana to stop the flooding.

It was the first of six gigantic dams on the Missouri, which eventually succeeded in turning this once wild and unpredictable river into the world's largest plumbing system. Although the dam was located upstream from the reservation, hundreds of Sioux and Assiniboine families, including Frank Kicking Bird's paternal grandparents, were evicted from the bottomlands that had sustained their ancestors for a thousand years.

It was a bitter blow, and it rendered those families incapable of maintaining the subsistence existence they'd always known. Forced to work for wages for the first time in their lives, many of them had to suffer the indignity of helping build the dam that destroyed them, as if they were digging their own graves.

The dam tightly regulated river flows and controlled those pesky annual floods. It also severed the river's connection to the floodplain, and in doing so, diminished the river's fish and

wildlife habitat. And the cottonwood trees, those lovely adorn-
ments to the river's banks, were no longer regenerating the way
they used to when spring floods would commonly inundate
their habitat along the river.

But the views were still satisfying among the trees. And it
was here on the riverbank, a half mile from the reservation
town of Poplar, Montana, that Robert was meeting with Mason
Tomlinson, the editor of the tribal newspaper, the *Wotanin
Wowapi*. Mason had been hounding Robert for information for
the past two weeks, ever since they had convinced him to help
invent the story of Frank's death.

"You owe me that much, damnit!" Tomlinson said, throwing a rock into the river's muddy waters.

They were sitting on the bank enjoying the sunshine reflecting off the water onto their faces. It was warm for early February, and the bright winter sun had melted most of the snow. A
lip of opaque ice extended from the bank several feet into the
river.

"I don't owe you a thing," Robert said, throwing a rock
about twice as far as Tomlinson did.

"Let's aim for that log." Mason jumped to his feet. He and
Robert threw a barrage of stones at a chunk of driftwood float-
ing lazily by about a quarter of the way across the river. Mason
was the first to hit it and he celebrated by prancing around like
a boxer who had just scored a knockout.

"Let's put a bet on it," Robert said. "Next one to hit it gets
a buck."

"Tell you what. If I hit it first, you give me the information
I want. If you hit it, I'll get it out of you some other way."

"Heads I lose, tails you win?"

"Right. Let's go for it." Mason threw a handful of gravel
that fell around the log like rain. It dimpled the surface of the
river, but not a single piece of gravel hit the log.

Robert bounced two stones in a row off the driftwood before it floated out of range. Then he sat back down on the bank.

"I just can't talk about this stuff yet. I'd be in serious trouble if it you printed a story on it now. And we haven't found out what we need yet. It's too early."

"I'm not going to write it up for the paper until I get your okay. I just want a head start on the story."

"I know you're interested in what's going on. I just can't tell you much yet."

"Do you have any idea how tedious it is to always write about basketball games and 'domestic incidents?' This sounds like a real news story for a change."

"Tell you what. I'll give you an exclusive interview when I can finally talk, and you can get the Pulitzer for your story."

"Fuck you!" Mason said, throwing another rock into the river. "You come into my office, tie me up, beat me—"

"Wait just a goddamn minute. We never laid a finger on you."

"Bullshit. I had a scab on my cheek for two weeks."

"All that was your idea, including the sandpaper."

"Trivial details, Robert. Stick to the point."

"You're a journalist. You're supposed to care about details."

"Somewhere in this stupid conversation, I had a point. Don't confuse things."

"Then don't push me too hard yet."

"I was pretty goddamn accommodating when you needed me," Mason said, chucking another rock into the river. "And I've been awfully patient since. But now I need you. Talk to me!"

"Ask me some questions. I'll answer them if I can. But no story until I say so. Agreed?"

"It's a lousy deal, but I'll take what I can get," Mason said. "For starters, what do you know about the guy who was just in our local hospital with a bullet hole in his gut?"

"People get shot around here all the time. Which guy?" Robert wanted to find out how much Mason already knew before he answered the question.

"Christopher Buckley, CEO and controlling owner of Pipe Butte Corporation, formerly Crown Pipe Mining Corporation. He's easy to spot, Robert. He's the only multi-millionaire white guy with a bullet hole in his stomach in the Poplar, Montana, hospital. At least I'm pretty sure he's the only one."

"My, my. You have done your homework. What do I know about him? I know he was here for about ten days until he was stable, and they flew him back to New England."

"Who put the bullet in him?"

Robert shrugged."

"I can't believe you'd shoot him. You just don't strike me as the type. So my guess is that it was Frank who plugged him. Why?"

"I can't say anything about the shooting. Try a new line of questions."

"I can understand you're not wanting to divulge anything about a possible attempted homicide."

Robert didn't like the sound of "attempted homicide." Suddenly the phrase carried more meaning than it used to.

"Let me ask you this. Why did you and Frank lure Buckley to the reservation with that phony story about Frank's death?"

"Do you know what Buckley's company does?"

"Yes, I do. Do you know where he lives, Robert?"

"Somewhere in Maine."

"Near Acadia National Park. He's practically a next door neighbor of Delvin Beersteen, former Secretary of Defense."

Mason was sharper than Robert thought. "What's the connection?"

"I thought I was supposed to be asking questions," Mason said. "But I'm the one giving out all the information. You ought to be a reporter yourself with all the questions you ask." He threw another rock in the river.

"Buckley's companies thrived off government contracts, hauling nuclear wastes, mostly. So, naturally, he wanted to stay close to the Secretary of Defense. I'd guess their relationship was mutually enriching."

"You mean he paid Beersteen off?" Robert asked.

"Maybe. I do know that Beersteen got a fat consulting contract with Buckley after he retired from government service."

So that's how things work, Robert thought. Mason was turning out to be very helpful. He decided it was time to share a few things with him.

"I don't have much to offer you yet. We thought Buckley was responsible for the bomb that killed Frank's wife, Anna." Just the mention of her name set off a little bomb of grief in him. The pain wasn't as constant as it had been the first weeks after her death, but it was nearly as intense. Dozens of little reminders of her would crop up during the course of a day, and, still, there was no one with whom he could share his grief.

He continued with his story. "Buckley dumped tons of nuclear wastes on the reservation. Frank and I and a whole lot of other people will never forgive him for that. But Buckley was not acting alone. He had some inside help setting up the dump site."

"Look at that!" Mason pointed across the river. A bald eagle glided along the water in front of them. "I love eagles. Now what were you saying about inside help?"

"A former reservation kid, a half Indian who drove a truck for Buckley, talked Buckley into using the reservation for a dump site." Once Robert started in on a story, it was hard for him to stop—a dangerous habit when talking to a reporter. "This kid planted the bomb that killed Anna."

Again he felt an almost primal urge for vengeance, an urge that scared him in the weeks after Anna's death. But now it felt like an urge that needed to be satisfied, like hunger or sexual longing.

"Why would he want to plant a bomb?" Mason threw another rock at a forked cottonwood branch bobbing down the river. "Bombs are so, well, so messy. They really chew up bodies and buildings and things. Yuck! I hate explosions."

"He wanted to either kill us or scare us off because he has something to hide. Apparently he's spent years squirreling away—"

His sentence was interrupted by a loud blast, a deep-throated explosion from the center of town about a half mile away.

"I'll be goddamn!" Mason shouted, jumping to his feet. "We were just talking about bombs, and whoosh! There goes one." He was very excited. "I wish we'd been talking about sex." A cloud of smoke and dust rose from Main Street. Some debris fountained in the air with the smoke.

"Speaking about chewing up bodies," Robert said as he stared at the flying rubble. "I hope no one was hurt."

"Oh, shit!" Mason slumped back to the ground. "I can't tell for sure, but that looks like the sign from my office. I think someone just blew up my newspaper."

Sure enough, Robert saw the sign cartwheeling in the air.

"C'mon, Mason," Robert said. "Let move it. I think Newt's back in town."

He ran toward town with Mason puffing along far behind him. The footing was treacherous as he picked his way through the brush and jumped over fallen limbs. He was almost out of the wooded area when suddenly, the air exploded from his lungs as someone hit him across the sternum with a heavy piece of wood. He went down hard, grabbed his ribs and struggled for air as he rose to his knees.

Then he heard the metallic click of a pistol's hammer and felt a cold ring of steel against his skull behind his right ear.

"You have no idea how much trouble you've caused me, Mr. Botkin."

Robert gasped as he finally got some air into his lungs. He took another breath. The second one came much easier.

"Sorry, Newt. I was only trying to find out why you killed Anna, you son of a bitch!" Robert stayed on his knees with his back to his attacker.

"You're right. It's my turn to apologize," Newt said. "I never met the woman and had no intention of harming her. I hate killing people, especially the wrong ones."

"So it was Frank you planned to kill?"

"Yes, it was. But he got even, you know. That was my brother he killed at the dumpsite."

"Frank always gets even. You'll have to forgive him for his actions at the dump. He tends to lose his head when someone's pointing a gun at him. So do I. So why don't you put the gun down?"

Newt ignored the request. "I had also hoped to get lucky and kill you with the bomb," Newt said. "I know how close you and Frank are, and I assumed you were working with him to get me in trouble. But my plans have changed. I don't want to kill you anymore. I just want you to come with me."

"Why?"

"You'll find out. If you do join me, you won't regret it, and I'll never harm you again."

"And if I don't?"

"I'll kill you right here. That's a promise, and I always keep my promises."

The threat didn't scare Robert, even though he took it seriously. He was so filled with anger that there wasn't any room for fear. Besides, the trip might give him some information about what Newt planned to do with his nuclear stockpile—but only if Robert kept himself from killing Newt.

"So what changed your mind about killing me?" Robert asked.

"Because I hate killing people. I really do."

"Yet you just blew up another bomb on Main Street in the middle of the day?"

"It was mostly a concussion bomb. Lots of noise, but very little real damage. I doubt anyone was hurt. Speaking of killing people, I would encourage you not to hurt me, curtail my freedom to move about, or turn me in to the police."

"Give me a good reason," Robert said. "I was just thinking about doing all the above."

"Because if you do, a lot of innocent people will die from a bomb I rigged up."

Newt's voice was high, slightly effeminate, and very precise and polished. His diction was measured, as if he was trying a little too hard to achieve an air of authority. "And believe me, this is no ordinary firecracker like the one I just set off in town." He coughed noisily. "Another reason I didn't kill you is that I need your help. I found out you're friends with a reporter."

Mason? Robert wondered. *Why would Newt be interested in Mason? And where the hell did he go?*

"She works for *Time Magazine*," Newt said.

"Oh, you mean Amy," he said, immediately regretting having mentioned her name. Amy Boston was a stringer for *Time* who used to write stories about one of Robert's former bosses. Robert had maintained a friendship with her ever since he worked with her on those stories ten years ago.

"I'm in need of some publicity, so I want you to contact her," Newt continued.

"I'm a reporter!" Mason said stepping around the tree behind which he was hiding.

Robert turned to look at him. *The idiot!* Newt had apparently not seen Mason or had forgotten about him. *He should have stayed behind his tree.*

"You're not a reporter, you're a typist who spits out local police reports," Newt said.

Mason surprised them both by picking up a rock and throwing it at Newt's head. Mason's arm was warmed up from having thrown the rocks at logs in the river, and he almost connected. Newt screamed like a skinny kid being picked on by the bully at recess. He ducked as the rock whistled past his ear.

Robert got his first chance to look at Newt. The man was very long and thin. His legs were like sticks inside his charcoal gray slacks. His body looked bony inside his red down jacket. A few dead leaves stuck to his black wool cap. The guy looked so pathetic, Robert almost felt sorry for him. There was no visible trace of the Indian blood he was supposed to have in him.

Newt pointed his gun and fired off a shot between Mason's legs.

"Jesus!" Mason shouted, jumping backwards. "You could have shot my pecker off!"

"Don't you ever try anything like that again!" Newt turned towards Robert. "I want you to invite your reporter friend to meet us," he said, sniffing and wiping his eyes with the sleeve of his jacket.

"I told you," Mason said. "I'm a fucking reporter! I want to write up this whole damn story."

"Make him shut up before I shoot him!" Newt cried in a panicked voice.

It struck Robert as funny that Mason, a middle aged, thin man with a receding hairline who by no means cut a powerful physical presence, could intimidate anyone. *This is the guy I've been hating all these months?* he thought. "All right, Mason," Robert said. "Shut the hell up for a minute."

"Do you always throw rocks at the subjects of your interviews?" Newt said.

"Not if they're cooperative," Mason replied.

"Okay," Robert said. "I suppose I can call my friend. What kind of danger will I be putting her in?"

"She'll be in danger of missing the story of her life if she doesn't come."

"I don't want to put her at risk by meeting you."

Newt glanced up at a red tail hawk flying overhead. He raised his pistol and brought the bird fluttering to the earth with one shot. It fell dead in a bloody bundle of feathers a hundred yards from where they stood.

"Goddamn you!" Mason shouted. "That's a federally protected species." Mason took a step towards Newt but backed off when Newt pointed the pistol at his chest.

"Robert, I promise I will not harm or threaten your reporter. She'll be in no danger from me whatsoever. I give you my word."

"I think there's ample reason to question your character. Why should I believe you?"

"Because I don't lie. And, as a further incentive, I'll shoot you if you don't agree to call her. I already had her name before you blurted it out, but I'd like the introduction to come from you. It would make our first meeting less awkward."

"And what will happen to me when I call her and you no longer need me?"

"A fair question. You'll be free to go."

"I don't care what other reporter you get, I'm coming along," Mason said. "I'm not going to miss this story. No sir."

Newt stood about six and a half feet tall but did not weigh over a hundred and fifty pounds. Stringy yellow hair spilling from his wool cap hung limply to his chin, almost covering the acne scars on his cheeks. His huge head seemed to be perched precariously on top of his impossibly long, thin neck. An Adam's apple large as a baby's fist bobbed up and down his throat even when he wasn't talking. Robert knew from Buckley that Newt was in his mid-forties, but it was very hard to tell the age of his still somewhat adolescent face.

Newt looked down at the gun in his hand, then pointed it at Robert's chest. "See that van over there?" He pointed with his other hand to an older U-Haul parked on a nearby road between the town and the river.

Robert and Mason nodded.

"Climb in the back while everyone's attention is diverted by my little bomb. You can go too if you behave," he said to Mason.

"What about my partner, Frank? Can he join us too?" Robert said.

"Frank Kicking Bird is a drunken, crippled, abusive Indian. He goes out of his way to live up to people's stereotypes of the "Lazy Red Man." I want no part of him. Now, go!" Newt shouted, as if to re-establish some authority.

Interesting, Robert thought as he headed to the van. *He knows Frank well enough to describe him accurately.* Robert made a mental note of the van's tags before climbing in the back. 2T-2623. Unfortunately, he didn't have a pen with which to write it down.

Mason climbed in the back with Robert just before Newt closed the swinging doors, leaving the two men wrapped in a blanket of darkness. A small hole in the floor of the van allowed them to see the road below, and a little light came in through a crack where the doors latched. There were a couple of sleeping bags on the floor of the van, and they crawled in them to keep warm.

Newt locked the doors before he started the truck and drove off with them. Robert and Mason sat next to one another against the wall nearest the cab. They huddled in their sleeping bags to keep warm.

"Nothing personal, Mason. But you're a goddamn idiot. You should have stayed behind the tree."

"And miss out on this adventure? No way."

"The guy's dangerous. You could end up dead."

"That'd still make a good story. The only difference is that I wouldn't be writing it." Mason coughed loudly to clear his throat. "The truth is that I'm already dying a thousand small deaths on the reservation while I wait for something big to happen. I'm bored, I drink too much just like everyone else there, and I'm tired of doing what I do. I want a real story, and I was willing to take the risk."

"I hope your gamble pays off."

"What a fucking nut case that Newt is!" Mason said. "I probably should have killed him down there by the river instead of missing him on purpose with that rock."

"Like hell you missed on purpose. I've seen you throw," Robert said.

"I may never find another human being I can intimidate like that. I'll tell ya, I'm beginning to see the thrill of bullying people around like your buddy Frank does. It's kind of exhilarating."

"Don't underestimate Newt. Anyone smart enough to steal weapons-grade uranium and maybe even use it to build a bomb and bribe a man like Buckley can't be all stupid."

"Do you really think he's built a bomb?"

"I know he can build conventional ones. I've seen two of his already."

"Don't remind me. He blew up my office. That's another reason I wanted to come along. Maybe the tribal officials will rebuild my office while I'm gone. I sure I hope no one was hurt in town."

"Was anyone working in your office when the bomb went off?"

Mason laughed. "Whattya think I am, a big city newspaper? No, there's just me and the occasional intern, someone who needs credit for a class at the community college."

"This is a big story, Mason."

"To tell you the truth, I wouldn't know a nuclear bomb from a conventional one. I only deal with small arms fire on my beat. I've got a lot to learn before I can do this story justice."

"I'm not sure this whole kidnapping thing is for your benefit, Mason. He probably didn't have your *Wotanin Wowapi* in mind when he was talking about the press. Nothing personal, but I think you're just along for the ride."

"Well, screw you too, buddy. I appreciate the note of support and encouragement." Mason sulked for a couple of minutes before speaking again. "Maybe he's going to take us to a test blast." Mason became more animated as he spoke.

In the darkness, Robert could sense rather than see his movements and body language.

"Maybe he's going to set off one of those sons of bitches."

"I thought you hated explosions."

"I do. But wouldn't that be a sight!"

"I don't think he'd waste a bomb on us," Robert said.

"I've heard that a nuclear terrorist would need at least two bombs. One to show people he can really make one and another to do the deed with. Maybe that's why he wants the publicity— to be taken seriously."

"I have the impression being taken seriously is his lifelong dream."

"Well, he's got a ways to go on that score if he's still letting someone like me scare him."

"I think he's going to show us his nuclear stockpile," Robert said. "He did this same thing to Buckley a few years ago."

Just then the van stopped. Robert could see through the hole in the floor that Newt had pulled over to the shoulder. A minute later, the back door of the van flew open and Robert and Mason shielded their eyes from the light. When they were finally able to open them, they saw a highway patrolman standing in front of Newt.

"Hello, boys," the cop said cheerfully. "Where you headed?"

Newt looked terrified. Robert saw his hand creep up towards his jacket. Neither Robert nor Mason said anything to the cop at first. Newt's hand stayed near his jacket, a thumb hooked in his belt, and Robert could see a bulge where he thought Newt might be hiding a gun.

The last thing Robert wanted to deal with was a dead policeman. He'd already been involved in Buckley's shooting, and that was plenty. So he spoke up. "I'm sorry officer. I just woke up and I'm kind of groggy. What did you ask?" he said to buy time.

"I was just wondering where you boys are going."

"We're helping our friend with a move," he said, nodding towards Newt. "We're on our way to his place to pick up another load."

"I see," the officer said, glancing around the inside of the van. "If you don't mind my asking, why are you riding in the back? There's plenty of room up front where it's warm. It'd be a lot more comfortable."

"Hah!" Mason said so loudly it startled Robert.

My God, he thought. *Was Mason going to tell the truth? Would they end up with a dead cop before this was over?*

"That's what you think," Mason continued. "Newtie ate beans for breakfast. I'd ride in the back here in ten below weather before I'd sit in the cab with him."

Newt exhaled deeply and took his hand from his belt.

"What did Newt do wrong, officer?" Mason asked. "I know he's a shitty driver. Did he kill someone yet?"

"He's fine. There was an explosion in town, and we're stopping some of the outbound traffic is all."

"I think we heard the blast a while ago when we were stopped to eat," Robert said. "What's the damage report? Anyone hurt?"

"The tribal newspaper office was pretty much destroyed. We think there was only one person injured, but we can't say for sure."

"Who was it?" Mason asked.

"Some debris caught the local sheriff in the back of the head and knocked him out cold. He'll be all right, I guess."

"That poor bastard," Mason said. "Charlie always seems to be in the wrong place at the wrong time."

"How well do you know the sheriff, Officer?" Robert asked.

"Why do you ask?"

"I was wondering about the sheriff's goldfish."

"Don't worry. Golda's just fine."

Robert smiled.

"You boys have a good day, now," the officer said as he returned to his car.

When he had driven away, Newt thanked Robert and Mason.

"Were you really going to shoot him?" Mason asked.

"Get in the cab," Newt said. "You can ride up front with me for now." They pulled into a Conoco station a couple of miles down the highway. "Call your reporter friend now, Robert," Newt said. "Here's a couple of dollars of change."

"She has an 800 number, Newt. She's big time."

Mason stayed in the cab while Robert and Newt went to the

booth. The phone was outside. The wind was raw and cold, and the sound of the occasional passing semi made it difficult to hear.

Robert got a recording. "Hello. This is Amy Boston." She had such a lovely voice. "Please leave your name and number, and the time of and reason for your call. I'll get back to you as soon as I can. Thank you." The machine beeped loudly in his ear.

"Hello, Amy, this is Robert Botkin —"

"Robert!" she said on the other end. "How are you, dear?"

"Still screening your calls?"

"Of course. You never know what kind of lunatic might be calling."

"I'm glad I made the cut."

"Always. You're one of my favorite lunatics. What's going on?"

"I just might have a story for you."

"I'm getting that same knot in my stomach I used to get when you'd say that about your old boss."

"But you always got a good story, didn't you?" Newt was bouncing impatiently from one foot to the other. He gestured for the phone. Robert shook his head at him.

"Tell me, Amy," he said, trying to get her back on the subject. She liked her conversations to wander, but in a controlled way. She could keep track of a half dozen trains of thought at once until she found one that really caught her interest. "Do you know anything about atomic bombs, nuclear terrorism and such?"

"For crying out loud! Nuclear terrorists don't live in South Dakota!"

"I know that, but I'm in Montana now," Robert said.

Newt grabbed the phone from him and covered the receiver. "Get back in the van with what's-his-name. I'll be there soon."

Robert took a pen from the plastic holder in Newt's shirt

pocket and scribbled him a note that said he was going inside to buy food. Newt cupped the phone and said, "Stay where I can see you. I don't want you out of my sight for more than ten seconds."

Robert entered the station where he bought four ham and cheese submarines, a large sack of king-sized Fritos, two packs of powdered sugar donuts, and a couple of quarts of Coke. Newt was still on the phone when he returned to the van. Robert woke up Mason, and climbed into the back with him.

A few minutes later, Newt checked to make sure they were still in the back, slipped the lock on their door and headed down the road again. Off to an unknown destination, chauffeured by a madman on their way to witness who knows what, maybe an atomic detonation.

Well, Robert thought, as he settled into as comfortable a position as possible. *This sure beats ranching.*

CHAPTER 9

Newt drove for hours as Robert and Mason lay huddled in old sleeping bags in the back of the van. The whine of their tires, passing cars, and other highway sounds echoed inside the nearly empty compartment. Robert couldn't see the walls of the van because of the darkness but he sensed their presence from the way the sounds bounced off them.

He had a touch of claustrophobia, and just knowing there were walls around him, whether real or imagined, terrified him. That was one of the reasons he loved the open prairie of his native South Dakota and the Fort Peck Indian Reservation.

He made up games to control his claustrophobia. He tried to imagine he was a hobo who had just hopped a freight train on his way to the harvest in Yuma, Arizona, or some other warm southern location. But the creeping cold of the late February afternoon altered his images until he saw himself in a crowded boxcar with other Jews on their way to Terezin.

Soon, he found himself breathing hard and sweating profusely, despite the cold. Then he'd crawl out of his bag and make his way unsteadily around the van on his hands and knees until he'd touched all four walls. He would spend a couple of minutes with his mouth to the hole in the floor, breathing the air that blew past at sixty-five miles per hour before crawling back in his bag.

Mason was no help at all. Most of the time, he slept soundly, rolling along the floor of the van like loose cargo and snoring loudly.

The hardest part about traveling in the van was not the fantasies about concentration camps, but rather his thoughts of Anna. In the absence of light, she seemed more real. He hadn't slept well since she died, largely because her face, her mannerisms, even her smell became so much more vivid in the darkness. Her presence was like a star that came out at night, and the darker it was, the more vivid she became.

He was haunted by her memory, by the feel and smell of her skin, the sound of her laughter, her brooding nature. Memories of their time together came flooding back to him, like the one time he'd come to visit Frank and her last summer. Frank was sleeping with the wife of a fellow tribal council member at the time, and he was gone every night for a week, leaving Robert and Anna alone in the evenings. They spent most of their time at the house, or on the butte at Fort Peck Lake, the same butte they visited the night she died.

He remembered lying on a blanket with her one hot night at about dusk, watching the sun drop behind a low bank of clouds on the horizon as the wind dried the sweat from their naked bodies. When they'd cooled down, he began slowly stroking her hip as she lay on her side facing him, her hair draped over her neck and flowing down her throat.

"You know, Robert," she began after a minute of stroking. "I used to think about killing him."

"Hush, darling. I don't like hearing you say that."

"Seriously. I used to dream about shoving a knife into his fat belly."

"I mean it, damnit! Don't say that stuff around me."

Anna stood up and began putting on her clothes. He could tell she was upset and he stood to comfort her when she wheeled around and slapped him hard across the face. Shocked by her reaction, he shoved her with both hands. She fell backwards, jumped up and started beating his chest with both fists as she cried and called him a filthy bastard, a stupid prick, and other names.

"Hold on!" he cried as he grabbed her arms. "What's going on?"

It took her several minutes to regain control before she could respond. "I spent years with someone who wouldn't listen to anything I had to say. I'm never going to do it again."

"Point taken. But Frank's still a friend of mine. Can't you see how it might make me just a bit uncomfortable to listen to his wife talk about killing him?" He was still holding her by the wrists even though she was no longer struggling against him.

"If you're going to love me the way I need to be loved, then you're not going to censor me. Ever. How can I work through the anger I've bottled up for so many years if I can't talk to you about it? If you can't handle it, then now's the time to leave. Just get the hell out of my life."

"I'm not Frank, darling. You don't need to be mad at me, too." He dropped to his knees and hugged her to his face. "And I'm not leaving you. Ever."

She took his hand and used his fingers for her pleasure. Afterwards, she lay beside him again on their blanket and kissed his fingertips. "Thank you, Robert," she said.

"The pleasure was mine."

"No, not that. I mean for staying with me. For not getting scared and running off when I shouted at you."

"You'll never drive me off, Anna," he said nuzzling her hair. "Till death do us part."

"Till death do us part—."

The sound of his voice jarred Robert from his memories.

"Where the hell are we?"

"I have no idea." Robert took a minute to let go of Anna's memory before saying more. "It's hard to get much of a sense inside this box. Newt's stopped twice. He probably gets about 250 miles per tank, so I'd guess we've gone about six or seven hundred miles."

"Any idea which direction?"

"Away from Poplar, Montana, is all I know."

"Well, he'd better stop again soon. I gotta piss like a race-horse." Mason turned around and pounded on the wall next to the cab. "We got anything to eat?"

"There's a sandwich in the corner, some chips and donuts. Help yourself if you can find them."

Mason ate his sandwich in silence as Robert mouthed a silent "good-bye" to Anna. He ended most of his days that way.

About twenty minutes later, the van pulled to a stop. They heard Newt jam in the hose as he filled the van with gas. Then he slipped the lock off the heavy rear doors and swung them open.

"Rest stop," he said. "Time for a short break. Don't try to leave, though. We're on a tight schedule."

"Where are we?" Mason asked again.

"A service station. Conoco, to be exact. But that's all you need to know for now."

Robert's legs felt like rubber as he stepped onto solid earth for the first time in many hours. It was night, but the lights from the station hurt his eyes. Mason bounced out of the van like he was jumping out of bed. In fact, he was.

Newt was standing stiffly beside the van. His stringy hair was in his face, his bony shoulders stooped noticeably, and the Adam's apple bobbed in his throat. His breath formed little clouds of steam.

Mason stood on his toes, put his face just behind Newt's head, drew a big breath and said softly, "Boo!"

Newt swung his arm around and hit him across the cheek with his pistol. Mason dropped to the ground, touched his cheek and saw blood on his fingers. "Jesus, man! You're awful touchy."

"You say one word to me, or to anyone in the station—one

word—and you're a dead man." He shook with rage as he said it. "The same goes for you, Robert. You go inside, you do your business, and then you return immediately. Do you both understand?"

An impatient rage had replaced the passivity they had observed during their first encounter with Newt. Robert and Mason nodded.

"Good. Now go inside. I'll follow you." He pointed the way with his pistol.

Mason raised his hand like a student.

"What is it?" Newt said, tapping his foot. He rubbed his enormous Adam's apple while he waited for Mason to speak.

"Hide the fucking gun before you go inside. Okay?"

Newt seemed surprised to find the gun in his hand and he jammed it angrily inside his coat. "Don't let anyone see your face. It's bleeding."

While Mason took his time in the bathroom washing up his face, Robert looked for clues to their whereabouts. He strained to see the receipt as he watched Newt pay for the gas and a few more snacks, but only the name of the station was printed, not the address. Outside, it was too dark to see any license tags that might identify their location. Soon, Robert climbed in the back of the van once again with Mason.

"Man, oh man, my face hurts," Mason said after the van started rolling once again. "I think he nearly broke my jaw."

"He's awfully edgy, much more so than he was on the reservation," Robert said.

"I think he's on speed. I've seen enough speed freaks to recognize the symptoms."

"Oh, great."

"Yep, Robert, I think we're dealing with a psychopathic speed freak." After a moment, Mason continued. "I sure didn't have much luck intimidating him that time, did I?"

Robert laughed. "None whatsoever."

"I liked him much better as a wimp. By the way, did you figure out where we are?"

"It's cold, a dry cold. There's snow on the ground, and the headlights from the cars on the highway lit up trees along the road. If we'd gone straight south, we'd be in Wyoming. But there are too many trees around here for northern Wyoming. And we damn sure didn't go east with all the trees."

"Thank God. I can't stand the Dakotas."

"I beg your pardon?" Robert said.

"Just kidding. I know where you're from."

"He paid sales tax on the Cheetos, so we're not in Montana."

"We're not in Kansas anymore, Dorothy?"

"I don't think I blame Newt for pistol whipping you," Robert said. "Your jokes aren't funny. If I had a gun, I'd whack you with it too."

"Doesn't work. You can't even shut me up with a pistol. Newt already tried."

Robert yawned deeply. "I think we're either in Canada or we just crossed a pass into Idaho. But who knows? Maybe he's driving us in circles."

"Tell me again what you know about this guy."

"Not much. We think he's at least half-Indian. Spent his early years on the Fort Peck Reservation, hated it and left as soon as he could. He was kind of a nerd."

"No!" Mason said in mock surprise. "Not our Newtie."

"People picked on him mercilessly in school. I get the impression he knows Frank, but Frank can't remember him."

"So he went to work for Buckley. How'd he get a man like Buckley to notice him?"

"Newt understood Buckley's desperation. That's what gave him the power. Buckley needed a place to dump his wastes and Newt delivered."

"This is going to make a hell of a story someday."

Robert was startled to hear Newt's voice say, "It certainly is." The cargo area had evidently been wired for sound. "Mr. Botkin is right. We are, indeed, in Idaho, about halfway to our initial destination of Tonopah, Nevada, where Robert's reporter friend, Ms. Boston, will be joining us."

"So what kind of show are we in for?" Mason asked.

"Don't be impatient. You'll find out in due time." A minute later he added, "A psychopathic speed freak? I can't say I'm fond of the characterization."

"Yes, but," Mason said. "If the shoe fits—"

"Let me ask you something," Robert said to Newt.

"Go right ahead."

"Why did you decide to turn Fort Peck into a nuclear waste dump? Do you hate the reservation that much? Enough to poison it forever?"

"I don't hate the reservation at all. In fact I love it dearly. It's the people there I can't stand."

"Like Frank Kicking Bird?" Robert asked.

"That, my friend, is none of your business."

"So you know him?" Robert pressed.

"As I said, that is none of your business."

"If you love the reservation so much, why *did* you poison it?"

"I did it to gain power. And, to a limited degree, I was successful. You may not believe me, but I feel very bad about the dumpsite. I plan to make amends in my own way, in my own time."

"You certainly left your mark, all right."

Newt laughed pleasantly. "Oh, no, Robert. Not yet. I have not even begun to leave my mark."

"Aren't your expectations a little inflated?"

"I'll let you be the judge of that. Now be a good boy and shut up. I need to pay attention. There's ice on the road."

"You got any seat belts back here?" Mason asked.

"No, of course not. You shut up, too. And don't call me any more names. We psychopathic speed freaks hate that. No telling what we're liable to do." Newt laughed in a loud, high-pitched tone.

That was the last they heard from him for the next twelve hours.

Robert tried to doze, but the van bounced over the smallest blemishes in the highway, and every time he began to drift, he would be jostled awake. Finally, he managed to fall asleep, but his dreams troubled him more than the sleep refreshed him. He dreamed of two vehicles coming together very fast in a head-on collision. As they met, they exploded in a flash of light so brilliant that he had to shield his eyes from it. He remembered covering his face with his hands for protection. Then he heard someone call his name and shake his shoulder.

"Wake up, Robert. Robert—" It was Mason. "You've been asleep for a while. Newt stopped the van about ten minutes ago."

The back of the van was open and the slanting rays of the dying light of the day flooded their space. It was warm, almost hot, and Robert peeled off his jacket.

"Welcome to Tonopah," Newt said.

Through squinted eyes, Robert saw that Newt had changed into a new pair of khaki pants and a pink, button down Oxford shirt. He wore a pink and gray striped silk tie with a crooked knot that was dwarfed by the enormous Adam's apple perched above it. He was freshly shaved, and his thin blond hair was slicked back from his face, exposing his high forehead. He had the uncomfortable look of a kid dressed up for a wedding.

"Very dapper, Newt. What's the occasion?" The time spent in the back of the van tempered Robert's anger towards Newt, though not his resolve to make him pay for what he did to Anna.

"I have a date with your reporter friend, Ms. Boston."

Robert jumped out of the van. "So we're already here?"

"Yes we are," Newt said. "We made it in a little over twenty-four hours."

"The hours just seem to fly by when you're being kidnapped," Mason also jumped from the van.

"You weren't kidnapped. You forced your way along for the ride."

Robert was stiff from the trip and moved unsteadily towards the nearby coffee shop with his two companions. His hair was dirty and matted with road dust and grime. He had a day's growth of stubble on his chin and he desperately wanted a shower and a toothbrush.

The Gold Rush Inn served breakfast, lunch and slot machines. At 4:30 in the afternoon, every machine was being used by patrons who pumped in nickels and quarters, pulled the handles and stared intently at the displays as if through them, they could learn some great mystery about themselves. Their movements were as automatic as those of the machines that took their money.

A low bank of smoke dimmed the overhead fluorescent lights. Half a dozen people sat at a counter reading newspapers and reaching for the fries on their plates.

Robert excused himself and walked to the bathroom where he splashed water on his face and under his arms. Mason joined him and began washing himself too. He still had some dried blood around his mouth.

"You don't need to primp too much here," Mason said. "No one cares what you look like in a casino. They're too busy trying to turn their fortunes around."

"How do you know about casinos?"

"I lived in Nevada a long time ago. Winnemucca. Ugliest place God ever created."

"That's a little harsh isn't it?"

"You obviously haven't been there. When's your friend arrive?"

"I have no idea." He borrowed a comb from Mason, wet it in the sink and combed his hair. Then he put two dollars and fifty cents into a machine that spit out a tube of bubble gum flavored toothpaste and a toothbrush whose bristles fell out while he used it. The handle snapped in his hand. Still, he felt much better when he returned to the table with Mason a few minutes later.

Amy Boston had arrived and was sitting in a booth next to Newt. Robert gazed open-jawed at her shoulder length auburn hair pulled back from her high forehead, green eyes that sparkled in the dim light, and deep olive Mediterranean complexion. She smiled with a sweet expression that masked her tough inner core. Amy was raised in the city, yet she could hold her own with the most intimidating, old school ranchers in the country.

Robert had seen her do it. The two of them had sat together in the old days when Robert used to attend meetings where cabinet secretaries made decisions about the future of public lands, powerful men decided to ruin a competitor's career, or ranchers discussed how to pay off politicians.

At first, they treated this little woman with a patronizing politeness and flirtation. When she started asking the hard questions, the men moved into a new phase of trying to intimidate her with anger or crude behavior.

Her tongue, as it turned out, was far sharper than theirs. She would parry any crude or cutting remark with a retort so clever, few people beside Robert would catch it. But they could always tell from her smile that she'd somehow bested them.

After a while, the men began to hate her. They stopped talking to her altogether. But gradually, her talents won them over, and they developed a grudging respect for her as they learned to appreciate her ability to comprehend complex aspects of resource management, an area in which she'd had no formal training.

Robert did not go through these stages with her. He recognized her talents early on and treated her with respect from the beginning. She was a reporter, and he needed her to help publicize the work of his organization, something she was remarkably successful in doing. But his impressions of her had evolved in certain ways.

For example, he had become so accustomed to her beauty, he no longer thought about how pretty she was when he was with her. His respect for her and the friendship that developed between them overwhelmed his natural inclination to wonder what she looked like naked. But now, though his heart was still pricked with grief over the loss of Anna, seeing her sitting at the table in a casino in Tonopah, Nevada, made his curiosity rise once again.

"Amy!" he said, rushing over to hug her. "You look gorgeous."

"And you, Robert. What can I say? You smell like a combination of body odor and cheap soap."

"Flattery won't work on me. You already know that." *She* certainly didn't smell like sweat and cheap soap. "I want you to meet a reporter friend of mine. This is Mason Tomlinson. He publishes the Fort Peck tribal newspaper. Mason, this is Amy Boston. She works for—what's the name of that outfit you write for?"

"Very funny, Robert."

"I already know you work for *Time*." Mason said. "Robert told me about you on the drive down here. It's nice to meet you."

She extended her hand to Mason. "A pleasure to meet you, too. By the way, Mr. Tomlinson..."

Mason cleared his throat loudly and looked nervous. "Yes?" he said in a voice higher than normal.

"I'm very interested in Indian water issues. Particularly as they've affected the Missouri River tribes."

"Well," he said, already loosening up. "We have a few things in common. We're both reporters and we're both interested in Indian issues. Maybe we can work on an article together sometime."

Robert was impressed with his chutzpah. This reporter for a small community paper had already forced his way into a major story about nuclear wastes. Now he was asking to co-author an article with a reporter from *Time Magazine*.

"That's an intriguing proposition." She handed him a business card. "The U.S. Army Corps of Engineers really screwed over the tribes when they built the dams on the Missouri. I've been thinking of doing a piece about it. Maybe we can work together on the story."

"Excuse me," Newt said loudly. "I didn't drive all this way and bring you together so you could plan your next writing project. And I certainly didn't bring you here to listen to you chat about what the Army did to the poor damn Indians!" He shouted so loudly, people at the adjacent tables and booths turned to look at them.

"Well pardon me for my liberal, East Coast, outsider, politically correct, Great Society sense of compassion, Mr. Nuclear Terrorist," Amy said. "But the tribes were unbelievably fucked over by the Corps. And it appears that they continue to be fucked over by people like you who try to make a name for yourself by threatening to blow up a nuclear bomb. So you and your indifference to their plight can go straight to hell for all I care."

Not her usual style, Robert thought. This insult was a little more direct.

A middle aged waitress appeared at their table and took their order. Amy ordered the chef salad. Robert and Mason requested burgers, and Newt said he wasn't hungry.

"Ms. Boston," Newt said in a much calmer voice. "My father was among those dislocated by the dam at Fort Peck."

"Say that again," she said, pulling a small notepad and pen from her purse.

"Six months after construction began on the dam—this was back in 1934—officials from the Corps showed up with a contract. Their offer was for five dollars an acre for the land my grandparents had lived on all their lives.

"My dad was about fifteen years old at the time and still living with them. My father and his family were given less than two days to choose between a low-ball offer of hardly any money and a clapboard house in a new community forty miles away, or having their property condemned and getting nothing but an eviction notice."

"Forgive me," Amy said. "I didn't mean to talk down to you."

"My grandparents were given twenty-five dollars for the

garden where they grew their vegetables and grains, forty dollars for the house and another twenty-five for their woodlands next to the river. They would have gotten more, the officials said, but the flooding from the dam would begin in a matter of months, and that greatly reduced the overall value of the land and property."

The waitress brought their food. Mason poured a dollop of ketchup on each half of the bun. Robert bit into his without doctoring it up. Amy poked at her salad with a fork and a cube of processed ham fell off the lettuce mound onto the table.

"Let me get this straight," she said. "The Corps was going to cause the flooding that they used as an excuse to lower the value of your family's land?" she asked.

"Yes, interesting logic, don't you think? Two days later, the Corps of Engineers torched their house. They wouldn't even let my grandparents salvage it for firewood. My father started drinking that very day and continued until he died thirty years later. My grandparents survived only about six months in what turned out to be something akin to a ghetto, or more accurately, a shtetl. You're familiar with that word?

"They had no wood to heat with, and no garden spot to grow their vegetables. They couldn't pay the electric bill, even though the dam that drove them from their home would eventually produce the cheapest electricity on earth. And they had to depend on others to haul water from the river, which was now forty miles away. Grandpa died of pneumonia and grandma just plain died. No one ever bothered to find out how. So please, don't lecture me about the plight of the poor Indians."

Amy broke the silence that followed Newt's speech. "Why did you bring us here, Mr.—"

"Newt, Ma'am. You may call me Newt."

"Yes, Newt. Why did you bring us here?"

"Why did you come?"

"Because you had kidnapped my friend."

"And?" Newt pressed.

"And because I thought I might get a good story out of it.

Now why did you bring us here?"

"You'll find out tomorrow morning if all goes well. I've taken the liberty of renting a room for the three of you at a motel outside of town while I attend to some personal business. Robert, you're officially un-kidnapped. You're free to leave. And Mason, I really don't care what you do. But if either of you want to stay for the main event, I'll pick you up very early, so please be ready at the hotel by 3:00 a.m. It's time to go now so that we can get some sleep."

Robert realized that Newt hadn't slept in at least twenty-four hours.

"I already have a room and a car," Amy said, standing and picking up her purse.

"I'm sorry you wasted your money. Now please come with me."

Robert was stunned by Newt's revelations. Yet his self-disclosure raised far more questions than it answered. Why did he remain so bitter towards the reservation, or at least to its people? If he was so damaged by the federal government, why wasn't his anger directed towards it rather than the reservation? Why didn't he help poison federal rather than tribal lands?

And what was the purpose of this gathering in Nevada, thousands of miles from home? Robert still had no idea what Newt's intentions were.

The others were similarly stunned by the conversation. No one said a word on the way to the van.

"You may all sit in the front," Newt said when they got there. He unlocked the passenger side door and held it open politely while they climbed in.

"It'll be crowded, Amy," Robert said, still disconcerted by his attraction to her. "You'll have to sit on my lap, unless you want me to sit on yours." She had been scribbling notes on her pad all the way to the van. He climbed in after Mason and helped Amy into the cab. She settled comfortably onto his lap.

The wind whistled noisily through the windows, which refused to shut tightly. They drove east of town for about ten miles. Robert shifted his position several times. He could feel the muscles in her thighs, and he was embarrassed to be getting an erection. But the pressure and the closeness of an attractive woman on his lap made futile his efforts to suppress the flow of his blood. Amy shot him a dirty look when she became aware of it. He shrugged helplessly in response.

"If you don't stop poking me with that thing," she whispered. "I'm going to make you switch positions with me."

"Don't take it personally," he said, trying to ease his way out of the situation. "The same thing happens when I sleep on my stomach."

"How flattering."

Newt dropped them off them at a cheap motel with a blinking neon sign that flashed "Trails End—Trails End—Trails End—" throughout the evening and into the night. Weeds grew in cracks in the concrete parking lot. Only two cars were at the hotel when they arrived—a mid-'70s vintage Volvo wagon and a Toyota Corolla of similar age.

The room had a broken TV, a window unit air conditioner that whined when the wind blew outside and occasionally dripped a rusty liquid on the mildewy carpet beneath it. There were two double beds each covered by molting chenille spreads.

"God, it's good to be home!" Mason said as he threw himself onto the nearest bed. Within a minute, he was sleeping soundly.

"Let's take a walk," Amy said. "The air's got to be better outside than it is in here."

"Okay by me," Robert said. The two of them stepped into the cool evening air. The sun had already set and the faintest trace of pink silhouetted a low bank of clouds to the west.

"You seem downright morose, Robert. What's up?"

"You noticed, huh?"

"I'm a reporter, Robert. I pick up on things. And you're not the best about hiding things anyway. What's up?"

"It's not easy to talk about."

"You can trust me," she said, tossing back her head and

giving her hair a shake. She reached behind and tied up her hair in a Scrunchie. "What do you think I'm going to do, publish your problems in *Time*?" She smiled at him and punched him lightly in the arm.

"You might want to after you hear the story."

"Seriously, tell me what's going on with you."

"Do you remember me talking about a friend named Frank Kicking Bird who lives on the Fort Peck Reservation?"

"No."

"I've known him most of my life. We grew up together in South Dakota before he got chased out nearly thirty years ago."

"What did he do?"

"Confronted the sheriff who was raping a local teacher. Frank busted a bottle over the sheriff's head. Since Frank was Indian, no one was going to believe his part of the story."

Amy shook her head. "How many times has this story, or one just like it, been repeated throughout our history? It makes me ashamed to live here, even though no place is any better."

"Speaking of ashamed—" Robert stopped and cleared his throat. He wanted to talk to her about Anna, but he'd never spoken of her to anyone besides Buckley who was bound and gagged at the time. Robert's throat constricted every time he thought about mentioning Anna's name as if he had swallowed her and was trying to keep her inside.

Amy put her hand on his shoulder. Then she rested her forehead against his arm. "You've been keeping something in, haven't you? Something so big it's having a hard time getting out."

"I fell in love with Frank's wife."

"Oh, my! That is awkward."

"I mean deeply, passionately, obsessively in love. So much so, it drove me to do crazy things."

"Does your friend, Frank, know about this?"

"Yes. Apparently he's known for some time, but we've never talked about it. Usually, he was too busy sleeping with other women and treating Anna like shit to notice much. But to tell you the truth, I'm surprised he hasn't killed me yet."

"Robert, I don't need to tell you that falling for another man's wife is a very stupid thing to do."

"No, of course you don't. I wish it had never happened. I'm so miserable. She's always on my mind. I smell her on my clothes, I taste her in my food, I see her in my dreams, at least when I'm able to sleep."

"Is this love or obsession?"

"I don't know. And I don't think that distinction matters at this point. All I know is that it's changed me forever, not necessarily in a good way." His voice was shaky and he was fighting back tears as he spoke.

"I'm sorry, Robert." She slowly stroked his back as she spoke. "I knew you seemed different when I saw you, but I didn't realize how much pain you were in."

Hearing someone acknowledge his pain was too much for him, and he began to cry. Amy seemed slightly embarrassed by his tears, but she turned and hugged him. It was a little awkward because she was so short.

"I'm sorry, Amy. It's just that I've been sitting on this so long."

"And I'm sorry for you. On the surface, this relationship looks like it's not very good for you. Tell me, where are you going with it?"

"Nowhere. She's dead."

"Dead?" she said, stepping back. "How? When?"

Robert couldn't speak yet. Tears made shiny tracks down his cheeks. The sky was now dark and the air had grown cold. He began to shiver. Awkward as it was, the hug felt good and he wanted her arms back around him. A minute later he began to talk again while she stared at him incredulously.

"She was killed in a car bomb that paralyzed my friend, Frank."

"A bomb? Who planted it?"

He felt her suddenly switch from friend to reporter, yet he

didn't resent her for it. It's what she did; it's who she was. He'd finally told a friend about Anna and his love for her. He'd shed tears with another person over her, and he began to feel an extraordinary sense of relief at having done so.

He went on with the story, telling her about the ambush at the dumpsite and the guy Frank killed there. He talked about luring Buckley to the reservation, only to have Frank shoot him.

"My God," she said. "I think your friend, Frank, has an anger problem."

"You don't know the half of it."

"Handgun or rifle?" she asked, jotting down notes, always the reporter.

Robert told her how he'd learned it was Newt who planted the bomb in Frank's truck.

"Newt killed your girlfriend?"

"Yes. I thought I'd want to kill him the moment I saw him. But he's such a pitiful character, I don't think it would give me much relief." Finally, he told her about the nuclear stockpile Newt had accumulated over the years.

"Do you think he's really going to set off a bomb?"

"Maybe."

"Wow." That was all she said for a minute, uncharacteristically inarticulate. "How'd you find Newt?"

"I didn't. He found me. He kidnapped me yesterday when I was having a talk with Mason. Mason just horned in on the ride."

"I can't believe that tomorrow morning I might be writing a story about having witnessed a nuclear detonation. I think I'm glad you called me on this one." She touched her lips and wrinkled her forehead in thought. "What should a person do when they're faced with the choice of writing the story of their life or taking steps to stop a terrible thing from happening? Maybe I should turn in the lunatic."

"He said he's rigged a bomb to go off if anything happens to him, and lots of people would be killed."

"Great!" she said, almost cheerfully. "That certainly makes

my decision easier. I guess I'll write the story."

"Let's get back. I'm getting cold."

Amy put her arms around him once again and hugged him tightly. This time it was much less awkward. "You really fucked up, you know. Sleeping with another man's wife."

"I know that. But it happened."

"I'm sorry you're in pain, though. I hate to see you like this. What do you need to help you heal?"

Was that an opening? he wondered. From many other women the line might have seemed like an invitation. But not from Amy.

"I don't know. I just want to follow this story all the way, same as you do. Hell, Amy. We've got ourselves a front row seat. Let's enjoy the show."

CHAPTER 10

Newt knocked softly on their door about three the next morning. Robert had been lying on his back in one of the beds with Amy curled up asleep next to him. Random, disconnected thoughts of Anna, Frank, nuclear explosions, his ranch, and his future had chased away all hope of sleep. He had never felt less ambition, less drive, less zest for living. Nothing appealed to him. The thought of returning to his ranch bored him for the first time in his life.

He still hated Newt for killing Anna, but his general listlessness softened the feeling. Except for the few faint stirrings Amy had aroused in him, Robert couldn't even get excited about the thought of being with another woman.

During the early morning hours as he lay awake on the hotel bed, he thought about his mother. She had died after having lived a life she neither chose nor desired, and yet, at the end of her life, she had been an extraordinarily happy woman.

It was not always that way for her. She left her family in Cincinnati at a young age to live with her new husband on a farm in South Dakota. From the moment she arrived on the farm built and paid for by her now dead father-in-law, she was miserable.

She hated the flatness of the prairie and its people. She missed trees and symphonies and ethnic food and noise and stimulation. Her husband was reserved even by rural South Dakota standards, and he had little tolerance for her anger. Her moods terrified him, and the only way he knew how to deal with them was to work harder. Maybe if they sold a little more wheat or raised fatter cattle, she'd be happier.

What she craved, however, was human intimacy, not fatter cows. Robert was born about seven months after they were married, and he provided some of the intimacy she so desperately needed. But it wasn't enough and she continued to be angry about her circumstances.

Robert fought the gloom of his childhood by being funny. He thought about how he would use his humor like a foil to ward off the unhappiness he knew was killing both his parents. Now, with Anna dead, his parents gone, and no burning ambitions, he felt like he was falling prey to the same insidious depression from which he'd run all his life.

Newt seemed almost apologetic about waking the crew so early. After a couple of minutes, they piled into the van and Newt drove them about thirty miles east of town on Highway 6. Then he turned off onto a dirt road that headed generally southeast, staying on the same dusty road for almost an hour during which time they saw no other cars.

It was a slow trip. The U-Haul was not equipped with good shocks to handle the washboard road. It was very dark outside and there was no moon in sight. Robert watched the black shape of pine trees shooting past his window and heard boards groaning under the weight of the van as they crossed arroyos on wooden bridges. They were climbing steadily and eventually began slogging through small patches of snow and slush on the road. No one spoke as they drove.

At last, Newt turned off onto a couple of tracks, which he followed for two hundred yards. They passed through a gap that had been cut in an eight-foot high security fence, drove another quarter mile and then stopped.

"We're here," Newt said flatly.

"Where's here?" Mason asked.

"Where I want you to be. Now get out." He was all business this morning, neither polite nor edgy.

Their legs were stiff from the long and bumpy trip. They had all crowded into the front seat of the van, but this time, Amy sat beside Robert rather than on his lap. Newt returned to the back of the van, opened it and pulled out a daypack, which he threw over his shoulder.

"Follow me," he said as he stepped away from them. A flashlight emitted a small beam of yellow light that bounced on the ground in front of him as he began climbing a small butte. The four of them made it to the top of the hill in about ten minutes. Robert could barely make out the shape of several boulders strewn randomly across the top of the butte.

Once they had stopped, Newt spoke. "As you have guessed by now, I brought you here to witness the detonation of a nuclear device." He chuckled softly. "Listen to me. 'Device' is what they called it in the Manhattan Project where secrecy was paramount. This isn't a device. It's a bomb.

"I have succeeded in duplicating the structure of the Little Boy bomb that destroyed Hiroshima. The fissionable material is a small portion of the uranium I've acquired over the years. After the detonation, I'll tell you how I built it, and what I intend to do with this technology. Meanwhile," he began fumbling in his backpack. "Put these on in a couple of minutes," he said, tossing them each a pair of welder's glasses. "You'll go blind if you look directly at the blast."

"Where is the bomb?" Amy asked.

"To the south, on top of a mountain about seven miles away," he said pointing at it with the flashlight beam. "We're in luck. The breeze is from the north, so the cloud will drift towards the Air Force Range."

"What now?" Mason said.

"We wait."

132 ~ Elemental Threat

"How long? It's cold out here."

Newt flashed the beam of light on his wrist. "It's about a quarter to six now. We have about forty-five minutes. I'll tell you when it's time to pay attention."

The minutes passed slowly. Cold air seeped like water through Robert's jacket. His shoes were wet and muddy from the walk and his toes ached from the cold.

Knowing he was half an hour or so away from witnessing a nuclear explosion increased his desire to live for another couple of days. It had been a generation or more since anyone had witnessed an open-air nuclear test on U.S. soil. He doubted the test would succeed, and he wasn't sure if he wanted it to or not.

Fifteen minutes had passed when Mason asked the obvious. "What if it's a dud?"

"It won't be," Newt said.

"But what if it is?"

"I'll remake the bomb, I'll fix whatever went wrong, and I'll drag another reporter out here to witness it."

A faint glow from a weak dawn appeared to their left. It was so dim, Robert thought he was imagining it until he could make out the features of Amy's face staring intently at the place where the bomb sat. As the sky brightened, he could barely make out the outline of a mountain to the south.

"Time for your goggles," Newt said a moment later. "You might want to put on some of this, too." He handed Robert a tube of sunscreen. "Cover your face and hands with it."

"How bright will the flash be?" Amy asked.

"Six to ten times brighter than the sun," Newt said.

"Unless it's a dud," Mason said.

"Be quiet and focus your attention on the top of that mountain over there. We only have a couple of minutes."

Robert, Mason, Amy, and Newt secured their goggles around their eyes. The goggles fit tightly around their heads, blocking out the dim morning light that came from the east. All four of them crouched behind boulders and peered at the spot where the bomb sat atop the distant mountain. The seconds passed slowly. Robert could hear the blood pulsing through his temples.

"Any second, now," Newt called out from behind a rock.

Robert strained to see the outline of the mountain through the darkened goggles.

And then, with an intensity he could not have imagined, a blinding flash wiped out everything, including all his thought and concerns.

It started as a brilliant yellow spurt of fire, brighter than anything meant to be seen on this earth. In no time at all, there was a column of smoke and fire a thousand feet high with a mushrooming fireball atop it. The whole smoky structure was rising into the atmosphere hundreds of feet every second with an unearthly force. Flames and smoke and debris danced in the column as if creatures from Hell had been released from the bowels of the earth.

Robert thought about the movies he had seen in school as a child, practicing the "duck and cover" routine, hearing about Cuban-based Russian missiles which could destroy every major American city, his nightmares of mushroom clouds, waking up in a cold sweat screaming for his parents, seeing the round green bomb shelters pop up in people's backyards like some sort of fungus. He thought about how much of his childhood had been spent in fear of the bomb. Yet nothing, not even his most vivid dreams, could capture the sheer, unholy power that was unleashed in an instant on this lonely winter morning.

The cloud was over a mile high now and less bright, and Robert peeled off his goggles. He could see the shock wave traveling towards them. It looked like a shimmering heat wave, a three dimensional ripple on a pond.

The wave hit him like a sharp wind that lasted for about ten seconds. The force of it blew his head back and forced open his lips. It almost knocked him over. And then came the heat from the flash. It wasn't as intense as the shock wave, but it felt as if he was sitting too close to a wood stove.

He wondered if his cells were being re-arranged by radiation, which would later cause his skin to blister, sores to fester, and organs to malfunction.

The cloud was now over two miles high, maybe three, and it had been only a minute or two since the bomb detonated. Red and black flames danced through the thick column of smoke that supported the mushroom cap. He never heard the explosion. He did hear another unearthly sound though, the cackling of Newt shouting his excitement over the spectacle he had created.

"I did it! I did it!" He jumped up from his place behind the rock. "I made the bomb. I can do it!" He pumped his skinny arms in the air like a boxer.

Amy was snapping pictures of the blast. She stepped back and got a few of Newt dancing on the rocks with the column of fire behind him.

Mason was standing up, staring open mouthed at the mushroom cloud.

Robert began to shake. He felt as if his life could never be the same after having witnessed this event. Atomic power was a force that had won a war but changed forever the way human kind thought of itself, and he now understood how much innocence had been destroyed by The Bomb. Individual courage, manliness, grief, joy, love—they were all completely irrelevant to this thing, this force which had the power to turn human beings in an instant into mere shadows on stone. The community of mankind was now closer to both God and eternal damnation. It was a terrifying responsibility, one that he doubted humans were up to.

"Let's get back to the highway before the military gets here," Newt said.

Amy let the camera drop to her chest, walked up to Newt and hit him squarely on the mouth with her fist.

Newt recoiled in surprise. He took a handkerchief from his pocket and dabbed at his bloody lip, which was still curled up in a smile.

"You fucking bastard!" she shouted. "I should kill you! You're fucking with something we don't have the right to play with." She stooped to pick up a rock.

"Whoa, Amy. Get a grip." Robert grabbed her hands from behind. "There's more to this story," he whispered in her ear. "Let's keep our seat on the front row."

She shook herself roughly from his grip and stood staring at Newt. The light from the blast made ghostly shadows on her face.

"I mean it," Newt said. "Let's get out of here. I'll have more to say when we get to the van."

They returned to the U-Haul and crowded into its front seat. Newt drove back to the dirt road and began to talk.

"Please don't interrupt me unless you have very specific questions." The enthusiasm was gone from his voice and he was now remarkably calm for having just become the first civilian in history to have successfully built and detonated a nuclear bomb on his own.

"For the purposes of your story, let me say a word about nuclear fission." As he drove, he conducted a confusing monologue about the difference between protons and neutrons, how neutrons lack an electrical charge, making them relatively easy to remove from the core of an atom. He was not a good lecturer.

Amy was busy scribbling notes on a pad. Mason said, "Yes, but what does this have to do with the fact that you're a lunatic who just blew up a whole goddamn mountain? Get to the point and tell us what your next move is."

"I asked you once not to interrupt me. Let me continue. I'm oversimplifying, of course, but when uranium atoms are broken up and reformed into lighter elements, their neutrons give up some mass. In doing so, they release a tiny amount of energy. Mass is converted to energy."

"Ah, yes," Mason said. "The old 'E equals M C squared' thing."

"Exactly, with 'E' meaning energy, 'M' being mass and 'C' being a constant which happens to be the speed of light. Albert Einstein gave us a simple equation to estimate how much energy would be reheased in a nuclear explosion. The amount of mass converted from the individual neutrons is infinitesimally small, of course.

"But the speed of light is a big number, especially when you square it. So a very tiny amount of mass lost when you fission a uranium atom converts to a very large amount of energy, as you have just seen. The amount of mass lost in the explosion you just saw is only about half a gram, less than the weight of a penny. So much for theory. Now let's talk mechanics."

The morning light was brighter now as Newt sped down the dirt road towards the highway. The color had begun to drain from the eastern sky, but the mushroom cloud to the south blossomed nearly ten miles into the atmosphere. Newt was talking with the boring, self-assured demeanor of a professor, one who'd taught too long. His Adam's apple bobbed in his long neck continuously, even when he wasn't talking. His stringy blond hair hung to his chin. He seemed to have lost interest in the gigantic cloud that dominated the horizon.

"Building a bomb is easy," he continued. "All you need is a source of uranium 235 and a reflector to direct discharged neutrons back into the core of fissionable material. The hard part is getting hold of fissionable material. Making the stuff is very expensive because you have to separate Uranium 235, which is easily split apart, from Uranium 238 literally atom by atom. I don't have a billion dollars to set up a gaseous diffusion plant to separate it out, so I've been stealing the stuff for years. I have tons of it now, more than I'll ever use.

"If you have a critical mass of uranium 235 in one place, you get a chain reaction from all the neutrons flying around. To make a bomb—here, take the wheel for a second," he said to Mason so he could use his hands to explain.

"You take two sub-critical masses of uranium, fire them together so that the two pieces become one." He slammed together his two fists. "A critical mass is achieved, you begin the chain reaction and an enormous amount of energy is released." He spread his fingers wide to indicate the explosion. Then he took back the wheel. "The mass heats up instantly to several times the temperature inside the sun."

Robert remembered using similar expressions when he described his relationship with Anna to Buckley, the man Frank had shot—two coming together as one, the release of energy, the power, the danger, the toxicity.

"To enhance the reaction, you surround the uranium with material dense enough to reflect the neutrons back into the mass. I used an old bazooka for the gun barrel. I put a powder charge behind the smaller mass to fire it into the larger stationary mass at the other end of the barrel.

"That, basically is the design of the Little Boy bomb that destroyed Hiroshima and the bomb you saw detonated today. The Nagasaki device was a plutonium bomb, which uses a different construction. I don't like plutonium. It's too dangerous."

"And what is weapons-grade uranium?" Amy asked. "A play toy?"

He pulled to a stop at the highway. "Get out for a second, I have one more thing to show you."

Robert, Mason and Amy stepped out of the van and stood alongside it on the highway. Newt opened the glove box, rolled down the passenger side window, and handed Amy a small manila envelope.

"My plans for the future," he said as she took it. "I trust you'll be able to catch a ride soon. This place is going to be crawling with military agents. I have to get back now. I set another nuclear device to go off in about—" He glanced at his watch. "About four and a half days from now. Unless I get back to reset the thing, a lot of people will die. Let's hope I don't have an accident on the way home. And speaking of that, don't turn me in to the police. Any delays in my return could be costly. Bye."

"Wait," she yelled as the van sped off. "Bastard," she muttered. "I had some more questions."

She tore open the envelope. Inside it was a note, which she read aloud. It said the following:

> You have seen what I can do. And you have heard what the government did to my people on the Missouri River when they built their dams on it. Who is more destructive? That is the question.

I believe the jury is still out. But just as the government drove my people from the land, so will I drive out others. My target is the city of St. Louis, Gateway to the West, mouth of the Missouri River. This is the point from which the exploitation of the West began, and it is the place where it will end. I don't wish to kill people indiscriminately, so I give you ample warning. Be forewarned that I will destroy the city of St. Louis this coming April 11.

I also feel compelled to tell you that at all times, I have in a secret location a nuclear device which is wired to detonate in four days. Every morning, I reset the clock to give the world another four days. Do not look for me, and do not hold me in custody. Otherwise, you will lose both St. Louis and another location to the bomb. Indeed, all concerned citizens should pray to God for my continued safety and welfare.

May God bless.

Newt

"My God," Robert said. "He means every word of it, and he can pull it off."

"I always wondered what happens to nerds when they grew up," Mason said as he watched military vehicles speeding in their direction. "Now I know. They either become software magnates or nuclear terrorists. Get out of sight before they spot us!"

CHAPTER 11

"You what?" Frank slammed a can of beer onto the sticky kitchen tabletop.

"I witnessed an atomic explosion," Robert said calmly. "I was kidnapped by Newt. Mason Tomlinson tagged along for the ride. He thought maybe he could get a story out of it."

"'He thought maybe he could get a story out of it,'" Frank said, mimicking Robert's voice. "A nuclear terrorist with enough uranium to destroy North America sets off an atomic bomb. I'd say there's probably a story in there somewhere."

"The three of us met my friend Amy Boston, the reporter for *Time Magazine*, in Tonopah, Nevada."

"Toe Nail Paw?"

"Close enough. Newt drove us a couple of hours out of town and then blew up a mountain seven miles south of us. I thought he'd split the earth in two. My God, Frank, I've never seen anything like it. The power of it was—I can't tell you how terrifying."

Robert shivered as he talked about it. He knew it was a terrible thing he'd witnessed, but he couldn't stop replaying the flash in his head the way people obsess over injuries. Awful as it was, the blast was the most thrilling thing he'd ever seen.

"Bet it gave you a hard-on to see it."

"Shut up, Frank." Frank was closer to the truth than Robert he wanted to admit.

"I thought you'd flaked out on me. You disappeared without a word. I assumed you'd gone back to South Dakota, that things were getting a little too hot for you." Frank sipped his beer, set it down on the table, and flipped his braid back over his shoulder.

"Actually, things got a couple of hundred million degrees hotter for me after I left you. Did you know that the temperature at the blast site is several times hotter than the sun?"

"It did give you a hard-on, didn't it?"

Robert ignored the comment and continued. "Anyway, we hitched a ride back to town, diving into the dry creek bottoms when the military police would drive by. There were helicopters flying overhead, but we were always in someone's car when they appeared. The military's going to be a uptight for a few weeks. They probably think someone blew up one of their bombs.

"Amy and Mason holed up for a couple of days to write the story. When they were done, she bought us tickets home. I took the bus from Great Falls. Sat next to a skinny, twenty-year-old lonely guy with acne, who talked my ear off the whole way, I mean for hours. Then, my car in town wouldn't start, and I had to wait for someone to come jump it. I'm exhausted, Frank. I need a beer and then I need to go to bed."

"Grab one from the 'fridge. And bring me one too while you're at it."

Robert grabbed two beers and joined Frank at the table. It was six o'clock in the evening, nearly three and a half days since the explosion. Robert had heard nothing about the blast in the media. He guessed that the military was sitting on the story to spare itself the embarrassment of announcing that someone had sneaked undetected into one of its high security Air Force test ranges and detonated a nuclear bomb. It had probably put out a small, unnoticed press release about an accidental explosion at an old munitions dump, the same story the Army used after the test blast at the Trinity site in New Mexico over fifty years earlier.

That tactic might hold for a day or two, but surely some foreign country with a satellite would begin asking tough questions about the mushroom cloud that loomed over Nevada on an otherwise normal February morning.

Outside, the temperature was twelve below and dropping, a far cry from the sixty-degree weather in Nevada. There was no snow at all on the ground or clouds in the sky. Frank had nailed cardboard over the windows and added some staples to the tarp over the doorway that used to separate the kitchen from the living room, but now led outside. The wood stove radiated heat, and the house was either too hot or too cold, depending upon which part of it you were in.

"Do you have any leads yet tracking down Newt?" Robert said. "I know what he looks like, but I still don't have any idea where he lives."

"A woman I know on-line said she was having cyber sex with a guy about a week ago who turned out to be a real pervert." Frank shook his head. "You wouldn't believe the kind of creeps that hang out on computers."

"I'm talking to one of 'em."

"She asked the guy what really excites him. Know what he said?"

"If it has anything to do with fruit or animals, I don't want to know."

"Listen to this, I saved the file somewhere around here. Goddamnit!" he shouted. "What the hell did I call it?" He was shuffling through floppy disks with lightning speed. "Ah, here it is. Read this."

Robert crowded next to Frank to look at the monitor. Frank kept his computer on the kitchen table because it was in one of the warmest areas of the house.

> TWEN532: A nuclear explosion. That's what would really get me excited.

REDBRAT: You're speaking metaphor-
cally, of course.

TWEN532:   Not at all. I mean a real-life,
actual spontaneous fissioning of a critical mass
of uranium 235.

REDBRAT: That's one of the sickest things
I've ever heard on-line. And that's saying a lot.

TWEN532:   No really, I think it would be
one of the most thrilling sights in the universe.
Think of it, the fireball, the mushrooming cloud,
the smoke, the flames, the colors—

REDBRAT: The burning bodies, the radiation—

TWEN532:   I don't mean dropping it over a
city, I'm just talking about watching a test blast.

REDBRAT: Oh my, look at the time. Gotta
go pick up the kid for a dentist appointment.

TWEN532:   But wait! We were just getting
started—

REDBRAT: We'll pick it up later. Bye ::::
Kiss::::

TWEN532   Bye :(.

Robert read the conversation twice. "Could be him. He
sounds sick enough."

"That's what she thought."

"Does he have a profile?"

"No. I can't find out anything about him. My friend, Red,
had never seen him on-line before."

"Weird name, TWEN. Are you sure it's a guy?"

"Spell it backwards, idiot."

"N-E-W-T. 235 NEWT. I'll be damn, that probably is him.
But that was a pretty flimsy cover he used."

"It fooled you."

"Oh, I almost forgot." Robert slapped his forehead. "My friend, Amy, said she was going to email you a picture of Newt as soon as she could. She snapped off a couple while she was shooting the blast. I gave her your email address. Have you checked your mail lately?"

"Let's see." Frank clicked onto a new screen. There were about three dozen unread pieces of mail in his box. "You know what her screen name is?"

"No. Hmmm, lemme look for a second. AMYBOS. That has to be her. Check it out."

A picture slowly came into focus on Frank's screen. It showed Newt pumping his skinny arms in the air with a mushroom cloud as his backdrop.

"Hmmm," Frank muttered. "I thought that's who it might be."

"You know him?"

"Yes. His name's Iron Bear. Denny, I think. I did go to school with him for a while when I was back on the reservation between my times in South Dakota. He just kind of disappeared. He never looked much like an Indian, but he was one. What did Buckley tell you Newt's last name was?"

"I think he said it was 'Nori.'"

"That's 'Iron' spelled backwards, as in 'Iron Bear.'"

"You're right," Robert said. "Newt gave me the impression you picked on him at school."

"Of course I did. I picked on everybody. I knew his brother, Leonard, better."

"How many brothers did he have?"

"Just one, I think."

"Guess what, my friend. You killed Leonard."

"Get outta here!"

"Really, you did. At the dump site."

"I'll be damned. Leonard Iron Bear. The boy who gave me my first joint. We smoked it in his car one afternoon before math class. Who'd-a thought I'd end up bashing in his skull with a crow bar?" Frank shut off the computer and rolled back from the table a couple of feet.

Just then, the phone rang. Frank answered it on the second ring. "Just a minute," he said. "It's for you." He handed the receiver to Robert.

"Hello. What? Where are you? Oh, my God! We'll be there as soon as we can. Okay, sooner then." He hung up the phone. "Grab the keys, Frank."

"Who was that?"

"It was Newt, or Denny, or whatever the fuck his name is."

"Where is he?"

"He's in jail in Hamilton, just south of Missoula. The other side of the state. The police got him on a stolen car rap."

"Well, let him rot in jail then. You can tell the police all about him."

"Come on, damnit! We don't have much time. You drive. Your truck's faster than my car. I'll explain on the way."

Frank wheeled around the kitchen grabbing his keys and coat. "This better be a good story, man," he said as they pushed their way through the flap in the tarp. "It's fucking cold out here."

Frank pulled himself into the truck. Robert folded up the wheelchair and threw it in the back. Frank started the vehicle and let it run a minute while it warmed up. The pickup was a caricature of its owner—decrepit, rusty, and beat to hell, yet the damn thing ran like a Swiss clock even under the worst of conditions.

"So, talk," Frank said as he looked at Robert in the seat next to him.

"Newt wired another bomb to detonate if he doesn't get back to disarm it. This one's in Missoula. And if his identity is discovered, he won't disarm it either. So, if he doesn't get out of jail, or if the police find out who he is and continue to hold him, the next bomb goes off in about a day and a half."

Frank's mouth dropped open for a second before he peeled out of his drive with a force that was damn near nuclear.

* * * *

Robert couldn't believe the police didn't stop them during the 560-mile trip to Hamilton. Frank drove the whole way and made it there in a little over six and a half hours. To do that, he averaged eighty-five miles an hour, even with the pit stops, gas stops, and a beer run near Great Falls.

At Hamilton, they pulled to a stop in the parking lot of the Brass Rail Bar along the highway that ran through the middle of town. It was a little before 1:00 a.m. on a Thursday. "Get my chair," Frank said.

Robert met him at the driver's side door with the wheelchair. Frank dropped into it from the truck, tossed Robert the keys and said, "Hand me one of those rocks in the back of the truck."

Robert handed him a broken brick from the back end.

"Now get the hell out of here. You can pick me up in about an hour."

"What are you doing?"

"Just go," he said. Then he wheeled himself closer to the bar and heaved the brick through its front window. "I'll be at the police station," he added unnecessarily.

An hour later, Robert parked the truck a block from the police station and walked the rest of the way. It was tough to drive because of the way Frank had rigged it to accommodate his infirmities.

"Yes, sir," said the uniformed officer as Robert entered the station. The officer was seated behind a massive oak desk. Except for the crumpled cap, his uniform was crisp. "What can I do for you?"

"I'm looking for my friend, Frank. He's an Indian, he's in a wheelchair, and he's got a foul mouth. Pretty hard to miss him."

"He's here all right. I'd love to let you have him, but I'm afraid I can't do that yet."

"What are you holding him for?"

"Sit down, son. This may take awhile." The officer was about fifty years old and had a polite demeanor. He was of medium build and seemed tall, though it was hard to tell since he was seated behind the desk. The hair that showed below the cap was cropped close to his head. His teeth were white as pearls and looked as if he'd just polished them. His in-basket was empty, and he was working on a small, neat stack of papers from a desk that was otherwise cleared of debris.

Robert took a seat opposite him at the desk.

"Your friend tossed a rock through a window, took a swing at a couple of patrons, yelled obscenities in a voice loud enough to be heard in the next town, resisted arrest, refused a breath test, and crumpled my cap between his hands like it was an empty beer can."

"Sure sounds like him."

"Be tomorrow morning late before the judge can set bail."

"He can wait."

"Bail's going to be high."

"His always are, officer. Is he alone in the cell?

"No, he's got a drunk and a car thief to keep him company."

"Can I see him?"

"I suppose." He rose slowly from his chair and guided Robert around the corner. There were three people in the cell: Frank, a bald man snoring away on a cot, and Newt.

"If it's okay with you, I'd like to talk to him alone for a minute or two. I'm only one who can tell him he's an asshole and get away with it. I'll check in with you at the desk before I leave."

"Take off your coat for me, then, if you don't mind. I'll hold it for you at my desk."

Robert slipped out of it and handed it to him. When the officer left, Newt said, "Here's what I need. I'm sure you can get it at a supply house in Missoula. I need a couple of scraps of cotton, pure stuff, no synthetics. And some Q-Tips. I also need a small amount of concentrated nitric and sulfuric acid mixed together in equal proportions. Put the solution in a small mustard jar, or something you can sneak in easily. But don't spill any on yourself. Bring it to me tomorrow morning and then come back in the evening to pick up Frank. No later than 5:00 though. That gives us only about an hour to work with before I have to get back to Missoula. Got it?"

"Got it." Robert wrote down the list.

"Now go get some sleep," Frank said. "You look like shit."

"Thanks, partner."

"Newt and me are going to catch up on old times, aren't we Mr. Iron Bear?"

"No one's called me that for over twenty years," Newt said. He didn't seem to mind it. "And Robert, get that stuff back to me as soon as you can."

"Okay, don't stay up too late, kids," Robert said. Frank was acting pretty friendly towards Newt, considering the fact that Newt had killed his wife.

Robert spent the night at a Days Inn in Lolo, six miles south of Missoula. He fell asleep before he could wash. A call to the Thatcher Chemical Company the next morning revealed they didn't open until nine, so he took a shower, drove into town and ate a bacon and cheese omelet at a cafe on East Broadway.

He stopped at a store for cotton and was at the chemical supply house a couple of minutes before it was due to open. It was very cold and a raw wind blew from Hellgate Canyon east of the city. But there was no snow on the ground and very little in the hills around town. Robert purchased a half-gallon of each acid, way more than he needed, carefully mixed them together in a small canning jar, and headed back to Hamilton, forty-five minutes to the south.

At the police station, he chatted briefly with a different officer who let Robert through for a visit without even checking his jacket. Newt and Frank were now alone in the cell. The bald headed drunk had evidently been released earlier that morning.

"Perfect," Newt said. "When the sheriff puts his key in the lock to let Frank out later this evening, you're going to hear a small explosion. That's when you shove a gun, a knife, or something in the back of his neck and force him into the cell.

That's all there is to it."

"Oh, Jesus. I hate this shit. I've got to pull a gun on an officer of the law so I can help a nuclear terrorist escape from jail?"

"Think of the alternative," Frank said. "The bomb's hidden in a basement apartment near downtown Missoula. Half the people you saw there today will be vaporized if you don't do this. Newt's got us by the short hairs on this one."

"Did I say I wasn't going to do it? Did I? No, damnit. I just said I wasn't going to like it. Pulling a gun on a cop —"

"Hey, keep it down in there!" the officer yelled from his desk.

"By the way," Frank whispered. "Did you know that only a gram of uranium was fissioned in the bomb that destroyed Hiroshima?"

"Yes, Frank. Kind of gives you a hard on just thinking about it, doesn't it?"

Frank looked almost embarrassed.

On the way out, Robert asked the officer how much the bail was.

"Five hundred bucks. That's five times the going price for a Drunk and Disorderly. Your friend must be a real charmer."

"He is, but he also has a mean streak. I hope you never see it."

Robert stepped outside and the cold air hit his face like a slap. Puffs of frozen vapor came from his mouth, and he shortened his neck to bury his chin in the collar of his coat.

He drove to a pay phone. It was hard to make his icy fingers work well enough to dial. When he got the recording, he said, "Amy, this is Robert. Pick up the damn—"

She answered before he finished the sentence. "Give me a phone number," she said.

He read her the number on the phone. "What's so important that you can't—"

"Stay there. I'll call you back as soon as I can."

"But it's eighteen below zero and I'm in a booth—" She

had already hung up.

Robert stood in the booth for twenty minutes before she called back. His breath left a frosty coating on the Plexiglas walls. He was so cold that he'd stopped shivering. "Jesus, Amy, I almost froze to death out here," he said as soon as he picked up the receiver.

"They're monitoring my calls, Robert. All of them. I had to call you back from a pay phone. They've had me on lie detectors, they've grilled me with questions, people from the Pentagon have been here to interrogate me. My photos of the blast are now part of a U.S. Government Top Fucking Secret file. If I hadn't sneaked out the one roll of film, I wouldn't have a thing to show for my trip to Nevada. Want to hear how I hid it from them?"

"Some other time. When's the story hitting the streets?"

"The bastards are going to kill it. Seems like the military's having a hard time deciding what's more valuable—its reputation or St. Louis. The whole thing makes me sick. My bosses at the magazine caved big time on this one."

"Jesus, Amy. This is terrible. Where's Mason?"

"He slipped through undetected. I kept his name off the story byline to protect him, so the Feds don't know he exists. He called me yesterday and talked in code. He was smart enough to know my line was tapped. I wish you'd been. He's got the pictures for now. What's up with you? Make it quick. They have your number now since you called me at work. They're probably dispatching a squadron to your phone booth. And they know what you look like from my pictures."

"Newt's in jail near Missoula, Montana, with my friend Frank. We're breaking him out tonight, but I need five hundred dollars. Can you wire it to me?"

"I'll try, but I'm being watched pretty closely. Check the Western Union in Missoula in a couple of hours—"

Robert scraped a hole in the ice that had formed on the Plexiglas walls of the booth. Through it he saw three cars about half a mile away. They were driving much too fast.

"Gotta run!"

He dropped the receiver and ran into the nearest gas station.

The attendant was a burly fellow in his mid-twenties with a scar on his left cheek and curly black hair.

From the station, Robert saw the three cars screech to a halt in front of the phone booth. Six men jumped out with their weapons drawn. They checked out the booth and, finding it empty, scattered. Two of them ran toward the station.

"I never killed anyone," Robert pleaded to the attendant who was backing away. "I'm not a criminal."

"Those men aren't police." he said. "They're from the military."

The attendant picked up a tire iron.

"I'm not from California, for Chrissakes. You have to help me!" The last plea seemed to work.

The men were about a hundred yards away and coming fast. "You got an extra set of overalls?" Robert asked. "I'll pretend I work here."

"Quick. Into the shop."

"Thank you!"

Robert jumped into the back seat of a 1993 Ford Taurus. The attendant pulled a lever, which lifted the Taurus five feet in the air. He began loosening the lugs on the wheels just before the two men burst in.

"We're looking for an escaped convict."

"What'd he do?"

"Never mind that. Have you seen a Caucasian male about thirty-five, forty years old, about five-ten, black hair, medium build?"

"Yeah, there's one," the attendant said, pointing to the man's partner. "And you're another. You have to be more specific. This is Montana. Everyone looks like that."

"Here's a picture."

Robert could see none of the activity below him.

"What's that behind him? It looks like a bomb went off."

"Never mind that. Have you seen him?"

"Can I see some identification?"

There was a pause in the conversation.

"You guys aren't officers of the law. You're military men."

"Answer the question."

"No, sir. I haven't."

"Be on the lookout for him. He should be considered armed and extremely dangerous. Be careful, but don't let him out of your sight. Here's a number you can call."

"Okay."

A minute later, the attendant continued working on the lug nuts. Robert heard him remove the tire from the car, bust it from its rim and eventually fill it with air again. Then he replaced it, tightened the lugs, and lowered the car.

Robert looked through the windows, got out and said. "I can't thank you enough, man. You don't know what you—"

The man had his back to Robert. But he turned quickly and pinned Robert to the car with a tire iron across his throat.

"What the fuck did you do?" He pressed a little harder. "It's not too late to turn you in. One call is all it would take. Turn around. Put your hands behind your back."

He began wrapping electrical tape around Robert's wrists. "Okay, now turn around again. Talk to me. Tell me what this is all about. And you'd better be convincing."

"Alright. Tell me if you think anyone could make this up." Robert told him the whole story. "And that picture they showed you of me, what did you see behind me?"

"Well, it definitely wasn't a firecracker."

"No, it was an atomic explosion. And I'm trying to prevent another one."

"That's a pretty good story, I have to admit. Held my interest from start to finish." The attendant stuck a wad of tobacco in his cheek. "So what now?"

"Well, this evening I'm going to—Oh my God! I can't wait until then!"

"What?"

"Newt's picture. They have Newt's picture and they know we're in the area. They'll be faxing his photo to the police any minute. I have to go. Get me out of this tape. Hurry!"

"I want to hear the end of this one, man." He freed Robert's wrists. "I don't know if I believe you or not, but you tell a hell of a story."

"I'll keep you posted. Thanks for your help. Oh, and one more favor."

"You got nerve."

"Run over to the jail in about an hour. An officer over there is stuck in a cell. He'll need out, but don't go yet."

Robert drove the truck to the jail and marched inside. The same officer was still at his desk as if he hadn't moved in the past hour.

"I want you to let my friend out. The Indian in the wheelchair. I'll write you a check for the bail."

"We don't accept checks."

"How about credit cards?"

"You want to bail your friend out with a credit card?"

"It's a Platinum Visa."

"You stupid shit. We don't take cards. I don't care what color they are."

"Then take me back there for a minute, will you?"

The phone rang but the officer didn't answer. Two rings later it stopped. Robert heard a hum to his left and saw paper slowly coming from the fax machine. It was a cover sheet.

"It's back there," the officer said, pointing a thumb behind him.

Page two started coming through. "Can I get a cup of coffee?" Robert said.

"Over there."

Robert filled a cup and headed back to the desk. Newt's picture had just come through the fax machine. Blurry though it was, anyone could recognize him as the man in the cell around the corner. Robert dropped his coffee on the fax machine.

"Bastard!" the officer shouted. "Look what you've done. Get outta my way!"

As he pushed past, Robert stuck out his foot and the cop stumbled to the ground. Robert grabbed a pocketknife from his pants, jumped on the cop and pressed the unopened knife to the back of his skull.

"Don't move," he said in a shaky voice. "Put your hands over your head. That's it."

"Don't shoot. Don't shoot!"

"I don't plan to, if you behave yourself." His voice was steady now, though his insides were churning. "I'm going to take your gun now so we don't have any accidents while you try to be a hero."

"I won't, man. I just want to live through this."

"You'll be fine. Now get up slowly, and don't turn around. That's it. Walk to the cell."

"Well, hello," Frank said cheerfully. "Way to follow the plan."

"Sorry. We ran out of time. Okay, officer. Put your arms through the bars. My friend in the wheelchair is going to hold them while I get the keys off your belt."

It took Robert a minute to find the right key. He stuck it in the keyhole and it exploded. He yelled. The officer screamed, too, but Frank maintained his grip on the officer's arms.

"That stuff dried quicker than we thought," Newt said.

"Goddamnit, Newt. You should have warned me."

"It would have been a lot louder if we'd waited a couple of hours."

Robert unlocked the door and told the officer to enter. "Don't turn around yet," he said. Frank and Newt left the cell, Frank in his wheelchair. Robert slammed the door.

"I can't tell you how sorry I am about this, officer," Robert said. "I never would have done this if it hadn't been an emergency. Look," he said, showing the officer his hands. "I didn't use a handgun. I faked it. Remember that if I'm caught."

154 ~ Elemental Threat

"C'mon, Robert," Frank said. "You can kiss his ass later."

"You'll rot in jail the rest of your life for this, you bastard!" the cop said as Robert turned the corner.

"I said I was sorry, damnit," Robert yelled back to him. On the way out, he grabbed the coffee-stained picture of Newt from the ruined fax machine.

"Congratulations, Newt. You're finally famous. Your picture is being faxed to police stations all over the state."

"How did they get my picture?"

"Amy took a shot of you during the blast."

"When is her story coming out?"

"It may not. The military caught up with her and confiscated the pictures and threatened her superiors if they publish her story. It doesn't want people to know that a civilian constructed and tested a nuclear bomb."

"But, but—" he stammered. "I'll have to destroy St. Louis. Don't they understand that?"

"Gentlemen," Frank interrupted. "I hate to break up this pow wow, but we just stuffed a cop in a jail cell; we've got a nuclear terrorist on our hands; we're the subject of the biggest manhunt in years; the cops want to shoot us; the military folks want to kill us; we've got an atomic bomb that's scheduled to go off in a couple of hours; and all we've got on our side is a nerd, a cripple, and a clown.

"Do me a favor, Robert. Go get the fucking truck!"

CHAPTER 12

"That was a close one." Robert caught his breath inside the truck. His heart was pumping hard, and his lungs hurt from the run in the frigid air. But the excitement made him feel more alive, more like himself than he had in months. He felt a twinge of guilt that he had to hold a knife to a cop's neck to wake up from his torpor.

"It ain't over yet," Frank said. "Unlike you, I've never seen a nuclear bomb go off, but I hear they're pretty goddamn spectacular. Let's see if we can prevent another one from blowing up, okay?"

Newt sat between Frank and Robert. His attention was not on the conversation. He seemed to be staring through the windshield at a point miles away.

Outside, gray clouds hung low in the sky and formed a ceiling, which cut off the top two-thirds of the mountains to their left. Steam rose in wispy puffs from the Bitterroot River on the other side of the truck as they headed north to Missoula. The heater was overtaxed, and frost on the glass blocked most of their view from the windows.

Frank was driving. He seemed more angry than Robert and more worried than usual. "I've seen a lot of people like you, Iron Bear. You're not that fucking unusual."

"I'd prefer you to call me 'Newt.'"

"I don't give a fuck what you'd prefer!" Frank shouted. "I'd kill you right now if I thought I could get away with it."

"Oh, but you could," Newt said. "No one would miss me at all. Especially now that my brother is dead, thanks to you."

"But folks might miss the thirty or forty thousand people your bomb would kill."

"Oh, my," Newt said. "This is a warm, human side of you I've never seen." He scratched his enormous Adam's apple with his bony fingers. "I think you play the role of a prick much better." He glanced down at his watch. "Actually, I'm embarrassed to admit this, but I made a mistake in my calculations. The bomb's scheduled to go off in about forty-five minutes."

"Just a minute," Robert said. "You mean to tell me that if I had waited until 5:00 tonight to spring you from jail, I'd have been too late?"

"I'm sorry. I usually set the remote timer for 7:00 in the evening. But this time, with the travel and all, I changed my schedule and set it for an afternoon detonation. The timer is a rather crude device, and this was all the extra time I could squeeze out of it."

"Nuclear physicists are supposed to be precise, dammit," Robert said. "That was nearly a pretty costly error."

"But it doesn't matter now, you see. We're out of jail and on our way."

Suddenly, they heard a loud "pop!" and the truck swerved crazily into the oncoming traffic. Frank managed to swing back into the correct lane and then he guided the truck onto the shoulder. "How fast can you fix a flat tire?"

"I've never fixed one," Newt said.

"Not you, you," Frank said, pointing a fat thumb at Robert.

"Well, it's about fifteen below zero. Your nuts are probably rusted, maybe even frozen."

"You can say that again."

"With any luck, I'd guess I could do it in about fifteen, twenty minutes."

"That would put us into downtown Missoula at about," Newt glanced again at his watch. "I'd say about 1:15 or 1:20."

"Does that give us enough time?" Frank asked.

"How shall I put this?" Newt said.

"You only have two choices, for chrissakes," Frank said.

"The answer is somewhere between maybe and no."

"Get out and hitch a ride, damn it!" Robert opened the door and stepped out of the truck.

"We've gotta go with him," Frank said.

"No. We can't risk being seen. There are military police all over the place looking for me, and you just broke out of jail, remember?"

Before Newt stepped out, Frank grabbed him by the shirt. "I was going to kill you the second you disabled the bomb, you know."

"It wouldn't have worked," Newt said. His voice was tinny with fear, though he seemed to be making a great, if unsuccessful effort to mask it. "I can only reset the timing device, not disarm it."

"Then I would have made you take the bomb apart." Frank released his grip on Newt.

"Oh heavens," Newt said. "I wasn't taking you to the bomb. I was only having you drive me to the timing device. The bomb's several blocks away."

Newt stepped from the truck. When he was safely out of Frank's reach, he added, "You've been threatening me for almost thirty years. And I'm still alive. Maybe you're just full of talk, like so many people in the world. You just talk about what you'd do instead of actually accomplishing anything. At least I made something. I've accomplished something that nobody else has ever done. So compare that achievement with your useless, crippled, drunken existence, and tell me if you still think yourself superior."

He picked up a rock and heaved it at the truck. It bounced off Frank's window, leaving behind a complicated spider web in the glass.

Robert braced himself to stop Frank, who even in his crippled state, might lunge after Newt. But Frank remained calm. All he said was, "Iron Bear, you're an Indian. You can deny it; you can run from it. But our ancestors hunted together. They sang together. They suffered together. You are Indian to your core. Don't forget it. Now, get the fuck out of here or I really will kill you."

"You're lecturing me about being Indian. You're a drunk. You're what white people make fun of. You're a caricature, a cartoon. I on the other hand, am willing to give my life to improve our people's way of life. So don't you tell me what it is to be Indian."

"What the fuck are you talking about?" Frank said.

"Let's discuss this later," Robert said. "Go now, Newt. We'll catch you some other day. What time's the bomb scheduled to blow?"

"One thirty this afternoon." Newt stepped a few paces ahead and stuck out his thumb.

"Newt!" Robert shouted. "If we're vaporized, I'm going to hold you personally responsible."

A minute later, a blue Nissan pickup pulled to the shoulder about twenty yards ahead of Newt.

I never got rides that fast, Robert thought as he pulled on some old cotton work gloves. The right front tire had blown a sidewall and was useless. He crawled into the back of the truck and unscrewed the wing nut that held the spare tire to the side of the pickup bed.

The cold air made his lungs ache and his fingers were stiff. He tossed the spare onto the shoulder where it landed upright. Instead of bouncing, it leaned slowly to the side like a felled tree until it tipped over. "Your spare's flat," he called to Frank, who continued to stare ahead in silence.

Robert tossed the lug wrench and jack to the shoulder. The jack was an expanding type better suited to small imports than a three-quarter ton truck. The first four nuts loosened easily. But the fifth put up a fight. Robert's fingers were numb from the cold by now, and he worked clumsily in the frigid air.

"Hurry up!" Frank shouted from the cab.

"You got any WD40?" Robert asked.

"Of course," Frank said. He reached under the seat and tossed him a can. "Never travel without it. Duct tape and WD40 will fix almost anything."

Robert sprayed the nut with oil and waited for a few seconds. Then he positioned the lug wrench so its arm was parallel to the ground, and he leaned onto it with his full weight. The wrench slipped off the nut and mashed his knuckle. The cold made it hurt twice as much. He thought he'd stripped the nut, but the next try loosened it.

It's a good thing, Robert thought. *The gas station attendant in Hamilton has probably set the cop free by now. I bet there are a dozen police looking for us.*

The jack slipped twice as he hoisted up the truck. He almost told Frank to get out to lighten the load, but he managed to jack the truck high enough to remove the tire. He finished taking off the nuts, pulled the tire, and replaced it with the spare. Then he sprayed the bolts with oil, replaced the nuts and hand tightened them. He slowly cranked down the truck until he could pull the jack from it.

The tire sagged until the rim almost reached the ground. He threw the flat tire, the lug wrench and the jack into the back of the truck and then jumped inside. His hands ached from the cold. His nose hurt, too, as did his feet. His lungs still ached from the frigid air.

"Let's get out of here," he said. "They're probably looking for us by now."

Frank shook his head. "That son of a bitch," he said. "Know what he told me?"

Robert was shivering uncontrollably as Frank sat behind the wheel, evidently in no hurry to leave. "Tell me later. Let's get going."

"He said he loved the reservation more than I ever could. Can you believe that shit?" Frank started the engine. "Does that make any sense to you?"

"No, but I don't think like an Indian or a nuclear terrorist. Move it, will you?"

Frank put the truck in gear and pulled out into the traffic without looking. Luckily, there was no one coming behind him. "I mean, the guy was miserable when he lived there. He fit in about as well as a FBI agent on Pine Ridge. He left during high school, and no one's thought about him ever since. How can he say he loves the place?

"Sure he's got Indian blood, his grandparents were in the same clan as mine. But considering how he's lived his life these past few decades, why he's about as Indian as Ronald Macfucking Donald."

"I like that, Frank. Next time I stop by the Golden Arches, I'll be sure to order a Chicken Macfucking nuggets. Or maybe a Double MacFuck."

"You changed that tire in a little over thirteen minutes. Not bad, my friend. Not bad." Frank pulled a handkerchief from his pocket and blew his nose. "Let's head into town and replace that tire."

"What time you got?"

"About a quarter till one."

"You think Newt was lying about the timer business?"

"Maybe."

Robert thought for a minute. "Frank?"

"What?"

"Is there any way to get back to the reservation without going through Missoula?"

"What? Are you scared of a little old nuclear bomb? Don't be a pussy, man. Let's go."

Frank drove into town. Robert hoped the police didn't know about his truck. The traffic was slow. The two lane highway was full of old pickups like Frank's that spewed black smoke, and big, shiny new cars driven very slowly by old people who could barely see over the steering wheel. Frank cursed every vehicle they passed. They got to Missoula half an hour later, drove straight through downtown and stopped at a Conoco station on East Broadway about six blocks from downtown. "Let's get that tire replaced," he said.

"Couldn't we find a station in the next town?"

"Shut the fuck up."

Robert sat in the station while the tire got fixed. Frank stayed in the vehicle and rode the hydraulic lift as it hoisted the truck in the air.

Robert watched the seconds tick away on the clock on the gas station wall. The clock hung next to a calendar featuring Corvettes from the years 1958-1963.

All these people, he thought. *They live their lives, do their jobs, dream their dreams, hope for a better future.* He realized he hadn't thought about his future since Anna died. He used to miss her when he was away from her for a few weeks or a month. He never dreamed about how hard it would be to never see her again. Tears began to form in the corner of his eyes.

However, this time he felt something new. It was boredom, boredom of the self-pity he'd been stuck in for months. He was tired of the depression, tired of having no hope, and tired of living like a pig on Frank's floor or in cheap hotel rooms. He was tired of doing nothing. Suddenly, he wanted it to be springtime. He wanted to re-enter the world, become a player, a participant once again. He wanted to live. He missed his ranch, and he was tempted to quit this entire quest for revenge and just go back to work.

But wait, what time was it? He looked up at the clock. One thirty-five. "Hot damn!" he shouted. "Frank!" He ran into the working area of the garage. "Do you know what time it is?"

"It's about 1:25," the attendant said.

"But the clock in the waiting room says it's 1:35."

"I set it a little fast so I can shut down early."

"What are you shouting about?" Frank yelled from the suspended truck.

"Nothing. I'm just in a good mood is all."

"I don't understand you sometimes."

"Five minutes, Frank. That's all we need is five more minutes."

"Would you mind waiting in the other room?" The attendant was a middle-aged man with a paunch that stretched the material of his greasy coveralls.

"Sure, I'd be happy to."

Robert entered the office, which smelled of stale cigarette smoke. He put a plastic cone into the holder and poured himself a cup of thick, burnt coffee that somehow tasted wonderful.

Maybe it's the lack of sleep, he thought. Or maybe this is what everyone feels in the final minutes of their life. They say that presidential candidates who are about to get crushed in the voting booths get a frenetic rush of energy at the end. They run on pure adrenaline, and nothing, not the papers, the polls, their friends or advisors, can convince them they're doomed. That's how he felt now. Like a man refusing to accept the notion he was doomed—like he was throwing out his chest to meet the firing squad's bullets. Let them fire away, damnit. They can't rob my soul!

He stepped outside into the cold and faced downtown. A minute passed, and then another, and finally, another. Eventually, the cold took the edge off his euphoria, and he went back inside.

"Your truck's ready to go," the attendant said.

"So am I," Robert said. "So am I."

"What is with you, man?" Frank asked. "I haven't seen you like this in months."

"We just saved the lives of thousands of people. You need to celebrate your victories, however small."

"I'm still about half tempted to turn around and kill that little fucker, Newt. Let the chips fall where they may."

"If you'd seen the bomb go off in Nevada like I did —"

"If you'd seen what I saw—" Frank said, mocking Robert's voice.

"Shut up and listen. To think of unleashing that much raw power on human flesh is—it's unthinkable. I mean, just the light from the bomb is so intense it would sear your eyeballs."

"In Hiroshima, after the bomb," Frank said. "They found open books. The heat had burned through the black letters but hadn't touched the white part of the page."

"Where'd you learn that?"

"None of your business."

"You learned it from Newt, didn't you?"

"Shut the fuck up."

"This stuff does excite you. I bet you could scream because you're so jealous of me for getting to see the blast."

Frank said nothing.

"Let me tell you," Robert went on, "it was the most terrible thing I've ever seen. And yes, I was fascinated by it. I had a girlfriend once—"

"Oh, don't start that. I hate it when you talk about your old girlfriends."

"She was terrified of flying. We went on a plane trip once, and I thought she'd tear my arm off. She damn near did. It turns out that she didn't believe that people were meant to fly. She thought that if she died on an airplane, her soul wouldn't know how to make its way to God. I thought it was endearing at the time and didn't think much of it. But when I saw that bomb—"

He paused for a minute to re-visit the explosion. "I don't know for sure if we have a soul, Frank. But if we do, there's no way it could survive an atomic blast. No way at all. The bomb kills more than bodies. It destroys souls. I'm sure of that."

"That's crazy talk for a white man."

"Pull over at the next station. I want to make a call." When Frank finally pulled over, Robert jumped out of the truck and ran to the phone booth outside an Exxon station at the far edge of town. He called the attendant who'd saved him from the military police earlier in the day.

"Did they come back?"

"I can't believe the shit you caused me, man," the attendant said. "They were with me until about twenty minutes ago."

"What happened?"

"I went to the police station like you said. Those same agents had just gotten there and they'd let the cop out of the cell. They were all over me when I showed up."

"What'd you tell them?"

"The truth, that you pulled a gun on me."

"I did not."

"Well, they think you did. I said you were muttering incoherently the whole time you were here."

"Very flattering."

"I told them you said something about Idaho, your friends in Idaho. That's what you said, wasn't it?"

"Must be, if that's what you told them," Robert said. He owed this guy a couple of favors.

"What happened with the bomb?"

"Not to worry. The world's still safe for democracy for another four days. Thanks again for your help."

"Keep me posted."

Robert returned to the truck. "Let me know if you want me to drive. I feel great."

The next thing he remembered was waking up to the cocking hammer of a .38.

"Congratulations, you managed to sleep for over 400 miles," Frank said. "Thanks for the help driving."

"I must have dozed off."

"Charlie, our beloved sheriff, has a gun in your ear, case you hadn't noticed."

"Hello, Robert. Where you boys been?"

"Hi, Charlie." He turned slowly to look at him over the barrel that was now pointed at his nose. Charlie's head was bandaged with white rags. "When did you become a Muslim?"

"Very funny, Robert. You boys want to follow me to the

station? I got enough shit on you to keep you in jail for years."

"Why do you have the gun pointed at my head instead of Frank's? He's driving."

"Oh, you know Frank. He hates it when I threaten to shoot him. He might do something stupid and I'd have to actually kill him."

"This guy's afraid of me," Frank said.

"Unless you fuck with my fish."

"I'm sorry about the explosion at the newspaper office, Charlie," Robert said. "I know who did it."

"Really?" He snapped the gun barrel into the air, then pointed it back down and holstered it. "Now you got my attention. Let's talk. Follow me."

Instead of leading them to the station, he drove out to Frank's house in the county.

They stepped inside and were welcomed by a rush of cold, neglected air.

"Jesus, Frank," Charlie said. "Light a goddamn fire, will you? This place is an icebox."

"You light it, Mr. Officer of the Law," Frank said. "In case you hadn't noticed, I'm a fucking cripple. You're supposed to wait on me hand and foot."

"And in case you hadn't noticed, Mr. Prima Fucking Donna," Charlie shot back. "My head was split open by debris from an explosion which I suspect you had something to do with."

"Why don't you both shut up a minute," Robert said. He began tearing the pages from an old magazine and stuffing them into the wood stove.

Suddenly, he realized he was using an issue of *Architectural Digest*, one of Anna's old subscriptions, and he was appalled find himself tearing pages from something that was once an important part of her life. The action felt like a violation, as if he were shredding her memory. He closed the magazine, set it down on the nearby counter and smoothed its cover with the palm of his hand like he was stroking her hair.

Anna would have helped Frank and him prevent Newt from detonating another bomb, and she would have been thrilled by the adventure. But she may have given up before the job was finished. Robert decided that he would not give up before his task had been completed because that would be an even greater violation of her memory than tearing the pages from one of her favorite magazines.

The kindling he placed on the crumpled paper caught easily, and moments later, he had a fire roaring in the wood stove. The heat began to radiate to the far corners of the kitchen where the three men sat. Robert retrieved three cans of Bud from the refrigerator. The temperature control dial in the refrigerator was set too low and the cans were frozen, so he heated a pot of water on the wood stove and dropped them in to thaw the beer.

"Not too long on the stove," Frank said, as if he were directing the preparation of an exquisite meal. "They'll blow up if they get too hot. Be sure to stir the water so they heat evenly."

"Okay," Charlie said when Robert returned to the table with the beers. "Tell me what you know."

"The guy who set the bomb was named 'Newt,'" Robert said.

"That's it? All you got is one name? And a lousy name at that?"

"Hold on, Charlie," Frank said. "We've got more things to share with you. This 'Newt' character was a former resident of this reservation. He's a half-breed Sioux who used to be known as Iron Bear. Maybe you've heard of him?"

Charlie gaped at Frank, his fat lips parted obscenely and his chins folded atop one another below his jaw. "Tell me you're shitting me."

"No, sir," Frank said with uncharacteristic courtesy. "I can't tell you that. It's him. I've seen him."

"Frank, you've been holding out on me," Robert said. "What's going on? How well did you two know this guy?"

"Ask Charlie."

Robert turned to Charlie for an answer.

"This goes back about thirty years when me and Frank were in school together. It must have been senior year, because he was back from South Dakota. I was just about as much an asshole as he was back then, and between the two of us, we had the whole school terrorized."

"You're giving yourself too much credit, Charlie. You were never the asshole I was."

"I stand corrected. One night late, we were both drunk from a party earlier that evening. We were cruising the streets looking for someone to beat up because we needed some sport. All of a sudden, we heard this terrible racket coming from a side street. Frank drove down to see what it was. You were driving that old Plymouth, remember?"

"It was a Chrysler. One of those with push buttons for the automatic transmission. It was my grandma's car."

"We turn the corner and here's this gangly kid, Iron Bear, running down the street."

"I didn't realize Newt was the same guy until I was in jail with him last night."

Charlie looked at Frank and shook his head. "That's another story of yours I don't want to hear about. Anyway, Frank and I used to kick Iron Bear's ass every now and then, so this seemed like a good opportunity. Except the kid had a baseball bat. Not that that scared us. We were just curious to see this shy, awkward kid running down the street bashing in garbage cans and mailboxes.

"So Frank pulls up beside him and asks him what's up. The kid has the nerve to turn around and smash the hood of the car with his bat. Put a good size dent in it. A pretty gutsy thing to do for a kid who used to crap his pants every time he saw us."

"I told him to get in the car," Frank said. "I wasn't sure whether to kill him or compliment him on the only brave thing he'd ever done in his life."

"He got in, all right," Charlie continued. "We asked him what was going on, and he told us they'd just discovered coal on his dad and grandparent's land."

"The same land the government had moved him to after

they kicked his dad off of the homestead flooded by the dam?" Robert asked.

"That's right," Charlie said. "How'd you know about that?"

"It's a long story. So what was the problem about finding the coal?"

"The problem," Frank said, "was that when the bastards at the Bureau of Indian Affairs found out about the coal, they changed Iron Bear's allotment. They sent his dad a notice that due to a clerical error, the land they'd moved his family to years ago no longer belonged to him. The government, because of this alleged clerical error, traded his allotment for one fifty miles away that was about two-thirds as big and less than half as productive.

"And the federal government ended up with the mineral rights on the original parcel which they could sell at any time to the highest bidder."

Charlie blew his nose loudly into a handkerchief. "Jesus, Frank," he said, peeling off his jacket. "It's either too cold or too hot in here." Beads of sweat dampened his high forehead.

"What happened after Iron Bear, or Newt, or whatever his name is told you the story about the coal?" Robert asked.

"I haven't told anyone this in thirty years," Charlie said, taking a drink from his beer. "Whoa! That one had a lump in it. I hope it was just ice." He took another drink, crushed the can and tossed it over his shoulder onto the floor.

"Do you mind?" Frank asked.

"Yes, but I'm going to tell the story anyway. I don't re-member whose idea it was, Frank's or mine, but we decided to egg him on. I mean, Iron Bear was already pretty hot, so it did not take much work on our part. We told him we'd drive him to the house of the BIA official who signed the letter to his folks. He was more than game, so we gave him a few beers while we drove him to Wolf Point. Along the way, we kept urging him to kick the guy's ass with the baseball bat."

"Newt was a basket case, even more than usual," Frank said. "He was babbling and blubbering the whole way."

"He wasn't making any sense. He talked all the time, sometimes screaming and sometimes just kind of whimpering. But I never understood anything he was saying. I could tell how upset he was, though, and Frank and I were damn sure playing on it."

Robert brought out another round of beers and set them on the heater for a moment before serving them. "I can picture Newt losing it. I saw him practically faint because Mason Tomlinson from the newspaper tossed a pebble at him."

"Probably brought up some old memories," Frank said.

"That reminds me," Charlie said. "You're supposed to call Mason Tomlinson. He says it's an emergency. I got his number back at the office. Now back to the story. We got to the guy's house about ten-thirty that night. Frank and I parked around the corner where we could just see the guy's front door. We pointed it out to Iron Bear and sent him on his way while we watched. We were all giggles as he stood there knocking for a couple of minutes until someone finally answered. And then—" Charlie's voice trailed off.

"And then what?" Robert asked.

"You tell him, Frank."

"And then he pulls a gun out of his pants, a gun we didn't know he had, and he pumps six bullets into the guy's chest. Never said a word, just started firing. We sat there, dumbfounded, while he ran the opposite way from our car. But then, he circled the block, came back and knocked on our window. Liked to have scared the shit out of us. Then he jumps in the back and we drive off."

"About two miles down the road," Charlie said to Frank, "You stopped the car and stomped the living shit out of him. If I hadn't pulled you off, you'd have killed him."

"I wish I had," Frank said. "Funny thing is, he just took the pounding without a peep. The harder I hit him, the less impact it seemed to have. I could swear he was smiling through it."

"Then Frank told him to get his ass off the reservation for good and never come back. I think he probably graduated from high school, but this is the first I'd heard of him since then."

"Tell him the worst part, Charlie."

"Turns out, the guy Iron Bear killed didn't work for the BIA. We just picked out some house at random. The poor bastard who lived there ended up dead for no reason. I've never really gotten over that. Frank reacted to the incident by becoming even more like Frank. I ended up becoming an officer of the law. All because of what happened that night."

"Don't get all sentimental on me now, Mr. Rogers."

"Fuck you, Frank. I think that night's the main reason you're drinking yourself to death."

Frank tried to reach across the table for Charlie, but Charlie bounced up with his gun drawn and pointed it at Frank's head.

"Enough, already!" Robert yelled. "We've got a real problem here. I'm sick of fighting each other all the time. There's someone outside our little circle who needs to be stopped before he kills thousands of people.

"I've been spending half my time lately trying to hunt down Newt, and the other half trying to spring him loose from jail. I don't have time to watch over the two of you. Frank, you calm down. Charlie, put your damn gun away and let's talk."

Robert told Charlie the whole story, top to bottom. He told him about the men who tried to kill them at the dumpsite. He told him about Frank's shooting Buckley. And he told him about watching the blast in Nevada.

"The problem," Robert said, "is that he's got a bomb wired to go off in ninety-six hours. Every four days, he resets the timer. If we kill him, or if he ends up in jail or is otherwise unable to reset the timer, boom! The thing goes off. Right now we think the bomb's in Missoula."

"So what's the problem here?" Charlie asked.

"I'm not tracking you," Robert said.

"Who the hell in Montana's going to miss Missoula? Just a bunch of hippies and college students living there."

"Point taken. Nevertheless, we still can't afford to kill Newt outright," Robert said. "But wait, there's more." He proceeded to tell Charlie about the threat to St. Louis, and the fact that the military had killed Amy Boston's story about it.

"That explains a lot," Charlie said. "Like why I've had about half a dozen calls from Army intelligence asking if I knew where you were."

"Oh, shit," Robert said. "Those guys don't give up easily."

"They must not have ID'd my truck when we escaped from the jail in Hamilton," Frank said. "Otherwise, they'd have been here when we got back tonight."

"Wait, wait, wait a minute," Charlie said. "What's this about breaking out of jail?"

"You should have been there, Charlie," Robert said. "We've been having ourselves a time. I had to hold a fake gun to a cop's head and force him into a cell."

"I didn't hear any of this," Charlie said, putting his fingers in his ears. "I want to remind you that I'm an officer of the law."

"Have the police been asking about Frank?"

"They know he escaped from jail," Charlie said. "I got a call about him earlier this evening too, and I'm supposed to keep an eye out for him. I think they just want him on an escape charge. Hopefully they don't know that you two are working together on this."

"You've had lots of calls about us?" Robert said.

"Yeah. And I'm damn sick of them, too."

"So what's our next move?" Frank asked.

"Can I get back to you on that one? It looks like we have some company."

Through the one remaining window in the kitchen, Robert saw a pair of headlights bouncing along the road to Frank's house. They were about a mile away.

"Get in the trunk, Robert," Charlie said. "Frank, you get in the back of the car and act drunk. I know that's a stretch."

Charlie helped wheel Frank out of the house to Charlie's police car. Then he opened the trunk for Robert who climbed in immediately. Charlie shut the hood after him.

Frank lifted himself into the back seat. Charlie stayed just outside his police vehicle until the other car pulled up. Robert could hear the voices through the trunk.

"Special agents Kruck and Meinhardt. Can I see some ID?"

"Sure, if I can see yours, gentlemen. Okay, thanks. I suspect we're looking for the same person. No one else lives around here for miles."

"We're looking for a Frank Kicking Bird, two words in the last name. And a partner of his named Robert Botkin. Do you have any ideas of their whereabouts?"

Damnit, Robert thought. *They do know we're working together.*

"Frank lives here, in a manner of speaking. That's why I came. I want to arrest the bastard for generally making my life miserable over the past thirty years. Why are you here?"

"Official business. Who's in the back of your PV?"

"PV?"

"Patrol Vehicle."

"Oh, well that's our LD. I found him on the road on the way out here."

"LD?"

"Local drunk. His name's Freddie Kick-In-Rear. That's three words in the last name. Hyphenated, though."

The men peered in and saw a middle aged Indian man with his head thrown back on the seat, snoring loudly. "Here's a card. Call us if you see Mr. Kicking Bird or his partner."

"Sure thing."

Robert heard the car drive off. Charlie started his own car and drove for a mile or so before stopping. He let Robert out of the trunk and into the front seat.

"You boys can stay at my sister's. She's got a place on the edge of town. But keep a low profile, will you?"

"Sure thing, Charlie," Frank said.

"Thanks for your help," Robert added. "By the way, were

you going to arrest us earlier in the evening?"

"Now, you boys know I can't do that. I'm way out of my jurisdiction out here. I'll let the BIA cops handle this one."

CHAPTER 13

Charlie's sister lived in a clean, two-bedroom house just outside Poplar, the seat of tribal government on the reservation. She was gracious about putting the two men up for a couple of days. She had laid out blankets and towels for them before they had arrived and then had gone to bed.

Frank chose to spend the night in her overstuffed recliner. Robert got the couch, which proved to be one of the most comfortable beds he'd enjoyed in a long time. Robert and Frank were still sleeping at noon when Charlie came by for lunch. The blast of cold air from the open door woke Robert.

Frank, on the other hand, had to be shaken repeatedly before he finally stopped snoring, sat upright, and said, "Where the hell am I?"

"My sister's," Charlie said. "Remember? You're here until things cool down."

"What if they don't cool down?" Robert asked. "What if the Feds and the law are still hunting us after a couple of weeks?"

"Then I'm afraid I'm going to have to shoot you," Charlie

said.

"Or I will," his sister yelled from the kitchen.

"Come on out here, Janie. I want you to meet the boys."

Janie did not support as many chins as her brother did. She was about thirty-five years old with thick black hair tied in a ponytail that hung to the middle of her back. The skin of her face was smooth and the color of mahogany. She had no wrinkles aside from a few thin crows' feet at the corners of her eyes. Large, even white teeth showed through her big smile. She was a little thick around the middle, but her arms and legs were thin and strong.

"I know this guy," she said, pointing to Frank. "Lord God, Frank. I thought your snoring was going to bring down the roof. I was tempted to stuff a rag in your mouth."

"Where's that good lookin' boy of yours?" Frank asked.

"He's going to school up at the community college. I don't see him much these days."

"He's a good boy," Frank said. "Always has been."

"We're pretty proud of him," Charlie said.

"You talk like you're his dad," Frank said.

"Charlie helped me raise him, ever since Billy was a baby."

"Why, Charlie. You old softy, you," Robert said.

"Damn you, Robert," Charlie said. A rose blush colored his face. "I can't tell if you're giving me shit or not. But this is not a subject I want to be teased about."

"I'm not teasing you about it. I think it's great. You're a good man."

Charlie's face returned to its original color. "Oh, I almost forgot," he said. "Here's Mason's number. Can we use your phone, Janie? We'll pay you back."

"Help yourself."

Robert called the number and got a hotel operator. "Just a moment please, I'll put you through," he said.

"Mason?"

"Jesus, Robert! What the hell kept you? I've been waiting by the phone for almost twenty-four hours."

"It would take me twenty-four hours to tell you everything that's happened since I last saw you. What's going on?"

"I'm in deep shit. The police arrested Amy two days ago for withholding vital information related to national security. Can you believe that? The military's sitting on a story about a guy who's going to blow up St. Louis with a nuclear bomb, and it's accusing her of violating national security!"

"Damnit!" Robert said. "Amy's gonna kill me. She told me my leads always get her in trouble."

"This is serious, man. And I'm sitting in a cheap hotel room with an expired credit card and I don't have a dime. I don't know if the military police or my creditors are going to get me first."

"So what do you need from us? Money?"

"No! Forget the money. I need your help getting this story out. Amy's got a friend at the *Washington Post* who wants to print the story. That paper has more lawyers than the Justice Department, and it's the only one with the guts to stand up to the military. But I can't get the story to her friend. The military police have my name and picture now, even though they don't know where I am, and I can't get anywhere near the building."

"What's the guy's name?"

"Philip Montoya."

Robert repeated the name out loud. He turned to Charlie and Frank and touched his temple to get them to remember the name. "Can you fax the story to him?"

"I can't get out of my room to do it," Mason said. "I still can't show my face around. And the hotel doesn't have a fax machine."

"You sure you're not just being paranoid?"

"I tell you, man. This isn't a game. You saw the blast. You know what it can do. The military's desperate to kill this story, and you know how important it is to get it out. We're running out of time, and Amy's in jail."

"Reporters are supposed to be protected by dozens of laws," Robert said.

"Not when there's a choice between First Amendment rights and national security."

"Where's the story now?"

"It's on the laptop Amy lent me. We wrote it together. I got it right here."

"Let me put Frank on. He's the techno-whiz. He might have some ideas."

Robert brought the receiver to Frank.

"Hello, Mason. What kind of computer you got? What? That's a fucking dinosaur, but I think we can work with it. You have two phones in your room? Good. Hang up. Call downstairs and tell them you need two outside lines, one on each phone, and ask them to send up an extra length of phone cord so you can hook up to your modem. They'll know what you're talking about. People ask them that all the time. Call me back as soon as you get the stuff." Frank gave him Janie's number.

After hanging up, Frank told Charlie to run over to the community college to borrow a laptop. "Make sure it has an internal modem."

Ten minutes later the phone rang. Frank was eating a bowl of Janie's chili when he answered. "Yeah, you got it?" he said. "Huh? No, I wouldn't be interested in sponsoring two children to attend the fucking circus in Wolf Point, but thank you for calling. Have a nice day."

He slammed the receiver onto its cradle. "I just spared you a phone solicitation, Janie. I don't think they'll be calling you back next year, either."

"Thanks, Frank. That makes up for the long distance charges. I think I came out ahead on this one."

The phone rang again. "Hello. Good. Now here's what you do. Unplug the jack from the second phone and stick it into one of the two jacks in the back of your laptop." Frank walked him through the process. Robert was surprised how clearly Frank gave the directions. Even more shocking was that he didn't yell, belittle or cuss into the phone. He was all business.

"You what?" Frank said. Holding his phone momentarily away from his face he said, "Mother-fuckers are at his door. The police."

"We'll have to work fast. Jam a chair under the door knob and tell them you'll be out as soon as you get dressed."

He wiped his forehead with the sleeve of his shirt. "Those bastards mean business," he said to Robert. Then he gave Mason a screen name and password to enter on his laptop. "Don't panic. Yes, I can hear them kicking down the door. Okay. You got through? No? Busy? Try it again. Yes, it takes a minute."

Beads of sweat appeared on Frank's forehead. "Great, you're in!" He ran Mason though the email program. "Hit the 'attach' button and search for the program in Word. Now hit the send button and we're done. Hit it! Hit it, Goddamn it!" Frank repeatedly jammed his finger onto the desk as if in doing so, he could help Mason send the file.

Frank slowly lowered the receiver back to its cradle. "They got him. I don't know if it went through or not. It sounds like they ripped the cord from the wall. Maybe if they didn't know what they were doing, they ripped out the phone he was talking on first. That might give the file enough time to get through on the second phone. It takes about fifteen seconds to transfer the file from the disk to the modem."

He mopped his brow again. "Robert, call the *Washington Post* for Mr. Montoya's fax number. We have about four minutes until the police trace Mason's call and send an agent over here."

"I'll hold them off as long as I can," Charlie said.

"This is a little more excitement than I bargained for, big brother," Janie said.

Robert called information for the number of the *Washington Post*. Then he called the newspaper and got the fax number.

"Step aside, Robert," Frank said. "Let the Wizard do his magic. You have another phone, Janie?"

"An old one somewhere out in the storage shed. It's

broke."

"Find it and bring me its cord if it's still attached. Hurry."

She ran outside to the shed. Robert saw various objects fly from its door: a rusted shovel, an old wind-up kid swing, two rust brown sofa cushions, a window frame without glass, several pairs of work gloves, some two-by-fours, a couple of irregularly shaped pieces of plywood, a box that spilled out baby clothes when it hit the ground, an empty gin bottle. Finally she emerged, victorious and smiling, holding a dusty phone. She stopped halfway to the house and stared at the road. Then she continued inside.

"Make it quick, Frank," she yelled from the doorway. "They're coming fast."

Frank began pulling and replacing wires and dialing numbers. "We got it!" he yelled. "Most of it anyway. There seems to be some crap at the end, but it's here. Remind me to buy Mason a beer fifty years from now when he's out of prison. Robert, come over here. Type a note to Montoya to tell him Amy's in jail."

"They're almost at the door!" Janie yelled. "Hurry!"

"Okay, now step back. Charlie, jam the door with a chair like I told Mason to do. Here goes."

Outside, two men pounded at the door.

"Shit, a busy signal!" Frank said.

Robert hovered over Frank as he tried to get through on the *Washington Post's* fax line. The men broke down the door, and behind Robert, Charlie yelled "Halt!"

"Got it!" Frank yelled at almost the same time, but his voice was drowned out by two ear splitting shots from revolvers. Robert dropped to the ground in fear and turned to see Charlie and one of the agents lying on the living room rug. The agent was moaning softly.

"Don't anybody move!" the other agent yelled.

Robert raised his hands in the air and slowly, very slowly, began to stand up. "I'm just checking on my friend. Don't shoot," Robert didn't want to be the next casualty. He couldn't believe how quickly this all happened. Poor Charlie was always in the wrong place at the wrong time. But, Robert thought, he'll probably survive this, just like he survived the bomb at the newspaper office. When he saw the hole in Charlie's chest and all that blood on the carpet, Robert suddenly grasped the seriousness of the situation.

"Oh, my God! My God!" Janie yelled hysterically as she dropped to her knees and threw her arms around her brother's head. "Charlie, don't die, Charlie! Charlie!" She put her head on his and sobbed. Her voice was full of terror, and Robert realized that Charlie was dead.

Janie began shaking Charlie's corpulent body as if to wake him. Robert dropped to his knees and put his arms around her.

"Oh, God, Janie! I'm so sorry." She turned toward Robert, threw a bloody arm around him and hugged him while she sobbed. He too began to cry. "I'm so sorry, so sorry," he whispered into her ear. "He was a good man."

"You two, freeze!" The other agent said, somewhat belatedly.

"Fuck you, Jack," Frank said from the desk. "You just killed my friend in cold blood."

The agent's hand was shaking. "My partner killed him. And your friend had a gun. He shot my partner!"

"Your partner shot a cop, you bastard!"

"He was my brother!" Janie shrieked. She tried to make a run at the agent, but Robert held her down.

There has been way too much loss, Robert thought. And unless he and Frank succeeded in stopping Newt, there would be much, much more.

CHAPTER 14

Charlie was dead, and there was no one available to look after Robert and Frank in the Poplar city jail. So the agents decided to hold Robert and Frank in the Bureau of Indian Affairs correctional facility at the tribal headquarters. The Bureau of Indian Affairs jail was a concrete, over-built facility more accustomed to holding drunk and disorderlies than threats to national security.

Robert and Frank each had their own cell, presumably because BIA officials didn't want them contaminating other prisoners with their ideas or jointly plotting an escape. Their cells were far apart, and they had to shout at each other to be heard, so they talked very little.

Robert asked for some reading material the first day, and after an hour's wait, a dumpy, ruddy faced BIA official brought him two issues of *Popular Mechanics* and a copy of Eric Segal's *Love Story* with a third of its pages missing. Robert read them all cover-to-cover.

To pass the time, he did exercises in his cell. But no amount of reading or exercise could take his mind off the question of whether the story about Newt's threat had gotten out, and if so, what effect it was having. It was nice, he realized, to be obsessed with something other than Anna's death.

Robert was used to having lots of time alone, which was either a hazard or benefit of running a ranch, depending upon one's perspective and frame of mind. But he wasn't lonely, and he was never bored. There was always some aspect of the ranch that required attention, a fence to be mended, a U-joint on the tractor to replace, an animal to doctor.

At night when he was no longer busy with chores, he spent his time thinking through the activities of the next day or week, methodically fitting each project into a specific amount of time. He was a master at scheduling and managed with amazing efficiency without seeming hurried or stressed.

All that changed with Anna's death. Now, he carried with him an enormous burden of grief and a lot of time on his hands. Instead of trying to restore some sense of order to his life, he'd quit working on his ranch, practically stopped living at home, and focused all his energy on stopping a half-breed psychopath from blowing up St. Louis. Granted, it was a worthwhile pursuit, but he knew enough about himself to suspect that avoiding his own emotional pain was one of his primary motives in trying to stop Newt.

With his back resting against the concrete wall of his cell, he replayed the events of the past few months in his head. There had already been three deaths: Anna, Newt's brother, and now Charlie. Four if he counted the truth as a victim. Again, the question nagged at him. Did Amy's story about the Nevada detonation get out? If so, it might have been worth the price. Publishing the story would save thousands of lives in St. Louis.

Frank was not nearly so quiet and contemplative during his incarceration. Every few minutes he was pounding on the bars with his shoe and yelling for food, threatening officers, or trying to bribe them for a drink of whiskey.

"You fucking, cornholed, ass-licking, son-of-a-camel, mother-fucking, pig humpers!" he would shout. "I'm missing *Seinfeld* on TV, goddamn it! My lawyer'll sue your asses for cruel and unusual punishment, you cock-suckers!"

Twice he threw his food tray at the BIA officials, covering them with gravy and milk. He reached through the bars and grabbed one by the sleeve for a second before the man got away. The BIA officials began holding a gun on Frank and making him roll back from the cell bars before they dropped off his food.

Two days to the hour after having been locked up, both Robert and Frank were abruptly released by the BIA cops. Another officer, this one a tall, dark-skinned Indian with skinny legs and a pot belly, unlocked Robert's cell. "Please follow-me," he said curtly as he led Robert away from confinement. "Wait here," he said as he unlocked Frank's cell. Frank wheeled his way out to the hall.

"What's up?" Frank asked. "We getting off early for good behavior, or are we headed for execution?"

"Your friend's a national hero, Mr. Chairman." the official said to Frank.

"Yes!" Robert yelled, pumping his fists in the air. "So the story got out?"

"It damn sure did, partner. You're headlines in papers all over the country. Follow me." He led them to a desk in front of the building and pulled two manila envelopes from a drawer. "Your possessions, such as they are. Man, you should see the shit your friend had in his pockets," he said to Robert. "He had a pickle that must have been two weeks old. Jesus, that thing smelled."

"That was my dick, man. You stole my dick, no wonder I couldn't piss the past couple of days," Frank said. "Give me that thing." He grabbed the envelope from the man's hands.

"We're all going to miss him," he said to Robert.

"I'm headlines?" Robert said. "But this isn't about me. It's about a nuclear threat to a major U.S. city. It's about the military trying to hide that threat from the public. It's about a psychopath who learned how to build a bomb and has enough fissionable material to make dozens of them."

"That may be, but the press is playing up your heroics in

outwitting the military, escaping from jail, figuring out all that computer shit. Man, it makes for a good story."

"I'm the computer genius," Frank said. "Not him. Did they say anything about me?"

"Sorry. You weren't mentioned."

"Well, goddamn it to hell," he muttered. "You'd think the Indian angle'd be good for a couple paragraphs, at the very least."

"This is no time for jealousy, Frank. I'd gladly give you my fifteen minutes of fame."

"I lose my wife, get my legs blown up, get myself put in jail, risk my life, and lose a friend while I'm on the computer shipping an illegal story, and I'm not even a fucking footnote."

"Don't feel bad, man. It's not everyone who escapes from jail gets to walk away like you."

"Walk?" Frank said. "Could you use a different verb?"

"Wheel from jail?" the cop said. "That just don't sound right." The BIA official took a Marlboro from his shirt pocket, tapped it against the desk, put it in his mouth. "Don't tell anyone. This is a no-smoking facility," he said as he lit the cigarette. "Prepare yourself for a few interviews on the outside. You got the press pretty curious over this bomb thing."

"They should be curious."

"And one other tip for you," the officer said.

"What's that?"

"It's a buyer's market in St. Louis. Prices are real depressed right now."

Robert and Frank were greeted by shouts as they stepped from the jail. There were almost as many reporters as there were people living in Poplar. Cameras flashed, arms and voices were raised. A little snow added texture to the stiff, cold breeze that slapped at their faces.

"Mr. Botkin! Mr. Botkin!" they all shouted at once.

Robert and Frank stopped as soon as they left the front door of their facility. They couldn't have pushed their way past the crush of people if they'd wanted to.

"Mr. Botkin!" one woman shouted louder than the rest. "Do you know where the bomber is currently living?"

He held up a hand to quiet the crowd. "He's a slippery one, ma'am. His range extends from Nevada, through Colorado into Montana, and apparently as far east as St. Louis."

"Do you think he can pull off his threat?" another reporter asked.

"I've seen what he can do. I witnessed the blast in Nevada. I understand he has a huge store of fissionable uranium. Anyone with the know-how and the material to make a bomb has to be taken seriously."

"Would he really kill innocent people and destroy billions of dollars worth of property just to make a political point?"

"As I said, I believe he should be taken seriously."

"Do you think the military was justified in trying to kill this story by arresting you and your friends?" This question was asked by a tall, thin man in jeans and a blue down jacket.

"You know better than to expect a candid answer to that question. Criticizing the military is a great way to find myself back in jail."

He was operating on automatic pilot, answering questions without thinking but somehow knowing what needed to be said. At least a hundred people crowded around him as he spoke. He pointed to people at random who were allowed to ask questions, and the power of his situation was thrilling. But he didn't allow his vanity to control the interview.

"Mr. Botkin! Do you expect any sort of ransom demand?"

"I have no idea. He never mentioned money to me."

"Do you intend to help find him before April 11, the date on which he's threatened to destroy St. Louis?"

"I've run into Newt twice now, and both times he's found me. I hope he plans to find me again before then."

"What would you say to him?"

"I'd like him to share his recipe for Gazpacho. I don't know what I'd say, but I'd try to reason with him."

"Is he the kind of guy you can reason with?"

"He's threatening to blow up a major U.S. city. That does not seem particularly reasonable to me."

"Anything else?"

"He's about my age and he still gets pimples. I don't think his diet's very good."

"What do you think about the article written by Boston and Tomlinson?" another reporter yelled.

"I've been in jail. All I've read lately is a six-month-old issue of *Popular Mechanics*. But I know Amy Boston and Mason Tomlinson to be first rate reporters, and you can believe everything of theirs you read."

Frank pulled on Robert's arm until he brought Robert's face down even with his. "Where do you come up with this shit, man?" Frank whispered. "You sound like you've been doing this all your life."

"I don't know, but I'm thinking of applying for a job as the President's press secretary."

"Mr. Botkin!" shouted another interviewer, a middle-aged man with a cigarette dangling from his lips. "Tell us how you managed to get the story to Mr. Montoya of the *Washington Post* before you were arrested."

"That heroic act is entirely due to the electronic wizardry of my friend, Frank Kicking Bird." He heard Frank mumble, "It's about time."

Suddenly, a new barrage of questions was directed to Frank. He held up a hand to the crowd and the questions suddenly stopped.

"I'd like to make a statement," he began in a baritone laden with self-importance. "See that bar over there?" He pointed across the street and a hundred heads turned in the direction he pointed. "Only people who buy me a Jack Daniels on the rocks get their questions answered."

The reporters made their way across the street, leaving Frank and Robert momentarily alone on the steps of the jail.

"See, old man," Frank said. "I've got some instincts for crowd control, too. Give me a push and let's move."

With the crowd gone, they could see the wide, empty streets of the town and the old frame administration building of the community college. A couple of teenagers had apparently grown bored with the crowd at the jail and were throwing rocks with mittened hands at the town's lone stop sign.

By the time they got across the street, there were a dozen drinks lined up at the bar for Frank. He wheeled his way into the crowd, took a drink, and began talking. Robert, forgotten by the reporters now that Frank had center stage, headed across the room and asked the bartender for a copy of a newspaper that had Amy's story in it.

"You've made quite a stir," the barkeep said. He was an older man with deep-set wrinkles in his face and nicotine stains in his bushy white moustache. "That bomb's all anyone's been talking about."

"What can I say? I was in the wrong place at the wrong time."

As he said this he realized that both Anna and Charlie were in the wrong place at the wrong time and that he'd fared a lot better than either of them. He tried to imagine Anna in front of the reporters who had greeted him outside the jail. She would have been terrified. She would have stammered for a minute and then frozen up like a faulty engine. He smiled at the thought of it, the first time since her death that her memory had brought a smile to his face.

"Give me a shot of JD too, while you're at it," he said to the bartender. "In fact, just hand me one of those in front of Frank."

"Take a drink from the tribal chairman? Are you crazy? He'd kill me."

"He's got a dozen there."

"He's down to eight. Forget it. I'll buy you a drink. I'd say you've earned it."

"Thanks."

"Hard to imagine this town without Charlie."

"He was a good man."

"I never pictured him as the heroic type," the bartender said, as he set a drink in front of Robert. Then he ducked under the bar and came up with a stack of newspapers.

"These are *Great Falls Tribunes*, not *New York Times*, but hey, this is Poplar, Montana. You'll find Tomlinson's story in there somewhere." He wiped the bar with a damp rag. "I can't believe that guy got a story posted all over the damn country. Gotta be good for his career."

"Don't underestimate Mason. Deep down inside him is a Pulitzer Prize winner dying to get out. I mean that." Robert began sorting through the stack of papers. It was easy to spot the one he was looking for from the picture of the nuclear explosion on the front page. Underneath it was a short AP article that read as follows:

Terrorist threatens to destroy St. Louis with nuclear bomb

> Early this week, two reporters witnessed the first detonation of a citizen-constructed nuclear bomb in history. The bomber has threatened to destroy the city of St. Louis, Missouri on April 11 to exact revenge for the exploitation of the Northern Plains Indians..."

The article went on to describe the size and location of the blast. (The military was now being very cooperative, apparently.) It summarized the letter Newt left with Amy and Mason, and it talked about the military's early efforts to kill the story.

> "Military spokesmen initially denied the blast was nuclear in nature, instead blaming the explosion on an old munitions dump..."

I knew it, Robert thought. *It's the same thing they did after the Trinity Blast, and nobody believed them then, either. They don't learn new tricks easily.*

The rest of the story talked about the three witnesses, Amy Boston, Mason Tomlinson, and Robert Botkin, being held by the military police for questioning. Below it was another article, this one co-authored by Amy Boston and Mason Tomlinson. Robert read it twice.

The Radiance of a Thousand Suns—

Dr. J. Robert Oppenheimer, when asked his reaction to having witnessed the world's first detonation of a nuclear device, a bomb he helped design, offered a quote from the Bhagavad-Gita.

He said:

'If the radiance of a thousand suns,
Were to burst at once into the sky,
That would be like the splendor of the Mighty One—
I am become Death, The shatterer of Worlds.'

"On a cold morning at dawn on February 27, we had the privilege and the curse of watching the radiance of a thousand suns burst into the sky. A terrorist, who claims to have enough weapons-grade uranium to build dozens of such bombs, detonated a thermonuclear device on an isolated mountaintop in the Nevada desert.

"The story begins years ago when a part Assiniboine Indian, who now goes by the name of Newt (short for 'Neutron,' the subatomic particles involved in nuclear reactions) lived on the Fort Peck Indian Reservation in Northeast Montana. Newt's family had been forced from land to which they had been assigned by the federal government sixty-one years ago, sixteen years before Newt was born. In 1933, the U.S. Army Corps of Engineers evicted Newt's father and grandparents from lands flooded by the reservoir that backed up behind the newly constructed Fort Peck Dam..."

Amy and Mason discussed Newt's early career hauling nu-

190 ~ Elemental Threat

clear wastes, his alleged role in helping arrange a nuclear waste dump site on the Fort Peck Reservation, and his meeting with Amy, Mason, and Robert in Nevada.

> "Then, as dawn was just beginning to add a wash of color to the eastern horizon, an enormous green fireball appeared to the south. It was a hellish light, a glimpse into raw power from the very bowels of the Earth. The spectacle was almost biblical, as if we were witnessing first-hand the wrath of the Almighty."

Mason and Amy devoted several paragraphs to the blast itself. There followed a transcript of the note Newt had left them. The article ended with a paragraph from Philip Montoya, the *Washington Post* reporter, who explained that the rest of the story had been lost in transmission. The line over which the story was being sent had been suddenly disconnected, presumably by someone who did not want the story to go to print. Mr. Montoya traced the phone number which had been used to transmit the story, and a telephone operator confirmed that there were 'technical difficulties" with that line.

Well, bless Amy's heart, Robert thought. She and Mason said nothing in the article about Frank killing the guy at the dump or shooting Buckley. Undoubtedly, they omitted these details to protect Frank and Robert.

Robert glanced at the crowd surrounding Frank at the other end of the bar. There were at least a dozen full glasses of Jack Daniels lined up on the bar in front of him, and almost that many empty ones. Robert could hear Frank's voice over the din of the reporters, who had tempered their earlier hysteria. Frank used the "F" word more than he should have with the reporters, but he was still new at this game.

Frank became the darling of the press in the week that followed their release from jail. Reporters were calling him at all hours of the day or night for a colorful quote, and Frank rarely disappointed them. His picture appeared on the cover of several prominent national publications, and he was touted as the wizard who outsmarted the United States military. Someone gave him a cellular phone that he strapped to the arm of his wheelchair with baling wire.

Two weeks after their release, Frank said to Robert, "I got something to show you. Take a look at my foot." Frank's body was loosely wrapped in a red bathrobe.

"I can see it from here. What's so special about it?"

"No, man, you gotta get close for a good look."

"What am I looking for?"

"I got a fungus under my big toenail in the shape of Jesus. I think it's a sign from God." The music of the Doors was blaring from a boombox on Frank's kitchen table.

"Get outta here," Robert said.

"I'm not kidding. Get down here and look."

Robert dropped to his knees. "I hope no one walks in on us now, with me bending down in front of you like this."

"It's a perfect pose for you. See it?"

"No. All I see is dirt under your toenail."

"Look closer."

Robert bent even lower. Suddenly, Frank lifted his foot and kicked Robert in the nose hard enough to make his eyes fill with tears.

"Frank!" Robert shouted, rubbing his eyes with his sleeve. "You can move your foot. That's great!"

Frank beamed like a proud father.

"This is wonderful news!" Robert blew his nose into a handkerchief. "When did this happen?"

"About two days ago, I noticed my toes wiggling. Scared the hell out of me at first. I thought there was a snake crawling on my foot. Get us a beer to celebrate. What do you say?"

"Sure! This is great, Frank. Just great." He returned shortly with two cans of Budweiser.

"I've been working my leg hard ever since, and I'm getting more movement in it every day."

"What about the other one?"

"Just yesterday I noticed some movement in my toes. Look." Sure enough, Frank's big toe moved like an inchworm. "My left leg'll probably start getting some strength back too in a couple of days."

"This is the best news I've heard in a long time. In fact, it's about the only good news I've heard. Cheers." Robert raised his can and tapped it against Frank's. Then they both pulled deeply from them.

"God, I love beer," Frank said, slamming his empty can down on the table. "It'll probably be the death of me. Get me another one, will you?"

Frank's drinking had long troubled Robert. Finally, here was an opening to talk about it, and best of all, Frank had brought it up. But the mood was so happy for a change that Robert decided not to ruin it.

Of course, there would always be an excuse not to talk. Either Frank was too happy, or too edgy, or Robert wasn't sufficiently focused, or he was feeling guilty about having slept with Frank's wife. It was always something.

"Are you going to see the doctor about your legs?"

"The fuck would I want to do that for?" He opened his second beer. "I'm getting better. I don't want some goddamn doctor to screw it up."

"Just a suggestion."

"A damn dumb one, if you ask me. Turn the tape over, will you?"

Frank had already played The Doors' first album a half dozen times that morning. "Don't you want to listen to something else?"

"No, man, I'm on a roll. There's none better than Van Morrison and company."

"Jim Morrison."

"Very good, Robert! I was testing you. You passed with flying colors. Now tell me this one. Who was Van Morrison's first group?"

"Give me a hint."

"I can't believe you don't remember Them."

"But I don't, so give me a hint."

"I just did."

"What?"

"It's Them. You know, G-L-O-R-I-A. Them."

"Okay, so you're a better man than I am." Robert turned over the tape.

"You can say that again."

"What?" Robert noticed something of a challenge in Frank's voice.

"You heard me."

"What's that supposed to mean?"

"It means I've got a score to settle with you."

Robert's heart pounded so hard, he could almost hear it and his stomach tightened in fear. He wasn't so much afraid of Frank as he was of admitting what he had done with Frank's wife. "What do you mean?"

In the background, Jim Morrison was screaming to "Break on Through to the Other Side."

"Are you talking about what I think you are?" Robert asked.

"Maybe." Frank glared at Robert over the can of beer he held to his mouth.

"You're talking about the fact that I was in love with Anna."

"I'm talking about the fact that you were fucking my wife!" Frank screamed, throwing his can against the wall. "Behind my back, you were fucking her!"

"I may have been fucking her," Robert shouted with equal force. "But I wasn't fucking her over like you were. I was in love with her!"

Frank grabbed Robert by the shirt, pulled him close and slapped him hard across the face with his other hand.

Robert touched the corner of his mouth with the back of his hand. "Feel better?"

"Not really," Frank said, looking at his feet.

"Is that something you've been saving up for me for these past few months?"

"I've tortured you in every possible way in my head, my friend. I've done everything but talk to you about it."

"She was going to leave you, Frank."

"Shut up!"

"She'd had enough of your abuse. We were going to tell you the night she got killed."

"I said, shut the fuck up!" He took a swing at Robert. He missed and nearly fell out of his chair.

Robert went to the refrigerator and took out two more beers. He opened them both and handed one to Frank. They sipped in silence for a minute or two.

"I didn't want to be so mean to her. It just happened." Frank took a long sip of his beer and wiped his mouth with his sleeve. "I think I grew to hate her after a while. She was so strong in some ways that I couldn't intimidate her. She was smarter than me, too. I hated that. So I began to look for her soft spots. And believe me, there were plenty."

It was good to hear him talk about his relationship with Anna. But Robert was still angry with Frank for treating her so badly. He held the cold beer can to his lip which was still throbbing from the slap.

"I used to pick on her for never finishing anything." Frank chuckled softly over her memory. "That woman started more things than anyone I've ever known. And she never finished a goddamn thing in her life. You ever think about what she'd do about this problem we've got with Newt if she was still alive?"

"Every day."

"Me too. I'd like to think she'd see this one through. Anyway, I did lots of other mean things to her, like cheating on her. That's no secret, I guess. I wanted to show her I could get my needs met from lots of women besides her."

"She had needs too, Frank. Lots of them."

"Not for me, she didn't. So I rubbed her face in the fact that other women wanted me."

"You ended up driving her straight to me."

"Serves me right, huh?"

"I don't know about that. I do know I feel worse about falling in love with Anna than anything I've ever done."

"You should, you bastard." Frank's voice was calm. "It damn near broke my heart. And it almost caused me to kill my best friend."

As the two men looked at each other, the phone on the side of Frank's wheel chair rang. He answered it automatically.

"Frank here. Who? Just a minute." He handed the phone to Robert who turned down the music.

"Yes? Amy! How are you?"

"I can't decide if I hate you or love you."

"That's funny, you're the second person in the last ten minutes who told me that same thing. When did you get out of jail?"

"Right after the article came out. I don't know how you got it out to the press, but I'm glad you did. Thanks."

"Frank's responsible, really."

"I don't think I could live with myself if that crazy bastard actually blew up St. Louis and I hadn't gotten the word out. Half a million souls on my conscience would have weighed awfully heavy."

"How was jail?"

"Scary. I've never been in one. They didn't tell me anything about the status of the news story, so I had no idea how long they were going to hold me there. I was lucky because I had my own cell, but there were some pretty scary looking women in there next to me."

"You'd still be in jail if we hadn't gotten the story out. So would I."

"I guess I owe you one, even though you got me into this

mess."

"I owe you one, too. You published a sanitized version of the story, leaving out a few small details which I don't want to mention over the phone."

"Mason and I didn't want to clutter the story with too many facts, if you know what I mean."

"Well, I appreciate that. Speaking of Mason, where is he?"

"He's been staying at my apartment since he got out of jail. We've been working on a couple of follow-up stories. He's really a very good writer, you know."

"I've always suspected that about him. All he ever wrote about around here were police reports and community events. Hard to win any awards for that kind of reporting."

"Listen, Robert. We have to find Newt again. We need to stop him before he does this thing."

"Amy, I'm done with this job. I've already lost a woman I love over it." He had forgotten about Frank momentarily. He glanced over at him, but Frank was sipping his beer as if he hadn't heard a thing. "I lost my friend, the sheriff, over it, and Frank's paralyzed. I helped get the story out. I figure my part's done. I just want to go home."

"You're not serious."

"The hell I'm not. I started off wanting revenge, but things have changed. I figure my job was to help warn the people of St. Louis that a crazed maniac was planning to destroy their city. I did that. Now it's up to the police and the military to find Newt. I'm through."

"You're not a quitter, Robert, I know you better than that."

"I'm glad to hear from you, Amy. And I'm happy you're out of jail. You got anything else to say?"

"Yes, I do. You're a goddamn, son-of-a-bitch, mother—"

Robert hung up the phone. "That was pleasant."

"I better not have heard you say you were walking away from this whole Newt thing," Frank said.

"That's exactly what I said."

"We're not done."

"Yes we are. At least I am. I need to go home, Frank. I have a ranch to run."

"You've had all the excitement. You're the one who got to see the blast. You're the one who got to spring us from jail. All I got outta this was a useless pair of legs and a dead wife."

"Anna was my loss, too."

"She was my wife, though, goddamnit! Or are you forgetting that again?" Frank stared hard at Robert. "Our job isn't done, and I still need you."

"I can't work on this anymore, Frank. There's nothing else I can do."

"You leave here, you're never welcome in my home again."

"Then you'll have to visit me in South Dakota."

"Fuck you!" Frank shouted as he headed out the door.

Robert stayed in Montana for nearly three more weeks. He wanted to leave Montana sooner, but Charlie's sister asked him to help her after her brother's death. Robert stayed on her couch and listened to her tell stories about Charlie hour after hour. He felt ever so slightly dishonest for listening and not talking about his own grief over Anna's death. But it was much easier for him to offer comfort to someone other than himself. He was a patient listener, though he began to miss his ranch terribly.

Finally, on a sunny morning in late March, Janie kissed Robert on the cheek. It was the only time the two of them had ever touched. "It's time for you to go now, Robert," she said.

"Are you throwing me out? Don't you like my cooking?"

"I didn't notice you doing any cooking. Seriously, I can tell you're getting antsy. You need to get back to your own life."

"But I'm worried about you."

"My son and I will be fine. That doesn't mean we won't miss Charlie. It doesn't mean we won't cry a lot, but we'll be fine. You've helped more than you know. Now get your bottom in that car of yours and get outta here!"

Robert gave her a kiss on the cheek and a quick hug. Then he threw his few belongings into his station wagon and started it up, reversed it down the driveway, and pointed it towards home.

CHAPTER 15

Robert was thrilled to be heading home. Despite the overcast sky and temperatures in the mid-forties, he rolled down the window to feel the wind on his face and catch the smell of last summer's hay in the fields.

It was late March and spring would be arriving soon. He could feel it in the air. The fields were speckled with calves, many of which were only days old and stood shakily on spindly legs. Cows would lick the suckling calves with eyes half closed. It had been a mild winter, and all of the ranches had leftover hay piled in gray stacks that looked like sod houses on the prairie. It was going to be a dry spring, but he didn't feel like complaining. He was heading home.

As he drove east, the country became more lush, the grasses taller, the fields smaller, more tame. A brief shower welcomed him as he crossed the state line into South Dakota, and it was the first time he'd seen rain since the fall. It smelled so good that he stuck his head out the window and let the fat drops sting his face.

He thought he saw a slight green tinge to the fields, but his mind was probably filling in the colors in anticipation of spring. Spring was a season of miracles with its violent flush of growth. The fields took on color, the rivers and creeks flowed faster and fuller, and the creatures became more animated as they reveled in the fact that they once again survived the long northern winter.

Soon, Robert was pulling into his hometown of Millington, South Dakota. He drove slowly past the feed store, by Pastor Erickson's Lutheran Church, past Old Man Headington's fields, fallow since his death three years ago, and arrived home at dusk.

The rain had stopped. To the west a thick layer of clouds trapped the setting sun just above the horizon, lighting up the landscape in brilliant highlights of yellow and gold. Tree limbs glowed like embers. Barns and houses were so bright from the sunlight it was hard to look at them, and the lengthening shadows made the world look bigger than it was.

He drove past the poplar windbreak, flushing a family of four whitetail deer from the trees. Pheasants skittered along the dirt driveway to his home. The two story, white frame house was in need of a coat of paint. Three dormers, two of which faced east and one to the south broke the sharp roofline.

His bedroom was behind a window facing east. A row of lilac bushes, not yet leafed out, lined the west side of the house, and a big picture window separated the kitchen from the outside world. Robert's mother used to sit there by the hour looking over their property, sipping coffee and watching birds through binoculars.

Robert stopped the car, fumbled with the house key and entered the house, which was cold and damp, almost cave-like from its lack of use through the winter. Sammy Carter had looked after the ranch in Robert's absence, but he had not given much attention to the house.

A thin film of dust dulled the surface of the oak table in the kitchen. He turned up the heat and smelled the musty air blowing through the vents, boiled water and sat on top of the waffled floor vent to catch the heat from the furnace. He had just settled down with a cup of Earl Gray tea when the phone rang.

"Hello."

"Mr. Botkin?"

"Yes?"

"This is Stanley Krupp, Army intelligence. I need to speak to you about the man who detonated the device in Nevada. We're less than a month away from his April 11 deadline, and we need to learn more about him."

"Oh, you must be looking for Robert. I'm his cousin, Seth. Robert's somewhere in Montana, last I heard. I just drop by from time to time to look after his place."

"I'm sorry to have bothered you, then. Would you please have him give me a call as soon as he returns?"

"I sure will, if he ever does come back. He's been gone a long time."

"Thank you. My number's 605-555-2195. Please have him give me a call as soon as possible."

"Okay. Bye." *Shit*! he thought after hanging up. *I can't get away from this stuff.*

There were a thousand things to do. He had to inspect the ranch, check on his new calves and lambs, catch up on things with Sammy Carter, read the mail that had accumulated in his absence, and balance his checkbook.

But all that could wait. After an hour in a hot bath, Robert crawled into bed with a book that he barely opened before he fell asleep. The sheets were crisp and cool, but they soon warmed up from the heat of his body. His bed was like an old friend, more welcome than ever after spending so much time on Frank's floor or couch. And it was clean.

Fourteen hours later, he woke to a clear, crisp morning, cold enough to make the coffee taste even better than usual, when he heard a knock at the door. He opened it and saw a tall, broad shouldered man who addressed him politely from the doorway. "Robert Botkin? I'd like to speak to you."

"If you don't mind, I just got home and I have to catch up on a lot of work around the place." He started to close the door, but the man blocked it open with his foot.

Robert looked down at the foot then up at the man's bronze, ruddy face. "You better have either a gun or a badge, Mister. Otherwise, you're going to lose that foot in about ten seconds. So which is it? Are you here to rob me or question me?" He opened the door a little wider.

"William Tomley, FBI." The man held an ID badge in his right hand.

"Mr. Tomley. I really don't want to talk about anything right now besides my chores and the weather."

"I understand, Mr. Botkin. Can I call you Robert?"

"I'd rather you called me 'tomorrow.'"

The FBI man ignored the comment. "You've been through a lot, but you owe it to society to help us solve this thing before that man blows up another bomb. His next one's going to do some real damage."

"I've done what I can. There's nothing more I can do for you. So, if you'll excuse me..."

"I'll fly you to DC for questioning if you don't comply voluntarily. How's that for an incentive?"

"Let's talk, but make it quick."

"May I come in?"

"For just a minute. You can join me on my errands and ask me questions then." Robert stepped aside for Tomley and then shut the front door. "Want a cup of coffee? It'll have to be to go."

"That'd be great. Cream and sugar if you don't mind."

"The cream's a few months old. I wouldn't recommend it."

"I'll be fine without." Tomley sat at the kitchen table, a claw-foot oak piece of furniture Robert's mother brought from Cincinnati shortly after she was married. Robert had wiped the dust off the night before, and the grain showed through handsomely.

"How much land do you ranch, Mr. Botkin?"

"Never ask anyone out west that question, Mr. Tomley,

unless you're in Texas. It's considered impolite." He put a kettle of water on the stove, struck a match and held it to the burner he had turned on. He jumped back when the gas ignited with a 'whump.' "I guess I'm a little jumpy when it comes to explosions," he said.

"Speaking of explosions, do you think the bomber will adhere to his April 11 date?"

"I don't know why he wouldn't."

"You don't think he'd set it off early?"

"I don't know the man's soul, and I'm not about to try to figure it out. I think I'd get a migraine trying to read his mind."

"Tell me what he said to you about the date."

"He didn't say anything about it. All I know is what he said in his note."

"And what he said was that he was going to destroy St. Louis on April 11 which is what, a little more than two weeks away?"

"That's right. I think his intentions are pretty clear."

"Maybe."

"What's ambiguous about saying he's going to destroy St. Louis on a specific date?"

"He doesn't say he's going to do it with a bomb."

"What the hell's he going to use? His wit?"

"I don't know. But I also don't know how he's going to smuggle any weapons-grade uranium into the city. There's almost no way for him to sneak it in undetected."

"Can't he shield it in lead?"

"Our equipment is pretty sensitive. It doesn't take many stray neutrons to detect a mass of weapons-grade uranium."

"That's good. Maybe you'll catch him," Robert said as the water began to boil. He poured it through a filter and dark, fragrant coffee collected in the pot below.

"We might. If he does what he says. Unless—?"

"Unless what?"

"Unless he doesn't plan to blow up St. Louis with a bomb."

"But he said—"

"He said he was going to destroy the town, not blow it up."

"I don't know where you're going with this one."

"Me neither."

"Grab your coffee. I've got to drive to a neighbor's."

"Hold off a minute. I've got a couple of other things to talk to you about."

"I told you already, we can talk while I work." Robert marched out the front door and was headed to his car when the FBI man shouted at him.

"Do you have any idea what it's like to be in St. Louis now?"

"No." Robert said without turning around.

"Well, I do. Read this."

Robert had a sense that this was an important moment, maybe even a turning point in his life. There was something in the FBI man's tone, a confidence that he had Robert where he wanted him. Robert knew he could keep walking and, at least for a little while, pretend that life was normal. He could check in with his neighbor and ranch caretaker, Sammy Carter, drive around his property and see his newborn calves and sheep, catch up on local news at the feed store the way his father used to do, and come back to sit at his desk and plan the next couple of days.

He knew that if he turned around, he'd be turning his back yet again on the kind of life he has planned for himself, the life he still needed to ground him and keep him from going crazy. But he couldn't resist seeing what the FBI agent had to show him. And he could not stop thinking about the deaths that had already occurred and the other people that Newt might kill.

He wondered if he could really do anything to help. Newt was clever to have succeeded this far. What could Robert do to stop a person who managed to remain invisible to the United States military establishment, hide a cache of tons of nuclear material, and cause millions of people to live in fear? In the end, Robert decided he owed it to the memory of Anna and Charlie to try to help. If there was the slightest chance to help save the city of St. Louis, he knew he had to try.

Robert had a relationship of sorts with Newt; he was probably the closest thing Newt had to a friend. *Strange arrangement*, Robert thought. *His only friend wants to kill him.* And then he recognized a similarity to his own relationship with Frank. Robert wondered whether he might be able to use his "friendship" with Newt to help save St. Louis. But what about his house and his need to settle back into his comfortable routine? That would have to wait, he decided. The ranch had survived his absence, thanks to his friend Sammy's help. So he turned, reluctantly but with deliberation, back into the house.

"I thought you might be interested in this note." Tomley took an envelope from his pocket and handed it to him.

The envelope wasn't sealed, and Robert pulled from it a crudely folded piece of paper that had been ripped from a spiral notebook. He unfolded the note and read the following:

> Dear Robert,
>
> I hope you can read this. My handwriting's so bad, even I can't read it half the time.
>
> I wanted to let you know I've moved. I'm living with Mason in a small basement in St. Louis. We haven't gotten out much yet. We can't. We're chained to the iron pipes overhead."

"Oh, My God!" Robert said. He sat down at the kitchen table before he read the rest of the note.

> "All we can do is drag our chains with us to the bathroom, heat up soup on a hot plate, and type on our laptops about what it's like waiting to die in a city that's supposed to be incinerated by a nuclear bomb in two weeks. Newt's paid some kid to come down every few days to pick up our

disks so we he can publish our stories after we die, presumably (I've never been into posthumous honors!). Newt himself will mail this letter, so I can't provide you with many details.

I hear they're evacuating the whole town. I can't see it, of course, because there are no windows down here. I can only imagine what's going on above.

I'm scared, Robert. It's so much worse having seen the explosion in Nevada because I can imagine quite vividly what it will do to us and everyone else around here who refuses to evacuate. But I want you to know that I don't blame you. I'm the one who put myself in danger, not you. All you did was to give me one hell of a good story to report.

If I don't see you again, thanks for your friendship. It meant more to me than you know. If I do see you again, I'm going to kick your ass.

Much Love,

- Amy

p.s. Hi Robert. I'm having the time of my life. Keep an eye on the newspaper office for me. I hear they are planning to rebuild it.

- Mason"

Robert read the note a second time. His right hand was curled in a tight fist, which he bounced on the tabletop as he read. After reading it again, he opened his fist and slapped his palm on the table. "Where'd you get this?"

"Your mailbox. It came yesterday."

"You've been reading my mail?"

The agent nodded.

"Is the note authentic?"

"We're pretty sure it is."

"Can you find them?"

"Maybe, maybe not. St. Louis is a big city, even empty. Things are kind of chaotic there now."

"What can I do?" So much for playing the friendship role with Newt. He wanted to kill him once again. Newt had promised he wouldn't harm Amy. Now he had locked her up in a basement in the city he was planning to destroy.

"Not much. Just be on the lookout for Newt. He may want to get to you next. I'll be keeping an eye on you for the next couple of weeks. Maybe we can nab him if he makes a play for you. Here's my number. Call me if you see anything suspicious. I won't be very far away."

Tomley marched out the door, climbed into his powder blue sedan and drove away, kicking up dust behind him.

Robert watched him drive off, then kicked his doorway hard. "Shit!" he yelled.

One by one, Newt was picking off the people Robert cared most about. Robert knew he was going to have to go to St. Louis. "I hate that place," he said to himself. "They stole the Rams from Los Angeles."

His friends were being held hostage in a city about to be destroyed. He had two weeks to find them and there wasn't much time. But he couldn't count on the police or the military. They'd be too busy helping with the evacuation and arresting looters.

He threw a few clothes and a toothbrush in a paper sack (he didn't want to use a suitcase in case he was being watched) and headed outside to his car to drive to Sammy Carter's house. Sammy lived about a mile on the other side of town.

Robert rolled down the window to smell the soil as he bounced along dirt roads lined with signs shot full of holes, fences strewn with old newspapers, and rusty beer cans in the barrow pits on either side. The sun was high enough to have drained the colors from the sky. It was almost fifty degrees, un-

208 ~ Elemental Threat

seasonably warm for a March morning in South Dakota, and there was no wind for a change.

Sammy lived in a white frame two-bedroom house that was always under repair. During Sammy's alcoholic phase, the house had almost completely disintegrated. But now that he was sober, he'd been fixing it up little by little, trying to stay ahead of the invisible destructive forces that make houses fall apart. It was an uphill battle saving it from ruin. The process of decay was strong and seductive but Sammy seemed to be slowly gaining ground.

Robert pulled up to the front door and knocked since the doorbell still wasn't working. That particular repair job was apparently not very high on Sammy's priority list. He could hear a voice inside, but no one answered. So he opened the door and stuck in his head.

"Hello!" he called.

He saw Sammy standing in the living room with the telephone receiver in his hand. "It's for you," he said softly.

"Tell them I'm not here, damnit!" he shouted, not caring if the person on the other end heard him or not.

"I think you'd better take this one."

Robert approached Sammy and grabbed the phone from his hand. "Hi, Sammy," he said before putting the receiver to his ear.

"Robert?" the voice on the other end said. It was a high pitched voice that sounded as if it might belong to a woman.

"Yes?"

"It's Newt. How have you been?"

"You son of a bitch! If I ever get my hands on you again, I'll kill you. I should have done it last time!" So much for taking the friendship approach.

Sammy looked startled to hear Robert talk that way.

"But if you had killed me," Newt said, "thousands of people would have been killed in Missoula. Would that have been worth it?"

"Where are you keeping Amy and Mason?"

"They are the least of your worries for now. Don't even think about them. Listen to this—"

On the other end, he heard a sound like two pieces of wood hitting together.

"Ow! Goddamn you motherfucking, son-of-a-cocksucking bitch!"

There was no mistaking that voice. It belonged to Frank.

"Frank and I were wondering if you could come back to the reservation. There's something I want to show you," Newt said.

"I told you, if I see you again, I'm going to kill you." Robert's anger was back in full force.

"I'm willing to take that chance. Would you like to say hello to your friend?"

"Robert. Stay the fuck away from here," Frank said.

"What's he doing to you, man?"

"He's got me chained to the fucking wheel chair."

"How'd you let him get the drop on you like that?"

"He slipped me a Mickey or something. He wants you to come down here, but don't do it. This fucker's crazy. He's—" The line went dead. Robert waited for the dial tone before he took the receiver from his ear and replaced it on its cradle.

"Welcome home, Robert," Sammy said. "It sounds like you had an eventful trip."

"I'm sorry I was gone so long, Sammy. Thanks for looking after my place. I'll make it up to you."

"Don't worry about it. We'll deal with that later. Was that him?" Sammy asked, pointing to the phone. "The guy who's going to blow up St. Louis?"

"I better not answer that, Sammy. You're liable to get questioned, and the less you know the better."

"How'd he know to call here? I didn't even know you were back in town."

"I don't know. But he knows my line is tapped, so he didn't want to call me there. He must have just gotten lucky with his timing."

210 ~ Elemental Threat

"You're leading quite a life. I could almost get jealous."

"Listen, Sammy, my girlfriend and a buddy of mine in Montana have already been killed. My friend, Frank, is paralyzed, and this wacko has kidnapped two other friends of mine. I'd trade lives with you in a second."

"What are you going to do now?"

"I don't have much choice. I'm going back to Montana. Mind if we switch rigs for a few days?"

CHAPTER 16

Montana, home of the crazies, Robert thought as he drove the lonely, deserted road between two isolated spots in remote western states.

It was late afternoon and cumulus clouds billowed on the horizon, while the wind ruffled the fields on either side of the road. It felt almost summer-like. The air smelled like rich, fecund soil. The cycle of life was starting anew, and despite his troubles, Robert celebrated the end of winter's dormancy as he drove west.

This was the time to be back on the ranch, nursing the calves and lambs through the first weeks of their lives. So why, he wondered, was he rushing away from the very things he should be celebrating, the things that would help him heal from the worst winter of his life? Why wasn't he throwing himself into work instead of racing back to Montana to meet with a crazy man who'd mastered the art and science of the Manhattan Project, a man who was planning to use that knowledge to destroy the lives of hundreds of thousands of people?

Was it a sense of duty that called him back to Montana?

212 ~ Elemental Threat

Was it the belief that he could prevent further tragedy? Was it for revenge? It was not for fame; he'd already had a taste of that. It was fun to have the press wave microphones under his nose and to see himself quoted in prominent publications. But the thrill was shallow and short-lived and it certainly did not sustain him. He would rather measure success in terms of miles of fence built or tons of hay produced than in minutes on prime time news.

Maybe his motive for returning to Montana was to save Frank from whatever plans Newt had for him. Robert still felt a great deal of loyalty to his friend, but his love for Anna complicated his feelings for Frank.

Guilt was also a likely factor. God knows he certainly had cause for it. Or maybe he was just plain curious and wanted to see things to their conclusion. It was a fascinating turn of events, and he felt fortunate in one sense to have been a witness to it all.

Robert eventually settled on the motive of curiosity because it was the easiest explanation and required the least amount of soul-searching.

The day soon faded into night, and his sense of smell grew sharper as the light dimmed. He picked up the scent of a rainstorm in the distance and the perfume of sagebrush. There was no moon, and an occasional shooting star streaked across the dark, speckled sky that flared in the distance with lightning.

Lightning, he thought. *Already in April?*

The morning sun eventually began washing the eastern horizon with pastel pinks and yellows, and many hours later, Robert arrived in Poplar, Montana, seat of the Fort Peck tribal government. He still had half an hour's drive to Frank's place.

Robert knew that calling the police would have been easier, but it would have made the situation even more dangerous. Surely Newt would kill Frank immediately if he knew the police were involved. And he probably hard-wired his plan for St. Louis like he'd done with the bomb in Missoula, so that it would proceed in his absence. A call to the police, therefore, would save no one but himself.

He parked half a mile from Frank's house and walked the rest of the way to avoid detection. New shoots of grass were poking up through last year's rank growth. The arrival of spring was subtler in Montana. Still he found signs of rebirth and renewal everywhere except Frank's house. The blue tarps flapping from it in the morning breeze, looking like a neglected dressing on an old wound.

Robert hiked up a draw until he was within about fifty yards of the house. Along the way, he spooked a couple of mule deer that bounded from their hiding place. A new wave of anger suddenly washed over him.

Damn! Robert thought. *This bastard killed Anna. I can't ever see her again until I'm dead. So what am I sneaking around like a thief for?*

Just then, as if to answer his question, a bullet slammed into the ground next to his foot, kicking up a small spray of dirt.

He didn't hear the shot. Newt must have equipped a pistol with a silencer. Robert instinctively rolled to his right, catching his breath as his heart pounded in his chest.

He looked for low ground to hide in, but he was already at the bottom of a draw. Newt must have ambushed him. He looked up to see Newt crouched at the lip of the gully pointing a pistol at him. Robert thought Newt was going to kill him right then. He closed his eyes and tried to picture Anna's face. He wanted it to be the last thing in his head before dying.

"Get it over with," he shouted. "Just pull the fucking trigger and get it over with."

Newt was wearing brown polyester pants and a maroon sweater two sizes too big. A black wool cap was pulled over his ears and a few scraggly strands of stringy blond hair stuck out from underneath the cap.

He started laughing. "Is that what you think? That I called you out here to kill you?"

He laughed some more, a high, squeaky noise that irritated Robert.

"You've seen me shoot a pistol before. That's one thing I do very well. I wouldn't have missed you from here if I had wanted to kill you."

"Damn you, Newt!" he said. "What's this all about?" Robert stood up and brushed the dirt from his pants.

"I thought I was doing you a favor. You seem to love a good show, so I wanted to give you a good seat."

"Don't do me any more favors."

"Then maybe I should just kill you."

"That might be better than watching you picking off my friends one by one."

"I'm sorry about Anna. She didn't deserve it. That bomb was really meant for Frank. But really, Robert. I've grown quite fond of you over the past several months, even if you are Frank's friend. I don't want to kill you. Play your cards right, and you'll come out of this just fine. Now walk to the house."

From twenty feet away, Robert could see Newt's bulbous Adam's apple bobbing in his throat as he spoke.

Maybe I should rush him now, Robert thought. *I could overpower him and set Frank free.*

While he was thinking about his options, Newt fired a shot between his legs. The bullet missed his crotch by inches.

"Jesus!" Robert shouted.

"Move it," Newt said. "Frank's inside. Why don't you join him."

Robert crawled out of the gully. He saw a shape on the ground between him and Frank's house. He turned to Newt and shouted, "Tell me that's not Frank. Tell me!"

"It's not. Your friend's still inside. That's just some military agent sent to watch the house. I killed him about half an hour ago because he was an extraordinary pest."

Robert pushed aside the tarp and entered. Frank sat with his arms handcuffed to his wheelchair. Dried blood traced a line from the corner of his mouth to his neck and stained the collar of his flannel shirt. His head drooped onto his chest, and his left eye was swollen shut.

"What the hell did you do to him?" Robert took a step towards Newt who had entered the house behind him. Newt fired another shot between his legs, and Robert jumped so high, he almost hit his head on the ceiling.

"You have two strikes already," he said. "Three strikes and you're out. The next one I fire will be about six inches higher."

Frank's head jerked up at the sound of the pistol. "Are you okay, Frank?" Robert said. "Frank?"

The big man strapped to the wheelchair opened his right eye and said, "Robert?"

"Yes, it's me."

"You dumb son-of-a-bitch. Didn't you hear me tell you to stay away?"

"I was never very good at following directions."

"See where it's gotten you?" Frank said. "Look out—"

Suddenly, Robert felt a hard object crash against the back of his head. Then the tunnel through which he viewed the world shrank to a pinpoint of light before disappearing completely, and he let go and sank into the darkness.

Robert awoke to a splitting headache as he bounced along a dirt road in a late model Suburban. He tried to speak, but the words came out thick and barely audible.

"Very articulate," Frank said. He sat in the front seat next to Newt, who was driving. "You ought to be elected to Congress. We're famous in Montana for our inarticulate representatives."

"Sorry, Robert. I hate to resort to violence," Newt said from behind the wheel. Frank's hands were cuffed to the rubber loop above his door. Robert's hands were also cuffed to the loop above the back seat door. His head still throbbed. Newt was out of breath and panting loudly, so he must have hauled Robert to the Suburban very recently.

"Where are we going?" Robert asked.

"On an adventure." Newt patted the top of his wool cap.

"I told you not to come, you stupid shit," Frank said. "This crazy bastard's going to kill me regardless. You could have at least saved your sorry ass."

Newt hit Frank in the head with the butt of a pistol. "Your friend is getting on my nerves," Newt said to Robert, wiping his forehead and neck with a handkerchief. "I can't figure out why you two are friends. Especially now that Anna's dead."

"Don't you ever mention her name, you bastard!" Robert shouted, leaning forward in his seat. The way Newt said her name so casually, as if he had known her, seemed like an insult to her memory. "Don't you ever say her name around me!"

"I told you I didn't mean to kill her. Let it go, Robert."

"You feel so bad about it that you're also planning to kill Amy Boston and Mason Tomlinson? That doesn't sound like remorse to me."

"Maybe not. You might be able to save them, but more about that later."

"Where are you taking us?"

"As I said, on an adventure. Please be patient. Before the day is done, you'll know my plans. I already told you I like you. That's why you're here. Don't force me to change my mind, or you might end up missing the finale. And I know how much you want to see it."

"This can't be the finale. Tomorrow's the first of April. You said the end would come eleven days from then."

"And which holiday would tomorrow be?" Newt asked.

"The Fourth of July?" Frank said, shaking his head as he woke up. Robert could see a fresh trail of blood from the left corner of his mouth.

"Beeeep! Thank you for playing!" Newt said, enjoying himself immensely. "No, that's incorrect. Nor is it Christmas or Easter, or Thanksgiving, or Passover. But it is April Fools Day, time for the Trickster to play out his pranks. Tomorrow is my April Fool's joke on the world."

"What are you talking about?" Frank said.

Suddenly, everything came clear to Robert. He understood what Newt's plan had been all along.

"You set April 11 as the date for destroying St. Louis," Frank said. "You're eleven days early. That's not fair. They haven't even had a chance to evacuate yet." Frank rattled the chains of his handcuffs. "You bastard! You fucking liar!"

"I'm not a liar at all, and I resent your accusation." Newt smiled as he drove through the afternoon light.

The pieces began to fall quickly into place as they drove. "Newt," Robert said.

"Yes?"

"I think I figured out your plan. You were telling the truth about St. Louis, weren't you?"

"I always tell the truth."

"And how many days does it take for water to get from Fort Peck dam to the mouth of the Missouri River at St. Louis? No, let me guess. I'd say about eleven days."

"You're a smart one, Robert. No wonder I like you so much."

"You're not planning to blow up St. Louis at all. Are you? You're planning to flood it."

"I get it!" Frank said. "You're going to blow up Fort Peck Dam. Goddamn!" he shouted. "That's clever. Everyone in the world's looking for an atomic bomb in St. Louis, but you're twenty-four hundred miles upstream. If I didn't want to kill you, I think I might even admire you."

Newt smiled as he drove along the isolated highway.

"So the water from Fort Peck will wash out the Garrison Dam in North Dakota" Robert said.

"Yes," Newt said.

"And Oahe Dam in South Dakota, and the three others downstream from that."

"Jesus, God!" Frank said. "That's a shitload of water. How much water do those dams hold, anyway?"

"About seventy-three million acre-feet at full capacity," Newt said. "Enough to bury a medium size state in about a foot of water. But I suppose that this time of year, there's about sixty-five million acre-feet behind them now."

"Sixty-five million acre-feet." Frank said. "Lemme see, there's 43,000 cubic feet in an acre foot, that'd be about... 325,000 gallons or, what, two point seven million pounds of water." Frank mumbled to himself. "Multiply that times sixty-five million. That's—my God, that'd be about seventy-seven million tons of water you'd be releasing down the channel."

"Very good, Frank," Newt said. "You always were good at math."

"He's a whiz at calculations," Robert agreed.

"I'd say that's enough water to do serious damage to St. Louis," Frank said.

"And Kansas City, Omaha, Pierre, Bismarck and every other town along the river," Robert added.

"Don't forget the towns along the Mississippi River from St. Louis to New Orleans," Newt said.

"What about the people in those other towns? You didn't warn them," Robert said.

Newt shrugged. "I gave the police a clue. I didn't want to give away my whole plan. Besides, the people farther down-stream will have a few days to evacuate. It's probably too late to up their flood insurance, though."

"When's the bomb going to blow?"

"At eleven tonight. In about five hours."

"That's your whole plan, you crazy bastard?" Robert said. "To blow up a few billion dollars worth of public works projects?"

"Yes. That's part of it. I want to get rid of them. Those dams should never have been built."

"But what about the people living there along the river?"

"As your friend Frank would say, F--- them." Newt apparently could not get himself to say the "F" word aloud. "They should not have built along the river. The corridor should have remained a floodway, home to native fish and birds and people. It wasn't meant to be a sterile ditch."

"But you'll kill all the fish in the river."

"You're underestimating the recuperative powers of the system, Robert. Once you restore the natural functions of the river, it will take care of itself. The flood in 1993 did millions of dollars worth of environmental improvements to the system. I expect my flood to multiply those benefits proportionally."

Frank interrupted Newt's speech with an hysterical outbreak of laughter. It came from deep in his belly and caused his whole body to shake.

Newt got angry and he tried repeatedly to hit Frank on the head with the butt of his pistol. But Frank kept laughing and shielding himself from the blows with his arms, which were already at head level because of the handcuffs.

"You sound like a hyena," Newt said. He stared at the road ahead of him. "What's so funny?" he asked irritably.

Frank wiped the tears from his eyes on his shoulders. "Robert's still trying to talk you out of this thing. He seems to have forgotten that you're a fucking lunatic. You can't talk logically to a crazy man, Robert. Logic and reason are foreign languages to this kook. The whole thing suddenly struck me as funny, that's all."

He started laughing again, but no one joined him. Newt and Robert sat sullenly in the Suburban.

Newt turned south at the tiny town of Nashua, drove through the even smaller town of Fort Peck, and then turned off onto a dirt road, which he followed for about half an hour.

The country was rough and broken, and the gumbo hills formed odd shapes on either side of the road. Steep cuts scarred the dark gray hills, and little vegetation grew on the clay soils. The dirt road was impassable when wet, but the little snow that had fallen in the region that winter had long since blown off. A few scraggly juniper bushes began to dot the landscape, and they grew thicker closer to the lake.

The sun was setting when they pulled up to the Pines Recreation Area on the north shore of Fort Peck Lake. The last rays of the day shot up from the hills and streaked the western sky. A few red, fleecy clouds were rimmed with bright gold. The surface of the lake mirrored the colors of the sunset.

"That's beautiful," Newt said, pausing to look at the lake from behind the wheel of the Suburban. "Better look at it now, gentlemen. This is the last time the sun will set on this lake." He drove a few hundred yards down a dirt trail to a cabin that had a small rowboat underneath a carport. "I'm going to leave you men here for an hour or two while I do some business. There's no one within miles, so don't bother shouting for help."

The immensity of the lake was startling. It was the fifth largest reservoir in the country, and no one was on it. The ice had come off early this year, but it was still too early in the season for people to begin returning to their cabins. They were in a bay. The lake was at least three miles across at this point and over a hundred miles long.

Newt stepped out of the car and came around where Robert sat. He opened the door. "I'm going to unlock your cuffs now, Robert. If you make one wrong move, I'm shooting Frank." He pointed the pistol at the back of Frank's head while he used his other hand to unlock Robert's cuffs from the loop above the door. As soon as the cuffs were loose, Frank yelled, "Get him!"

Newt jumped backward. "I almost shot you! You keep your mouth shut."

Robert couldn't have grabbed Newt if he'd wanted to. His arms were numb from being held up in the air so long.

"Now, get out and put your arms behind your back."

Robert stepped out stiffly from the car and did as he was told. The cuffs dangled from his left wrist. Newt attached the other end to his right wrist.

"Wait here. I'm going to borrow a boat from the cabin owner. I don't think he'll mind. There won't be any water to float it anyway, come tomorrow."

He went to the carport and pulled out the rowboat. He dragged it to the water's edge and then returned, panting, to the Suburban. "I checked it out a couple of days ago. It's seaworthy." He pulled a handkerchief from his pocket and used it to wipe his face. "Here's the plan. I'm going to unlock Frank and you're going to put him in the wheelchair that's in the back of the Suburban. Then you're going to use the duct tape I brought to tie his arms to the chair. Got it?"

"How am I supposed to do that with my arms tied behind my back?"

"I'll unlock you."

"How's he going to haul me around when I refuse to go anywhere?" Frank said.

"I'll take care of that, too." Newt approached Frank's side of the van, opened the door, and slammed the butt of his pistol against the side of Frank's head. Frank slumped down in his seat.

"Damn you!" Robert shouted.

"What was I supposed to do? Expect him to cooperate? You know Frank better than that. Here, let me help you out of those cuffs."

He pointed the pistol at Robert's back while Robert struggled to get Frank's heavy body into the chair. Robert then taped down Frank's wrists and legs. Newt inspected the tape job.

"Pretty loose, Robert. I'd almost think you wanted him to be able to escape. Step aside and I'll finish the job. Put your cuffs back on first. Keep your hands in front this time."

Newt ran a few more loops of tape around Frank's arms. "You get on one side of his chair and I'll get on the other. We'll lift him into the boat." The procedure was awkward, and they ended up dumping Frank on his side where he hit his head on the gunwale. The blow wasn't hard, but it woke him up.

"What the fuck's going on?" he asked as they picked him up in his chair.

"We're leaving for a short trip," Newt said. "Get into the boat, Robert."

Newt unhooked one of Robert's hands and used the cuff to connect Robert to the metal stern seat. Then he locked Frank's chair to the middle strut with another pair. He pushed the boat into deeper water until it floated, then he made his way to the bow and climbed in, wet from the waist down. He rowed about 200 yards from shore and threw out an old paint can full of cement that served as an anchor. The nylon rope to which it was attached played through Newt's hands as the anchor dropped about fifty feet and settled into the soft mud on the bottom of the lake. He tied the other end of the rope to his seat and leaned against the bow to enjoy what was left of the evening.

"I'll be back to pick both of you up in an hour or so." He looked east towards the dam. "You'd have a heck of a ride if I left you here when I pull the plug, wouldn't you? Don't think I haven't considered doing just that."

"What about Amy and Mason?" Robert said. "You promised you wouldn't hurt them, or at least Amy. I thought you said you never lied. Are you going to let them drown?"

"Probably not. I want to read more of their stories about what it's like to be trapped in a Sodom and Gomorra just before the fire storm."

"Are you going to tell me where they are?"

"Not yet, but here's my plan. Thanks for reminding me. On the afternoon of April 10, one day before the flood waters hit St. Louis, you'll get a call at your house in South Dakota. The caller will tell you the name of a city. That same day, in that same city's newspaper in the personal ads, you'll find out the name of another city. The ad will mention your name, so you'll have no trouble finding it once you get a copy of the paper.

"Then, you're to fly to the city mentioned in the ad to visit its downtown Post Office station. In box number 9013 will be the address of Amy and Mason's current residence. Here's the P.O. box key. Don't lose it." Newt pulled out a key for Robert who picked it up with his free hand and put it in his pocket.

"There won't be many people in St. Louis to help you on the eleventh, so you'll have to beat the flood to get to them."

"That's really sick," Frank said. "I got another question."

"What is it?"

"I can understand you're wanting to blow up these fucking dams. It'll ruin the reservation below it and kill most of the fish. But in a generation or two, the radiation will have been flushed and the river will be healthier than it's been in decades. That part makes sense to me. I almost support you in that, though I don't approve of your method."

"Thank you. What's your question?"

"I still can't understand why the fuck you poisoned the reservation with radioactive wastes. That, my friend, is a violation of nature."

"Maybe it was petty of me, but I had my reasons."

"Let me guess," Robert said.

"Go right ahead."

"Your dad lost his land the second time when the BIA thought there might be coal underneath it, right?"

"Yes, they forced my family to trade for some worthless land miles away, like I told you in Nevada."

"My guess is that the dump site is where your family's allotment was—the same spot the BIA thought had the coal under it."

"You're right, Robert. Again, I am impressed."

"So you were, what," Frank said. "Paying back the BIA for fucking over your family?"

"Yes, although I wouldn't have put it that crudely. They claimed the land was so valuable, let them have it now."

"Let me ask something else before you leave, Newt," Robert said. "How many more bombs do you plan to build? How much more damage do you plan to inflict?"

"You haven't been following the news the past two days, have you?"

"No."

"The Army found my uranium stash. I'd recently moved it away from the reservation."

"You were keeping your shit on the reservation all these years?" Frank said.

"Yes, at the dump site."

"You motherfucker! I'd like to shove a bar of uranium up your ass."

Newt rolled his eyes in disappointment the way a teacher

does when she gets a stupid answer from a student.

"As I was saying, I had to move the uranium after the two of you found the site. Too bad. The reservation was such a perfect hiding spot, no one would ever think to look there. I ended up moving the stash to an abandoned uranium mine in southern Colorado. Everyone expects a little radiation to escape from an abandoned mine. But the military stepped up its surveillance after my threat and found it. I'm afraid I only have one bomb left. So it's very important I use it wisely."

"What about the bomb in Missoula?" Robert asked.

"I had to move it here to the lake."

"Why, Newt," Frank said. "Without a big stash of nuclear material, you're just—like any other nerd!" Frank started laughing again, the deep belly laugh that irritated Newt.

"And then what?" Robert said while Frank continued laughing. "After the flood what are you going to do? Get a job at McDonalds?"

"I'm afraid my future is a short one." He pulled off his cap to reveal an advanced state of baldness. Only the scraggly hairs around his ears and the back of his head remained. He smiled broadly and in the fading light, Robert could see thin strings of blood connecting his upper and lower lips.

"I had an accident making the ingots for the bomb, you see. So this, in a very real sense, is my last shot. Now I must be off. I'll be back in two hours, maximum."

Newt dove into the icy waters of the lake, nearly upsetting the boat. "I'm an excellent swimmer," he shouted as he breast-stroked his way towards the shore. "I used to belong to the Colorado Chapter of the Polar Bears. This is nothing!"

For the next couple of hours, Robert and Frank sat quietly, careful not to rock the b. They knew they would drown quickly in the lake's icy waters. The air temperature also plummeted to near freezing and they shivered violently. They were both dressed in jeans and flannel shirts. Robert wore a down jacket and Frank had on a fleece lined denim coat.

Frank struggled to free his arms from the chair. Robert made sure that Frank's palms were facing each other when he taped his forearms to the chair. That way, Frank would have a little play when he laid his arms flat.

"This is another fine mess you've gotten me into, Stanley."

Robert didn't feel like playing along with the gag. He was too busy trying to stay warm and imagining the fireball that would vaporize the dam and release a hundred foot high wall of water that would travel over two thousand miles downstream.

"For a man who spent his life bullying people," Frank said. "I'm having a hard time adjusting to life as a cripple."

"Neither of us has the upper hand right now. Newt's got us by the balls."

"Speaking of which, I just pissed in my pants. It's downright embarrassing. I'm not hooked up to my catheter anymore, but my control's not very good yet."

"I'd say that wet pants are the least of your problems. I'm still trying to figure out how to get through this night alive. In my free time, I'm trying to figure out how to keep our friend from blowing up the dam. How are you coming with your arms? You get one loose yet?"

"I wish I was a little more limber. Maybe then I could bend over and chew my arm off at the elbow."

"You have any thoughts about how to stop Newt?"

"I told you, I'm a cripple. I don't have the power to control my own bladder, much less a nuclear terrorist."

"Stop feeling sorry for yourself."

"That's easy for you to say."

The two men stopped talking. A slight breeze brought with it the smell of sage from the nearby hills. A couple of coyotes yipped from the breaks. There was a faint humming that sounded like a distant airplane, but as it grew louder, Robert realized it was coming from an outboard motor. In about twenty minutes, Newt pulled up alongside the rowboat in a modified tug.

Newt was whistling a tune Robert had never heard. He appeared to be in good spirits as he tossed the end of a rope into the rowboat, jumped down into it and tied the little boat to his tug. The footing was treacherous in the darkness, but Newt was hopping around the decks like he'd grown up on boats.

"Nice rig," Frank said. "Where'd you get it?"

"I borrowed it from the Army Corps of Engineers."

He unhooked Robert from the stern seat and told him to go up the short ladder into the bigger boat. There was a handle mounted on the wall of the tug above the first deck. Newt tried to cuff Robert to it, but Robert had fouled up the loose cuff when he was chained to the rowboat. With his free hand, he'd jammed a couple of splinters from the rowboat into the female end of the cuff.

Newt, who still carried a pistol with him, had to settle for taping Robert's wrists to the handle on the tug. Then Newt tied a rope across the arms of Frank's wheelchair. He jumped back to the tug and swung its boom over the rowboat, playing out line with the winch. Once more he was in the rowboat, where he hooked the line to the rope on Frank's chair. Finally, he used the winch to lift Frank, chair and all, into the tug. The pressure of the line bent the arms of Frank's wheelchair, but Frank made it safely on board.

Newt continued whistling while he worked. In the dim light from the tug, Robert could see the Adam's apple bobbing in his throat. Newt untied the rope from the tug and tossed it into the rowboat.

The tug's deck was clean and orderly. A gaff and lifesaver were mounted on the port side of the elevated deck near the place where Newt had taped Robert to a handle bolted to the wall. A heavy wooden door covered the ship's hold.

Newt revved up the engine and took off for the dam. "We've got about fifteen miles to go," he shouted down from the flying bridge. The boat was fast, and they made good time on the smooth surface of the lake. The sound of the boat was amplified by the surface of the lake in the darkness.

Before long, they stopped a couple of hundred yards from the middle of the four-mile long earthen dam. Robert couldn't see the dam, but the streetlights strung along each side of the deserted highway that crossed it made the dam look as if it were decorated for Christmas. "This looks like a good spot to me."

He jumped down and swung the boom so it was centered over the deck, pulled open the heavy wooden hatch in the cockpit and lowered line into the hole. Then he crawled into the hold with a flashlight and emerged several minutes later.

"Here she is, boys." Newt slowly winched the bomb from the hold. "I made a fairly exact replica of the Little Boy bomb that was used at Hiroshima. I could have just used an old pipe, since I don't have to worry about aerodynamics, but I wanted to show some respect for history."

"Jesus!" Frank said. "Are we getting irradiated by that obscene thing?"

"No need to worry, the nuclear core is shielded in lead."

"Didn't Little Boy weigh several tons?" Robert asked. "How could you carry something that heavy on this boat?"

"This one's much, much lighter. The water itself will reflect neutrons back into the core, so I didn't have to use nearly as much lead in the reflector."

"Did that make any sense to you, Robert?" Frank asked.

"A little."

"I've already set the timer, so it's ready to go." He swung the boom out over the water and began playing out line. "In a strange sort of way, I'll miss it. It really is a thing of beauty."

After he lowered the bomb about sixty feet, Newt attached an inflatable buoy to the line to keep the bomb at that depth. Then he severed the steel cable with bolt cutters, and the boat was free of the bomb.

"I can't believe it's that easy to destroy a dam," Robert said. "You just pull up, dump in a nuclear bomb and that's it?"

"Sure it's easy, once you have the bomb. I guess we're ready to shove off. We have about two hours until detonation. Oh, there's one more thing."

Newt made his way behind Frank's wheelchair. "I owe you one, Frank. You killed my brother, remember?"

Without waiting for a reply, Newt shoved the chair through the handrails right over the edge of the boat.

"Motherfucker!" Frank yelled just before he splashed into the water.

"Fitting that would be his last word," Newt said, peering into the darkness as Frank slipped into the frigid lake.

"You son of a bitch!" Robert shouted. "You just killed my best friend!"

"Yes, but you're still alive, so don't complain." Newt climbed up to the flying bridge and began to rev the engine.

Robert pulled with all his strength against the handle to which he was taped when suddenly, the tape tore loose. He was free!

His wrists were sore and bloody, but he grabbed the life-saver from its hook on the wall and threw it overboard. A thick rope connected the lifesaver to another handhold on the boat like the one to which Robert had been taped. Robert threw another rope overboard that had been coiled on the deck of the boat. One end was tied to the railing.

Robert stripped off his jacket and eased his way quietly into the dark lake. The coldness of it took his breath away as he grabbed onto the rope. He heard Frank splashing nearby and found him in the darkness. Frank had freed one arm and was using it to tread water as best as he could, but he was still dragging that damn wheelchair with him, and the cold water was sapping his strength as quickly as it was Robert's.

Robert handed him the lifesaver. Then he tied the end of the rope to the buoy connected to the bomb. He held his breath and dipped underwater to pull on the arm of the wheelchair to which Frank was still attached. It had been bent and weakened when Newt lifted him with the winch into the tug, and it broke off easily. Frank was finally free from his chair.

Robert grabbed the rope attached to the buoy just before he felt the boat surge as Newt began the return trip to the Pines Recreation Area. Robert pulled himself back to the boat and crawled up the side ladder onto the deck. In the dark, Newt had not seen or heard Robert leave and return to the boat. Robert was almost totally spent, having been in the freezing lake for just over a minute. He could not believe that Newt had swum so far in the lake earlier that night.

The wind across the deck drained the remaining heat from his body, and his clothes began to freeze. He slipped his jacket back on and looked out over the deck. The two ropes were definitely pulled tight, very tight. But he didn't know if Frank was holding on to the other end, if they were towing a nuclear bomb, or if it was just the drag from the lifesaver in the water taking up the slack. How long would the rope hold? Frank was heavy, and the bomb was really a load.

Robert collapsed onto the deck and spent the next five minutes getting his strength back. Finally he stood up and held onto the handle as if he were still tied to it. Five minutes later, Newt slowed the engine to an idle.

"Damn you, Newt!" he shouted. "You killed my friend!"

Newt looked back over the top deck at Robert. "What's that? I couldn't hear you over the engine."

"I said you just killed my friend, you son of a bitch! And I'm going to kill you if I live through this!"

"Robert, please! I don't want to hear you talk like that. I'd expect that kind of talk from Frank, but not you."

"I'm going to wring your scrawny neck!"

Newt killed the engine. "Frank had death written all over him. I knew back when I first met him that he'd come to a violent end."

"He didn't have to. You're responsible for his death, not him."

"You didn't have to die either, Robert, but I'm disappointed in you. I can't possibly let you go now, or you'd kill me. Now that you're going to die, you've ensured that your friends, Amy and Mason, will die too. And it was all so unnecessary."

"You promised you wouldn't hurt her!"

"You're the one who's hurting her. If you hadn't acted this way, she would have lived through this."

"If you're going to shoot me, then get it over with. I think I'd rather die now than listen to you anymore."

"I hate guns, Robert. You wouldn't believe the nightmares

I've had about them. I much prefer bombs."

Robert couldn't see Newt in the dark. But his voice was loud.

"Do you see that little pinpoint of light over there?"

Robert nodded, a useless gesture since Newt couldn't see him either.

"It's the boat ramp where I left the Suburban. I'm going to swim to it. It's about half a mile away, which is my upper limit in cold water, but I'm sure I'll get there in plenty of time. I'm going to let you drift. There's a slight headwind. It might blow you back towards the dam, in which case, you'll die immediately from the heat and radiation. If that doesn't kill you, then I suppose you'll know exactly what a bug feels like when someone flushes it down the toilet."

"Just get the hell out of here, will you?" Robert wanted him gone so he could take over the boat.

"One last thing. I have a present for you." Newt jumped down to the lower deck and slowly approached Robert. "Don't kick, I just want to give you these sunglasses. Wouldn't want you to go blind from the blast."

He approached Robert in the darkness. When he got close, he slipped on the puddle of water from Robert's clothes. Robert took a swing at him, but Newt had already started backing away. Robert's reflexes were still slow from the cold. Newt grabbed the gaff from the wall and swung it at Robert, missing at first but catching him square in the temple on the backswing. Robert woke up a moment later lying face down on the deck with his hands taped behind his back. His one chance to kill Newt with his bare hands, and he'd blown it!

"There was no need for that," Newt said. "Everything you've done or said the past ten minutes has caused you trouble. Good-bye, Robert." There was a splash, and that was the last he heard of Newt.

A minute later he heard a low voice say, "Is he gone?"

"Frank!" he whispered back. "Is that you? Thank God!"

"I don't know if I have the strength to climb up the rope. I was just about to let go when he stopped the boat."

"Keep your voice down. He might swim back."

"Hold on. I'll try to climb up the ladder. I have to be careful; I can't swim a stroke. I couldn't swim even when my legs worked."

"Your lack of talents always show up at the worst times. I wish I could help you, but I'm all tied up again."

It was a mighty struggle, an epic one, but Robert never doubted that Frank would make it up. Despite what Newt said, Frank had life written all over him. No amount of self-abuse could kill him, and God knows Frank had tried. Frank was shivering and wheezing when he finally pulled himself aboard. He took a minute to catch his breath. Pieces of the wheelchair were still taped to his arm.

"I feel sick. I just spent over twenty minutes in freezing water."

"I'm sorry, Frank. Just get this tape off me and then I'll take over."

Robert's head throbbed and was still bleeding. He was shivering from the cold, though the down jacket helped warm him.

Frank crawled over to Robert and began pulling at the tape on his wrists. Two minutes later, Robert was free again. He found a flashlight, pulled up a seat cushion on the upper deck and found some wool blankets. Then he helped Frank off with his clothes and wrapped him in a wool blanket.

"You better haul ass, buddy," Frank said. "We're towing a nuclear bomb. We need to find Newt and make him disarm it. If he gets there first," Frank stopped to cough. "He'll take the Suburban and then we're really be up shit creek. I don't think either of us is in shape to outrun a nuclear explosion."

Robert jumped to the upper deck and started the engine. Newt undoubtedly heard them start, and he was racing to the shore. Robert slowly accelerated to full speed and headed for the light Newt had pointed out earlier. He didn't like driving fast. No telling what the strain would do to the rope holding the bomb, but he had no choice. He had to get to shore first, so he gave it full throttle. The light ahead grew brighter as he approached it. Suddenly, he hit a bump that almost threw him off the deck. He lost his balance and fell, but he pulled himself back up and idled the engine.

"The fuck was that?" Frank shouted from below.

Robert scrambled down and shone the flashlight beam behind the boat. Wrapped around the buoy was a piece of wet cloth. "I think we just beat Newt."

"Yuck!" Frank said. "I don't think I'll ever fish here again."

"While I'm here, I think I'll pull the bomb aboard so it won't drag on the bottom."

Frank was shivering on the deck. The winch still had some cable on it, which was fortunate since the bomb was too heavy to pull in by hand. Robert reached out with a long gaff to snare the rope below the buoy, but when he pulled on it, the buoy bobbed like a cork. Stunned, Robert realized the bomb was no longer in tow.

He used the gaff to snare a piece of cloth that had caught on the buoy and pulled it in to examine it. Sure enough, it was shredded maroon fabric, just like the stuff from which Newt's pullover was made.

"Want the good news, Frank?"

"Uh." Frank grunted.

"We got a positive ID on Newt. The bad news is that we lost the bomb somewhere in the lake."

Once again, Frank's hearty laughter filled the night.

CHAPTER 17

Robert drove as fast as he could to the shore, which was only a couple of minutes away. He pulled alongside the dock and used some extra rope to tie up, then got out to find that Newt had locked the Suburban doors. He figured that Newt had taken the keys with him and that they, like the bomb, were somewhere on the bottom of the lake. He ran back to the boat and climbed in.

"What's the story?" Frank asked. His voice was very weak, and Robert knew he had to get him to a hospital.

"Newt has the keys. We're taking the boat back to the town of Fort Peck. I should have thought of that sooner."

The town was very near the dam, but the trip there seemed longer than it had when Newt had driven them there earlier that night. Robert drove the boat right up the concrete boat ramp in town, tearing a huge hole in the boat's hull and making a hell of a racket. Soon the town's only policeman pulled up and came out of his car with his pistol drawn.

"Freeze!" he shouted. "Now come out slowly with your

hands in the air and show yourself." He sounded more mad than frightened, like he'd had to deal with this silliness many times before.

Robert followed the policeman's advice. "This is the second time today I've had a pistol pointed at me."

"You're in stolen property, son. You're in big trouble."

"The first guy to point one at me was a fellow named Newt. Maybe you've heard of him."

"The bomber?"

"Yes, and I'm Robert Botkin."

"The guy in the papers?" He lit up Robert's face with a flashlight beam. "I'll be go to hell. What are you doing up here on the lake?"

"We've got an emergency, officer. I found Newt. In fact I just ran him over in the boat. He's dead, but he left a nuclear bomb on the bottom of the lake. It's going to go off in less than an hour. Somewhere around eleven o'clock tonight."

"Holy Mother of God!" Now he sounded scared. He lowered his pistol. "Are you telling the truth?"

"Yes, I am. There's an injured man aboard. I need help getting him off. We've got to evacuate the town. Then we need to call Wolf Point, Poplar, Williston, and every other town down the line. We have to get people off the river. Who's the Corps of Engineers person here?"

"He lives in Glasgow."

"Call him at home. Tell him to get the Corps to start dumping water from the other reservoirs as fast as they can to make room for the Fort Peck flood."

"You call him. I'll start evacuating the town. Then I'll call the deputy at Wolf Point. He can call the next town. We'll start a phone chain." A small crowd of people had gathered and many of them began to shout and run off to spirit their families to safety.

"Good idea, but first get my friend, Frank, out of the boat. He can't walk."

"He the computer guy?"

"Yes."

"You better not be shitting me, boy."

"Are you willing to ignore me?"

"Okay. The station is just around the corner. Look up the number for Gerald Roundtree in Glasgow. He's the Corps person. I'll be up in a minute."

In twenty minutes, Fort Peck became a ghost town. The police blocked any incoming traffic from Glasgow so the people from the town of Fort Peck would have two lanes north for the drive. Glasgow was fifteen miles away and high enough to be out of the flood path.

Robert had a tough time persuading the local Corps of Engineers representative to make the call to his bosses in Omaha. But the sheriff got on the line and verified Robert's identity.

The sheriff drove Robert and Frank to Glasgow in his own squad car. They got there at ten-thirty, half an hour before the bomb was scheduled to explode. Frank wanted to go directly to the bar, but he was still naked underneath the wool blankets, and the sheriff took him instead to the hospital. Then the sheriff took Robert to a local bar and ordered a beer for each of them. Everyone knew about the bomb by now.

"Folks, let me have your attention," Robert shouted. "Do not look directly at the bomb when it goes off. It could blind you, even from this distance. You won't get radiation poisoning this far away, especially since the breeze is at our backs, but do not look at it directly."

Robert noticed a bulge in his shirt pocket. It was the pair of sunglasses Newt had given him. He put them on and went outside. The sheriff followed him, as did the rest of the patrons in the bar. As far as he could tell, everyone in the town was outside and facing south. No one was speaking. It was as if they were awaiting the arrival of God.

At precisely eleven, Newt's bomb exploded on the southern horizon. It was a mighty blast that sent up a brilliant ball of fire highlighted in ghostly hues of red and black surrounded by a thick, gray cloud of water vapor. The crowd recoiled from the sight. Several patrons were screaming, a few were crying. The fireball blossomed towards the heavens like a hellish flower, rising thousands of feet every second. The colors were surrounded in steam, but now and again, the flames would break through with blinding clarity. But the blast was not as big as the one in Nevada. Not nearly. Newt would have been disappointed, Robert thought.

A couple of drunks cheered the blast, but their neighbors quickly silenced them with angry looks.

After watching the cloud for a minute or two, Robert could only imagine what might be happening downstream. A torrent of muddy water, the consistency of a thin milkshake, might be tearing its way down the river channel, sweeping away houses, cars, trees, and everything else in its path. If the dam broke, it would scrape hundreds of feet of topsoil down to bedrock in an instant.

The scars would be visible for thousands of years. He knew this because he'd seen the scars left from when, tens of thousands of years ago, the ice dam holding back ancient Glacial Lake Missoula in western Montana suddenly broke, and the waters had cut a new path across the state of Washington to the Columbia River.

If Newt's bomb did cause such a flood, most people would have time to get out of harm's way. A few hundred families in some of the more remote stretches of the river might perish in the catastrophe, but most would escape. Those who did escape would lose everything they owned.

There was no way the Corps could empty enough water from the downstream dams to catch the initial rush of floodwater, so the flood would be continuous all the way down the river and beyond. How many tons of water did Frank say the dam would unleash? It would be a tragedy far greater than anybody could imagine. Damages would run into the trillions of dollars.

"Well, sheriff, what's say we go take a look at the dam, or what's left of it?"

"The road's blocked off."

"Aren't you an officer of the law?"

"Good point. Let's go."

With the siren blaring, they raced toward the town of Fort Peck, which was situated dangerously close to the mushrooming cloud. "I don't want to get too close," the sheriff said. "I don't know much about radiation, but I damn sure don't want to expose us."

"Caution's good, but let's at least get close enough to see if the dam held."

They rounded a bend and off in the distance, there was darkness where the town of Fort Peck should have been. The gigantic cloud was no longer throwing off any light.

"That's a bad sign," the sheriff said. "You can usually see the lights of town from here at night."

"I heard that a nuclear blast plays hell with electricity. Maybe it just gave the town a blackout. Let's go just a little further and hope to God there's still a lake to see."

A mile down the road, they came up over a crest, and below them, they could see sparkles of light from the moonlight reflecting off waves on the surface of the lake.

The dam had held.

EPILOGUE

In the weeks after the blast, it seemed the entire world marveled at the story of how the dam had held against the bomb. Nuclear scientists analyzed the blast and speculated that water had seeped into the bomb's barrel and slowed the uranium bullet that was fired into the core. Neutrons passed back and forth between the bullet and the core before the two units fused into a critical mass, and the result was a huge explosion by conventional standards, but a fizzle yield in nuclear terms.

The Corps of Engineers' boat that Newt had stolen had towed the bomb a little more than a mile from the dam before the cable snapped. Robert's quick thinking in the frigid waters of the lake saved the dam from immediate destruction. The hydropower units, five huge turbines at the dam's face, were destroyed. The blast itself ruined the wiring of the facility, and the huge slug of debris kicked up by the explosion clogged the outlets, literally shutting off the river for two days while the Corps worked feverishly to cut a new spillway. It was spring, and runoff into the reservoir was nearing a peak, so the lake was filling rapidly. This helped dilute the radioactivity, but it added to the physical stress on a dam likely weakened by the blast. No one knew for sure how much damage it had sustained.

Once the new channel was cut, the Corps released huge amounts of water to take pressure off the dam face. North and South Dakota wanted Montana keep the radioactive water for a few thousand years, but there was simply no place to put it. Levels of radioactivity in the outgoing water were indeed elevated, but authorities assured people downstream that they were in no danger of exposure, a proclamation that rang hollow and gave no one comfort.

Throughout the summer, the lake was kept at its lowest levels ever while authorities determined the extent of damage. The news was not good. The dam itself appeared to be in good shape overall. The blast would probably have cracked a concrete dam in half, but Fort Peck was an earthen dam, and the dirt had enough give to sustain the blast. But early that summer, ominous springs began appearing just below the outlet. The Corps of Engineers discovered several new springs below the dam. When authorities noticed little whirlpools dancing on the surface of the lake near the dam face, they decided to drain the lake.

It took months to evacuate all the water. By late fall, the Corps finally cut back its water releases from all the major reservoirs on the Missouri (the others had to be lowered to make room for the waters from Fort Peck). High flows downstream flooded fields and farmhouses. The flows were comparable to the levels seen during the flood of 1993 and remained high for an even longer period of time. There was no navigation season on the Missouri River that year because of the high water releases. Nor did any farmers plant crops in the lower basin floodplain because the soils had no chance to dry out all year. By winter, what used to be a lake in eastern Montana had become a gigantic mudflat. The next couple of years would likely produce some enormous dust storms in the area, but gradually, signs of life would began to appear in the former lakebed. First weeds would invade the flats. Then the grasses and shrubs, and soon, deer and antelope would move into the area. Closer to the new channel, willows would spring up and help define a new river bank.

The Corps of Engineer officials would probably continue to talk about someday rebuilding the dam, but people would not believe them. Private landowners and the state of Montana would argue with the Corps over ownership of the thousands of acres of land that suddenly appeared when the lake was drained.

A little over a week after the bomb blew, Robert got a call from someone who told him to look on page e25 of the Kansas City Star. He had the conversation traced for good measure and learned that the voice on the other end belonged to a fifteen-year-old black kid from St. Louis whom Newt had earlier paid to make the call. Robert flew to Kansas City, bought a paper and learned from page e25 that he was to stop in Columbia, Missouri on the way to St. Louis and use his P.O. box key to learn the address in St. Louis where Amy Boston and Mason Tomlinson were being held. In death, Newt had remained true to his word.

Robert rented a car in Kansas City and drove to Columbia, then on to East St. Louis where he found the two hostages holed up in a basement near the Mississippi River. They were delighted to see Robert, but they were generally happy anyway, having fallen deeply in love during their forced time together. A year later, Amy and Mason were still an "item" though they lived far apart. They both earned a Pulitzer Prize for their reporting of Newt's bomb blast in Nevada.

Mason used his Pulitzer Prize fame to raise enough money to rebuild the tribal newspaper office. He and Amy, who had returned to New York for her work, were collaborating on a book about the impacts of the Missouri River dams on the northern Plains Indians.

Frank Kicking Bird nearly died from pneumonia in the weeks following the blast. Robert stayed with him in the hospital for two weeks until Frank was strong enough to feed and bathe himself.

"You make a good nursemaid, Robert."

"And you make a pleasant patient when you're unconscious."

The illness delayed Frank's recovery from his paralysis. But two months after he was released from the hospital, he was able to pull himself up to a standing position and take a few small steps with assistance.

By the time Robert came to visit him again in the summer, Frank was walking with a cane. The first evening of the visit, they were sitting on the porch. Frank had rebuilt his house over the summer, and had even cleaned up the kitchen floor a bit.

"You know what today is?" Frank asked.

"Yes, I do."

"The first anniversary of Anna's death."

"I said I knew. I wish you wouldn't bring it up."

"But that's why you're here now, isn't it?"

"Yes."

"Well, the least we can do is drink a toast in her honor. Go grab us a beer from the fridge." He still liked to order Robert around.

On the way to the kitchen, Robert noticed a big, fat goldfish swimming in a bowl of water on the living room table. He stopped briefly to pay his regards to Golda, who seemed quite happy in her new home. When he returned to the porch, Frank said, "I have a couple of embarrassing confessions to make."

"Let's hear them."

"I'm gay."

"Fuck you. Tell me the truth."

"Okay. I'm down to one beer a day."

"Frank, that's great! How long has it been?"

"All summer. I got people trying to get me to go to AA, but I can't do it. Those people are so boring, they'd drive me to drink."

"I'm really proud of you."

"You sound like my dad, except he probably wouldn't have understood."

They sat in silence, slowly sipping their beers. Robert had spent years worrying about the effect of alcohol on Frank's health. He was happy about the change in Frank's lifestyle, and maybe just a little worried about whether a non-drunk Frank would like him as much.

"Guess where I'm going next week," Frank said, interrupting Robert's thoughts.

"Don't have a clue."

"Maine. I'm going to visit Buckley, the guy I shot." Frank took another sip from his beer. In days past, he would have already finished it and told Robert to get him another one by now. "I didn't tell you, but I spent a lot of time with him while he was in the hospital here. We sort of got to be, well, friends. He's not really all that bad a guy, it turns out."

Frank sounded almost apologetic about this admission. Robert said, "Strangest way I ever heard of to make a new friend, gut shooting him first. I'm glad that's not how we became buddies."

Then Frank said, "I quit Tribal Council."

"Why?"

"That brings me to my other confession. I'm runnin' for sheriff. I'm gonna take Charlie's old job. I figure I owe him that much."

"My God, Frank. You're sounding more like an upstanding citizen every day. Think you'll win?"

"Of course I will. I told my opponent I'd break his face if he beat me. He dropped out the next day."

"Is it too late to take back that remark about your being a good citizen?"

"Not at all, and don't ever call me that again."

"Well, here's to your campaign." Robert lifted his can of Bud.

"And to Anna."

"To Anna."

* * * *

Robert had returned to work the ranch in South Dakota immediately after Frank's recovery from pneumonia. Except for occasional trips to the Fort Peck Reservation, he stayed there all the time. His days were much less eventful now that the press no longer hounded him for interviews. He was happy that people's lives no longer depended upon his making the right decisions.

His memories of Anna, though still painful, no longer set off small bombs of grief within his heart. The sunrises became more colorful once again, the grass smelled as sweet to him as flowers, and the summer rain felt like tiny fingers massaging his face. He spent most of his time alone, but he wasn't lonely. He worked harder than ever, but found himself to be less tired. And while not exactly happy, he enjoyed the peace that for so long eluded him.

About the Author

Elemental Threat is the second of three books written by Richard Opper. His manuscripts have received recognition and won awards in the Pacific Northwest Writers' Association Literary Contest, the Rocky Mountain Writers Competition, the Dark Oak Annual Mystery Contest, and the National Writers Association Literary Competition. He is currently working on natural resource and economic issues in the Missouri River Basin, the setting for Elemental Threat. Richard lives in Lewistown, Montana with his wife and son.

Oak Tree Press proudly sponsors....

Dark Oak Mystery Contest

Timeless Love

The Grand Prize in each category is a publishing contract! Visit our website at www.oaktreebooks.com for information on previous winners, guidelines for the upcoming contests, and details on our other fine books.

Oak Tree Press books are available at Barnes & Noble, Borders and independent bookstores, Amazon.com and other internet booksellers, or direct from the publisher.

Mailing address: 915 W. Foothill Blvd., #411
                        Claremont, CA 91711-3356.